PRAISE FOR CAPIT

Very impressive - New Author for me

Wow, my first read in this series first read of this type of fiction. Really enjoyed it will definitely be carrying on with the next book and be sharing this series with other readers.

5 STARS, A MUST READ!!!!!

I really enjoyed this book and cannot wait to read more. It is fast paced and written very well. This is the first book I've read by this author and I really, really enjoyed it!!!

Highly recommend this series!

Once you start this book, you'll find it extremely hard to put it down. It continues to be an exciting story from the first page to the last. Andy is such a great character that you will be fighting with him the whole way. Hope the next book is not far away. Such a fantastic series.

Would make a great movie

Saw this advertised so thought I'd give it a go after reading the reviews - got to say reviews don't do it justice, halfway through book one and it's fantastic – please, please make it into a film ha-ha.

Lance Winkless was born in Sutton Coldfield, England, brought up in Plymouth, Devon and now lives in Staffordshire with his partner and daughter.

For more information on Lance Winkless and future writing see his website.

www.LanceWinkless.com

By Lance Winkless

THE CAPITAL FALLING SERIES

**CAPITAL FALLING
CAPITAL FALLING 2 – DENIAL
CAPITAL FALLING 3 – RESURGENCE
CAPITAL FALLING 4 – SEVER
CAPITAL FALLING 5 – ZERO
CAPITAL FALLING 6 – BREAKOUT**

THE Z SEASON – TRILOGY

KILL TONE
VOODOO SUN
CRUEL FIX

Visit Amazon Author Pages

Amazon US- Amazon.com/author/lancewinkless
Amazon UK- Amazon.co.uk/Lance-Winkless/e/B07QJV2LR3

Why Not Follow

Facebook LanceWinklessAuthor
Twitter   @LanceWinkless
Instagram @LanceWinkless
Pinterest www.pinterest.com/lancewinkless
BookBub www.bookbub.com/authors/lance-winkless

*ALL REVIEWS POSTED ARE VERY MUCH APPRECIATED,
THEY ARE SO IMPORTANT, THANKS*

CAPITAL
FALLING 6
BREAKOUT

Lance Winkless

25/5/2022

Lance Winkless

Published by Lance Winkless

www.LanceWinkless.com

For Zoe

Thanks for your patience and support!

Chapter 1

This fucker is going to lose his teeth in a minute! Josh seethes to himself. He dares the squaddie behind him to jab the muzzle of his rifle into his ribs once more, because that is all it will take to push him over the edge.

"He isn't worth it," Alice tells Josh from beside him.

Josh's growing anger hasn't gone unnoticed by Alice, who is struggling to keep herself in check as they are manhandled out of the building and towards the open doors of a waiting van. She tries to throw a reassuring smile Josh's way to calm him, but his attention has been drawn in another direction.

"Karen!" Josh says urgently upon seeing Stacey's mother being marched past him, in the opposite direction. Karen doesn't register him until she has been directed past him and is about to enter the building, the one that he and Alice have just been frogmarched out of.

"Keep moving!" Josh is ordered by the overzealous squaddie at his rear. Perhaps Alice isn't the only one who has noticed Josh's simmering anger, because the jab into his ribs that Josh expects to accompany the order doesn't materialise. Josh's clenched fist relaxes slightly as he decides that the young soldier can keep his teeth in place... At least for now.

Alice takes the lead and steps straight up and into the back of the van. She hopes Josh will follow suit before he loses his cool completely. Josh getting into a fight now with the squad of soldiers escorting them is not going to change matters. Apart from which they are outnumbered two to one... and outgunned.

The sudden and unannounced arrival of the four armed soldiers at their apartment door, only minutes earlier, had put the fear of God into Alice, and Josh. It only took a moment for them to realise what was happening and only a second more for Josh's protests to start. Nobody was listening to Josh's arguments though. They had been given a few minutes to gather their remaining kit before they were ordered out of the apartment and then the building.

Josh's head turns this way and that as he closes in on the doors of the open van, his eyes searching for options, his head plotting avoidance tactics. He is surrounded, however, with no way to avoid following Alice into the battered white van. Finally, Josh submits to his fate and lifts his leg to climb inside. His only option is to bide his time.

Alice is already sitting with her back against the left side of the van's interior wall. She is perched on a narrow fixed bench that runs down either side of the claustrophobic interior. Josh moves to slide in next to her but, before he has the chance, a hand grips his shoulder.

"That side," a young, but authoritative voice instructs, as a firm hand takes hold of his shoulder, pulling him away from the space next to Alice.

Josh feels blood rush to his face as his fist clenches, his anger threatening to boil over. *As if this tosser is now putting his hands on me!* Josh seethes. *Breathe*, Josh tells

2

himself, anger filling his gut. Somehow, he manages to control himself and simply sits down, opposite Alice.

"Where are you taking us?" Josh demands as the back doors of the van slam shut, locking them inside the vehicle's drab interior.

"Where do you think?" Josh's tormentor replies, smirking as he sits down right next to Josh, and too close for comfort.

"That's enough, Private Carter," a voice orders from next to Alice as the van jerks forwards.

Josh's attention concentrates on that voice and he focuses on the older, but nevertheless still tender in age corporal, whose job it is to keep the idiot next to Josh under control.

"We have orders to deliver every able-bodied squaddie to the front line," the corporal says finally, in answer to Josh's question. He realises that Josh won't release him from his stern gaze until he has an answer.

"But both of us were relieved of duty by Colonel Reed following our completion of a mission we undertook for him," Josh insists.

"We're just following orders, Private," the corporal informs Josh. "My superiors ordered me to take you to the front line and that's what we are doing. If you think a mistake has been made, I suggest you take it up with someone in authority when we get to where we are going."

The corporal looks away from Josh, ending the discussion, leaving him in the lurch. Josh doesn't protest any further, despite the overwhelming urge to do so, knowing that he will be wasting his breath. The corporal is only following his orders, as is the idiot sitting next to Josh. No matter what he says, it won't change either of their minds.

Alice looks at Josh sombrely. He can see the trepidation in her eyes, a feeling that is rapidly replacing the anger that was burning inside him only moments ago. He tries to reassure himself that this turn of events may not be how they had planned it back in Devon, but it is what he and Alice had discussed and decided upon: to report back for duty. That decision now seems ridiculous to Josh. It had been taken following a few drinks in the idyllic safety of a cosy Devonshire pub when anything had seemed possible. They are both now faced with the terrifying reality of the undead abyss, the full terror of which was brought crashing back to them on the trip along the River Thames into London only yesterday.

Josh's growing fear of facing the zombie horde again is one thing, but it is not his biggest concern. His sister Emily is his priority and the promise he made to his dad. He had promised to look after Emily and, my God, he meant it. Nothing is more precious than his little sister and Emily is no longer secure in Devon, she is back in fucking London, slap bang in the danger zone.

Josh curses to himself as he watches the barrier rise to allow the van out of Northolt airbase. Far from protecting Emily, he is being driven further and further away from her with every passing moment.

"Emily will be okay, Josh, she is with Catherine and she will never let anything happen to her," Alice says, reading Josh's mind and ignoring the prying ears sitting around them.

"Ooh, who's this Emily? Your woman? Don't worry, I'll look after her for you when I get back, mate," the sickening voice of Private Carter says from beside Josh.

In a red mist of anger, Josh whips round and goes for the young lad sitting next to him. Josh is totally out of control: his circumstances and the vile words spouting from

4

the bastard next to him cause his anger to erupt uncontrollably.

The two young men fall to the floor of the van, landing at Alice's feet. Josh has the high ground and his hands tighten around the neck of his foe. His arms are locked out straight, pushing his weight onto the soft neck in his grip. Josh has no thought of teaching the young prick a lesson: he is too far gone for that. He means to strangle the life out of the shit stain below him.

With bulging eyes and flailing arms, the squaddie in Josh's stranglehold finally understands the error of his ways as he feels his life beginning to slip away from him. Carter's gaping mouth finds it impossible to draw air into his lungs. Stars begin to form, twinkling in front of his vision. Will their bright light and shooting colours be the last things he sees?

Suddenly Josh's grip around the neck between his hands falters. He sees the redness in the face dissipate as air squeezes down the windpipe of the young squaddie beneath him. Josh tries to redouble his efforts and to squeeze the last morsel of life away but, instead, he feels himself rising, his grip slipping even more.

Alice took hold of Josh first, to try and drag him off the mouthy young soldier. She has met too many of these vile young men to be able to count them. They were meant to be her comrades in arms but turned out to be nothing but rude, sexist pigs. She admits to herself that part of her wanted Josh to strangle the life out of the ignorant twat, but the thought only lasted for a second. The last thing any of them needs is for Josh to be up on a charge of murder.

Josh's determination proves too much for Alice to tackle alone, despite her strength. Only when the corporal next to her decides enough is enough and also takes hold of Josh does Alice feel Josh begin to move.

"That's enough," the corporal shouts through gritted teeth, as he and Alice strain to pull Josh off the man below him.

Finally, Josh's grip is broken and he is dragged off, effing and blinding to be released. Great gulps of air are drawn down into the starved lungs of Josh's prey as he manages to push himself off the floor and onto his elbows.

"What's his problem?" Carter gasps between breaths.

"You, you bloody idiot," Alice snaps at him. "That was his young sister you were talking about!"

"Alright, alright. Keep your knickers on, darling. How was I supposed to know?" Carter retorts from the floor of the van.

This time it is Alice's turn to see red and, before she can stop herself, her leg kicks out. Her aim is true, her foot cracking into the soft nether regions of the idiotic man at her feet, landing right in-between his legs.

Once more, all the air is expelled from Carter's lungs as Alice's foot makes contact. Alice almost feels sorry for him as he curls up into a ball with his hands between his legs, crying out in pain.

"For fuck's sake!" the corporal exclaims as he finally feels able to release Josh. "Will you never learn, Carter? Why have you always got to be such a dickhead?"

Carter's only answer is a whimpering groan.

"Get him up," the corporal orders the other two men inside the van, who have been watching proceedings quietly. "And you two sit down over there," he orders Josh and Alice, pointing to the bench on the right side of the van.

Carter is hauled up and plonked onto the bench on the other side of the van by the two men. They sit him down as far away as possible from Josh and Alice. Next to the back doors of the van, where he bends forwards, breathing heavily with tears in his eyes.

"I'm sorry about Carter. I think he was dropped on his head when he was a baby," the corporal says to Josh and Alice when things settle down.

"I can believe that," Josh replies. "He definitely isn't all there."

"No, but he's part of my squad, so I'd prefer it if you don't strangle him," the corporal insists.

"I'll try not to, but that was my sister he was talking about," Josh replies.

"Yes, well, that's Carter for you. Speaks before he thinks."

"What's your name, Corporal?" Alice asks.

"Turner."

"Where are we being taken, Corporal Turner?" Alice questions. "Back to the quarantine zone?"

"You haven't heard?" Turner replies.

"Heard what?" Josh and Alice say in unison, sitting back in their seats with worried expressions.

"The quarantine zone has been breached," Turner tells them.

"When? Where?" Josh asks quickly in fear.

"As of an hour ago. I'm not sure exactly where it happened, but I do know that the infected are heading towards the Wembley area. That is where we are going to drop you off."

"Goodness, we had no idea," Alice says, her American accent coming to the fore.

"Cannon fodder," Josh states.

"Something like that," Turner admits with a guilty expression. "It's every man to the pump, I'm afraid. If we don't hold them back there, who knows where it will end?"

"And my sister is right on the doorstep," Josh tells Turner, who just looks at him, making no reply.

"Where exactly are you dropping us?" Alice breaks the silence.

"King Edward's Park," Turner answers.

"Is that the Forward Operating Base?" Alice asks.

"I assume so. It's where we have been instructed to take you," Turner replies.

"Do we get any weapons?" Josh pipes up.

"I expect you will be issued with them when you arrive," Turner says.

"Expect? Are we supposed to fight them with our bare hands?" Josh presses in frustration.

"I've told you all I know. I'm just following my orders," Turner fidgets.

Josh and Alice look at each other, both with the same expression of fear and worry. Alice attempts a reassuring smile for Josh but fails miserably. She is thankful when a loud bang hits the metal wall separating the back of the van from its cab, saving herself from her grimace.

"We are here. Look lively, you lot," Turner announces, ordering his squad to prepare.

Josh takes hold of Alice's hand as the van comes to a stop and gives it a reassuring squeeze. "We'll be okay. We've got through worse. We just need to stick together," he tells her. But his words fall flat, at least in his own mind.

Carter gets gingerly to his feet, with a visible wince. Turner nods at him and pulls the door's internal handle to let daylight stream into the back of the van. With the daylight comes the sound of commotion, a sound that both Josh and Alice are all too familiar with. Like a bad dream, the sound of the military preparing for operations greets them as their eyes adjust to the daylight outside.

Carter gently leads them out of the van, using the step fixed below the doors so as not to disturb his crown jewels too much. The other two men jump straight down onto the grass outside and then it is Josh and Alice's turn to make their exit.

"Attention!" a bellowing voice orders as Turner's boots hit the grass. "Form a line," the voice continues.

Turner salutes the sergeant major who is fast approaching them from a camouflaged tent situated only metres away from where the van has stopped.

"Two men escorted as ordered, Sir," Turner says, referring to Josh and Alice, as the sergeant major arrives in front of them.

"Corporal?" the sergeant major demands, ignoring Turner's information.

"Turner, Sir," Turner answers after a moment's hesitation.

"Corporal Turner, take your men and report to the supply tent," the sergeant major orders, pointing to a tent across the park. "Load up and then report to section B and prepare to move out."

"Sir, our orders are to drop these two off and then report back to RAF Northolt. We aren't here to move out," Turner frantically informs his superior.

"You're here to do whatever I order, soldier," barks the sergeant major. "We need every fighting man we can get, and that includes you lot of reprobates. So, gear up and prepare to move out, is that understood?"

"Sir. Yes, Sir," Turner replies, after a nervous short pause.

"It's time to get into the fight, lads. You have your orders. Now move it!" the sergeant major shouts, and that is exactly what all six of them do.

Corporal Turner leads them in double time across the grass and towards the supply tent, leaving the sergeant major where he stands.

"What do you think? Is there any getting out of this?" Josh asks Alice beside him, as they follow the members of their new squad across the park.

"No. Nobody is going to be interested in what Colonel Reed promised and I seriously doubt any paperwork was filed," Alice replies as she runs.

"Lieutenant Winters might be able to help," Josh argues.

"We will have moved out by the time he can do anything, even if he could," Alice observes.

"It looks like we are going into battle then," Josh replies.

"Yes, but on the bright side, at least we have Carter with us," Alice jokes.

"Fantastic. That fills me with confidence," Josh replies.

"I can hear you, you know," Carter says over his shoulder.

CAPITAL FALLING 6 - BREAKOUT

"I'm only joking, Carter," Alice answers.

"We're in this together now, mate, so just chill out a bit. How does that sound?" Josh asks, as they arrive at the supply tent.

"Me chill out. You're the ones attacking me!" Carter replies.

"Oh, for fuck's sake," Josh says in frustration, rolling his eyes.

Chapter 2

Josh follows Alice out of the supply tent, inspecting the SA80 rifle he has retrieved. The battered weapon has obviously seen more than its fair share of action and he wonders what happened to the soldier it was issued to before him. Nothing good judging by the bloodstains evident in the weapon's crevasses.

Josh's hopes of receiving a pristine fresh-out-of-the-crate rifle were dashed as soon as he walked into the supply tent. The hastily arranged outfit consisted of weapons piled on the floor in one corner and boxes of ammo stacked in another, with two incompetent personnel overseeing proceedings.

They had been free to choose their own weapons from the piles on the ground and as much ammo as they could carry. The only restriction was on how many grenades they could claim. Two grenades each was the limit, which was enforced by one of the jobsworth squaddies.

Both Josh and Alice have also managed to gain a bloodstained combat vest each. It was with reluctance that they had lifted the soiled vests over their heads, but beggars can't be choosers and even bloodstained protection is better than a bullet in the chest.

As satisfied as he can be that the SA80 rifle in his possession will actually fire bullets, Josh swings it over his back. He would dearly like the chance to strip the weapon down to check and clean its components, but there is no such luck. As soon as they leave the tent they are being ushered over to another section of the park, one with a sign stuck into the grass with a letter B printed on it.

"What do you think the infected will look like?" Carter asks Turner, as they make their way over to section B.

"Like they do on the television I expect," Turner replies.

"Have any of you seen action?" Josh asks urgently.

"Not as such," Turner replies.

"What do you mean, not as such? Have you come face to face with the undead or not?" Josh presses.

"Not yet we haven't," Carter answers plainly. "Have you?"

"Yes, both of us have, multiple times, and let me tell you this won't be like watching them on the television. They are vicious, terrifying creatures that are strong and lightning-fast. We are in the shit here and there's a good chance none of us will survive," Josh says, not holding back.

"They'll be no match for this!" Carter announces, waving his rifle in the air as if it were made of plastic and he were a seven-year-old child.

"That will stop them if you can hit a head shot for a target moving faster than Usain Bolt chasing after someone who's nicked his gold medals. Body shots don't slow them down and there will be hundreds of them probably, more even," Josh replies, trying to instil the gravity of their situation into this inexperienced squad.

"You're just trying to scare us," Carter retorts.

Josh grabs Carter by the shoulder, spinning him round to face him. "You should be scared, scared shitless. These things will eat you alive. I've seen it, seen my mates bitten into, fed upon and then left to turn into the exact same horrific creatures."

"Okay," Carter says weakly.

"We need to stick together. Stay in tight formation, fight as one and cover each other's backs," Josh says, looking at them all.

"Josh is right," Alice agrees.

"Let's do that then," Carter says, holding his hand up towards Josh in a peace offering.

Josh clasps hands with Carter, and then with Corporal Turner. Alice does the same and then the other two men introduce themselves.

"My name is Ant," the first tells Josh, offering his hand.

"And mine is Wrighty," the second announces.

With the introductions complete, it is Josh and Alice who lead the squad over to section B. Dozens of soldiers are milling about nervously on the grass around the sign. Some of them have formed small groups while they wait for further instructions, but many stand alone, unsure what to do with themselves.

The squad that Josh and Alice have found themselves entwined with stay together. Nothing much is said between them while they pace the same piece of grass over and over. They notice two more signs stuck into the grass. One away to their left is marked A and the area around it is empty. Another away to their right is marked C, and that sign has a few soldiers standing around it, with others joining them slowly. It doesn't take much debate between them to decide that section A must have been the first wave of the new offensive and that section C will be the one after theirs.

"What happens now?" Carter asks, directing his question at Josh, as if he has some insight.

"I don't know. We wait," Josh answers.

As Josh answers, the sound of heavy diesel engines begins to rumble in the distance. Everyone on the grass around sign B turns in the direction of the sound, craning their necks to see what is causing the noise.

"Whatever happens, we stay together," Alice says to Josh, putting her hand on his shoulder as she sees two military trucks heading in their direction.

"Absolutely," Josh answers.

"And if the worse happens, don't let me turn, Josh. I couldn't bear it. I don't want to hurt anyone," Alice says, looking at Josh.

"I won't let that happen and don't let it happen to me," Josh replies.

"We understand each other then," Alice tells Josh with a nervous smile.

"We do," Josh confirms.

The first truck comes to a juddering stop on the grass in front of sign B. Behind it, the second dark-green truck pulls up behind it. A single figure jumps down from the back of each truck and the congregated personnel on the grass wait for the inevitable.

"Make sure we don't get separated," Carter pleads, looking at Turner, but Turner doesn't get the chance to reply to his comrade.

"Load up!" a voice bellows from next to the back of the first truck.

Josh cannot see who gave the order, but he assumes that it came from the figure that jumped out of the first truck. Immediately everyone shifts forwards, ready to climb into the first truck.

"Turner," Josh says to the corporal in front of him. "Let's go for the second truck."

Turner nods and changes direction. He sees the logic in Josh's suggestion: the second truck is less busy and they have a better chance of all getting onto it so that they don't get separated.

As Turner changes direction to lead them to the back of the second truck, others follow suit. By the time they reach the open rear of the truck a queue has formed to climb onto it, but there is plenty of room for them all.

"Take a seat," Josh tells Alice, who sits next to Ant, who has already taken the opportunity. Josh remains standing; he takes hold of a strap hanging from the roof and stands over Alice.

"Where do you think we are heading?" Turner asks from beside Josh, his arm also in the air, clinging onto a strap.

"Somewhere in Wembley. I don't think this will be a long journey," Alice replies, looking up from her seat.

"No, me neither," Josh agrees, as more bodies shuffle around them to claim their spaces.

Thankfully, the back of the second truck doesn't get very crammed and the short back door is soon banged shut, ready for the off.

"Listen up, squad B," a voice shouts from the rear of the truck as it pulls off. "This is going to be a short trip so give me your full concentration.

"Squad A has been put into position just west of Wembley Park and will move east. We are going to be dropped on the north perimeter of Wembley Park and will move south. The infected are moving west and are heading for the stadium. The stadium's public address system is on at full volume and is being used to attract them to that point. Squad C will be placed south of the stadium and then all three squads will converge on the stadium, which is where we will make our stand.

"Once all three squads have converged to the east of the stadium and we have killed the infected in that area we will push east as one unit. The objective is to kill the infected, push east and plug the hole that has opened up in the quarantine zone.

"We are not alone in the fight; we will have air cover and more troops will be drafted in as soon as they arrive. Be under no illusions though, this is going to be a fierce fight. The infected are fast, strong and vicious. We will be outnumbered, but not outgunned. Use the stadium to get your bearings. Again, we will be to the north of it.

"I'm sure I don't need to remind you that head shots are the only thing that will kill these fuckers, or what is at stake if we fail.

"For Queen and country! Are you with me?" the voice shouts at the top of his voice to finish his briefing.

"Yes, Sarge," the whole squad in the back of the truck shouts in unison.

Josh looks at Alice as he shouts his reply with vigour, a shiver going down his spine as he does so. He couldn't see the person making the speech from his position. There are too many bodies in the way. But he knows now that it is a sergeant who will be leading them into the fight and that the man can make a pretty good speech.

Alice sees the determination in Josh's face as he shouts his reply, just as there is determination in hers. This is the reason she joined the army, to make a difference, and there will not be a bigger opportunity than this. Her adopted country depends on this fight, and possibly the world beyond too.

Alice looks around at the other men standing above her and sees the same determination in all their faces. Fear is present behind the determination too but, right now, determination to kill Rabids is overriding that fear.

"Are you ready?" Josh asks Alice, as the truck comes to a stop and the back is opened for them to move out.

"Yes, I am," she replies, taking the hand that Josh has offered to pull her up to her feet.

"Well then, let's do this," Josh says, pulling Alice up.

Carter jumps down in front of them, the effect of Alice's kick to his groin easing off or at least forgotten. Alice jumps down next, followed by Josh, Ant and Wrighty, and then finally Turner. They all see the sergeant who made the speech for the first time as they hit the ground. The confident-looking man in his late twenties waits by the side of the truck to give them each a nod of acknowledgement as they disembark. All of them return the nod, saying "Sarge" as they go.

The first truck, in front, is already empty and pulling off, presumably to pick up squad C. Corporal Turner helps to close up the back of their truck and it revs its engine and pulls off to follow the other truck.

"What's your name, Corporal?" the sergeant asks Turner through a cloud of diesel smoke.

"Turner, Sir," he replies.

"Mine's Noble. You are my second in command, understood?"

"Yes, Sarge. Thank you, Sarge," Turner replies with some surprise.

"Form a defensive perimeter. We move out in ten minutes," Noble orders Turner.

"You heard the sergeant! Form a defensive perimeter," Turner shouts, already settling into his new position.

"The stadium looks surreal," Alice says, almost to herself.

Josh turns round, having not even noticed the gigantic stadium behind him. He has been more interested in their orders. The stadium is impossible to miss once he is facing it, even though it is still some distance away. Part of the structure is hidden behind the new developments that have sprung up around the famous stadium, but not even those can hide the towering arch that stretches over the entire expanse of the stadium. The steel arch floats hundreds of feet into the air, with wires fixed to its underside and attached to the stadium's roof helping to hold it up.

"Yes, it does, like it's from another world," Josh agrees, as he looks down the wide, deserted walkway leading up to the stadium known as Wembley Way.

"It looks so peaceful, and the piped music is serene," Alice adds, referring to the elevator music carrying down to them from the PA system of the stadium.

"That won't last. All hell is going to break loose around here shortly," Josh says, as he takes a knee, his rifle forming part of the defensive perimeter.

"Thanks for ruining my peaceful image," Alice teases as she takes a knee next to him.

"Just saying," Josh smiles, glancing at her.

"Where are they?" Carter says from Josh's right.

"Hopefully somewhere else," Josh replies.

"They know they're in for a pasting, that's why," Carter says confidently.

"I hope you're right, but my experiences tell me different. This is going to get messy, very messy," Josh tells Carter and the rest of his new squad.

"Well, I'd prefer to get on with it, take them by surprise. What are we waiting for?" Carter asks impatiently.

"Squad C to get into position, idiot," Ant answers frustratedly.

"You'll get your chance, Carter. There's no rush," Wrighty adds.

"It'll be dark in a few hours. Do you think we'll be back for dinner?" Carter asks.

"Not a chance," Josh tells Carter, wondering if he is a bit simple. "We're in for the long haul. The only dinner you'll be getting is a ration pack if you're lucky and that's if you don't get eaten by a zombie first."

"No chance of that. I'm not missing dinner even if it is only a ration pack," Carter tells them all, in all seriousness, shaking his head.

None of them know whether to laugh or cry at Carter's gesticulations.

"I take it you don't like to miss your dinner then, Carter?" Josh jokes, and that tips the balance, sounds of laughter starting to rise along their defensive line.

"Keep the noise down! What are you laughing at?" Sergeant Noble barks from behind them.

"Sorry, Sarge, nothing, Sarge," Alice replies as the laughter is cut off.

"We'll be moving out soon, so keep your concentration and look for targets," Noble orders.

"Yes, Sarge," Alice speaks for them all as Noble moves down the line.

"Did anyone bring any ration packs?" Carter asks quietly when Noble has moved away. "I didn't. I thought we'd be back at base for dinner."

"Jesus, Carter. You're unbelievable," Ant says, shaking his head, as Josh has to stifle another bout of laughter.

Only moments later, Sergeant Noble orders them to check their weapons. His order stops any further banter in its tracks and tension rises as the squad follows his order, knowing that the fight is almost upon them.

Sergeant Noble and Corporal Turner step through the defensive line and signal for the squad to rise and follow them. Noble takes the left flank as they move onto Wembley Way and Turner takes the right. Josh and Alice manoeuvre to follow Turner onto the right flank, along with their three new friends and around fifteen other troops.

The pedestrianised Wembley Way is wide, and is watched over by tall office blocks, apartment blocks and hotels. Designed to accommodate thousands of fans as they walk to the stadium, the expanse is more than wide enough for the troops now stalking their way along it. Every building is deserted and locked up tight. Even the retail outlets built into the bases of the tall buildings have shut up shop. The area is like a ghost town. The only things moving are plastic bags and other litter being blown around by the breeze.

21

"It's deadly quiet," Turner observes from behind his rifle, despite the increasing volume of the music from the stadium.

"The quiet before the storm," Josh says from just behind him.

"Let's hope squads A and C are on schedule. I've got a bad feeling about this. It's too spooky," Ant says from Josh's side.

"They'll be here," Turner replies with confidence, as if his recently gained lofty position gives him insight.

Josh hopes Turner is right. He too finds himself on edge. He manoeuvres his rifle around to look for the enemy, trying to take his mind off the jitters he is beginning to feel.

Alice is quiet beside him, leaning into her rifle, prepared to fire at a moment's notice. She has a nervous expression fixed on her face and who can blame her? She knows exactly what to expect when the infected show themselves, just as Josh does.

Josh suddenly wonders how many of the troops around him have had contact with the enemy. He was surprised when Turner informed him and Alice that they hadn't. How many of the others have yet to? Will they stand and fight or turn and run with their tails between their legs when they come face to face with the horrific undead Rabids? Josh hadn't made any allowance for his comrades cowering in front of the enemy. A foolish mistake, especially because he has seen it happen before with his own eyes in and around the Tower of London. He can rely on Alice, he is certain of that, but they need to be prepared for others to falter in the face of the enemy.

"That music is beginning to get on my nerves," Carter moans as they approach halfway along Wembley Way, and the volume of the music increases.

Nobody answers Carter's comment, everyone is lost in their own thoughts, fears and trepidations. Josh himself is still concentrating on controlling his own anxiety and is starting to agree with Carter's earlier comment about getting this over and done with. Anything to quell the nervous tension tightening his stomach.

Don't be an idiot, Josh tells himself. *Have I got a death wish or something? The Rabids will present themselves soon enough, that's for sure. Stop wishing your life away.* He quickly wonders if the term "Stop wishing your life away" has ever been more apt. These could be the last minutes of his life and he can't wait to get them over with.

"Are you still with me?" Josh hears Alice ask.

"Yes, of course. Why?" Josh replies, glancing in her direction.

"Because I was talking to you and you didn't answer. You were away with the fairies," Alice tells him.

"Were you? I'm sorry, I didn't hear you; I was thinking. What did you say?" Josh asks, concerned. He hadn't heard a word she had said. *I need to get my shit together* he tells himself.

"I said, it looks like we are going up the raised walkway," Alice tells him.

Josh focuses and sees Sergeant Noble beginning to lead his squad onto the left-hand side of a two-lane sloping walkway that leads up to the outer perimeter of the stadium. Josh is familiar with the slopes leading up to the stadium, off Wembley Way, even though he has never been here before. He has seen them on television many times when cameras show crowds moving towards the stadium in the build-up to a big football match or concert. He wishes that was the case now, that he and Alice were off for an evening of

CAPITAL FALLING 6 - BREAKOUT

entertainment and fun, rather than their current task of going to fight the undead. *More wishful thinking* he scolds himself.

"Josh?" Alice insists.

"Yes, sorry. We need to take the right-hand one. It will take us up to the stadium level," Josh says redundantly, seeing as that is the way Turner is already leading them.

"You're beginning to worry me," Alice says honestly.

"I'm okay," Josh insists. "I just got caught up in my own thoughts for a moment. I'm back on track now."

"You had better be. I'm relying on you," Alice tells him.

"I'm with you. Don't worry," Josh replies.

"Good," Alice says, making her voice louder so that she can be heard over the music.

"Pick up the pace," Turner orders. "We don't want to get caught here."

Nobody questions Turner's order; he is completely right. They need to get up the slope and off the walkway as quickly as possible. If the infected were to suddenly appear now they would have the high ground and the concrete sides of the walkway would pen them in.

The squad moves at double time, its rifles primed, trained on the exit that they are rapidly approaching. As they near the exit they converge with Noble's squad as the two walkways filter into one wide one. Turner slows them down considerably and stays on the right flank, with Noble continuing on the left.

Josh must admit to himself that he is impressed with Turner's leadership so far. He is proving himself to be both intelligent and a capable leader. Moving off the walkway cautiously is the right strategy. They don't want to be

24

bowling out and into the arms of a horde of starving Rabids completely unprepared.

In the event, after Turner has recced around the side of the concrete wall on the right and Josh has positioned his rifle on top of the wall to scan the way ahead, they decide that the way forwards is clear. Sergeant Noble and his squad have been equally cautious with the left flank and the teams move off the raised walkway in unison.

Another walkway travels in two directions: left and right. Both directions slope upwards and will take them onto the main concourse adjacent to the stadium. Turner pauses for a moment, unsure which way to lead them.

"Take your squad right," Noble orders, after seeing Turner's hesitancy. "We will go left. Check our rear and then manoeuvre around at the top of the slope to meet up with us," Noble adds, pointing left to where he wants them to meet him.

"Yes, Sarge," Turner replies, and turns to the right immediately.

Once more, Turner doesn't hang around. The main concourse is above them and the squad's position is vulnerable. Josh is relieved to move. Anything could be above them and he knows for a fact that Rabids wouldn't think twice of flinging themselves down to attack from above.

The squad's boots hit the concrete below, throwing dust and debris into the air as they scurry up the slope. On their left, the grey wall hiding the concourse reduces in height the closer they get to the end of the slope. Gradually, they begin to get a view of the concourse and the bottom of the stadium is revealed. No nasty surprises are waiting for them, only more deserted concrete and the locked entrances into the stadium. Nevertheless, Turner slows them down as the squad moves off the walkway and onto the perimeter concourse of the stadium.

"It's clear, Sarge," Carter announces as they finally leave the walkway.

"Thank you, Carter," Turner replies sarcastically, not that his comrade notices. "Okay, let's double back and meet up with the sarge."

Josh lets the squad move off before he follows, taking it upon himself to cover the rear. Experience has taught him that the undead aren't averse to springing surprises of their own. Alice follows his lead, both of their necks straining to look behind them as they move.

"Who is that?" Alice asks as they pass a bronze statue of a man with one foot on a football who confidently looks out over Wembley Way, his arms crossed over his chest.

"That's Bobby Moore, of course," Josh tells her as they move.

"Who?" Alice replies.

"You Americans. Honestly," Josh says.

"If that's the way you feel, I'm sure I can turn round and get a flight home," Alice teases. "I could do with the rest," she adds.

"They'd never have you back," Josh jokes.

"They couldn't refuse me. I'm an American citizen," Alice smiles.

"It was Bobby Moore. The England captain when we won the World Cup," Josh tells Alice, not wanting to tempt fate. He'd hate it if Alice made good on her threat to leave.

"The soccer World Cup?" Alice asks, knowing full well her question will rile Josh.

"The football World Cup. The game actually played with your feet," Josh tells her exasperatedly.

"Yes, soccer," Alice laughs.

Josh rolls his eyes as they leave Bobby behind. He doesn't want to play anymore, knowing full well that Alice is toying with him.

Noble is exactly where he said he would be and is standing behind the defensive semicircle of troops that he has put in place to cover the way forwards.

"Anything back there?" he asks Turner as he arrives.

"Nothing, Sarge. It's dead," Turner replies.

"Great choice of words, Corporal," Noble jokes.

"It's clear. Sorry, Sarge," Turner rephrases.

"Good," Noble says, leaving his joke where it lies. "No sign of anything here: the undead or either of the other squads."

"What are your orders then, Sarge?" Turner asks eagerly.

"We move forwards in stages to the east end of the stadium and wait for the other squads," Noble tells him. "Lead us off, Corporal."

"Follow me!" Turner shouts at his squad.

This time, Josh doesn't hang around at the back to cover the rear. Sergeant Noble and his squad will be covering behind them and he calculates that the biggest threat is now from the front. Josh stays on Turner's shoulder as he passes through Noble's defensive positions and Alice stays on his.

Turner chases forwards a few metres before he drops and takes a knee, his rifle pointing forwards, looking for targets. Josh and Alice follow his actions immediately, as do the rest of the squad. The squad provides a defensive position to allow Noble and his men to move past them, which they do in quick time. Turner stays in position until he sees Noble mirror his action a few metres ahead and then he is up. The tactic only needs to be repeated a few times before both Turner and Noble's squads reach the east end of Wembley Stadium.

Nobody is waiting to greet them when they reach the rendezvous point at the east concourse. There is no sign of either squad A or C, but Noble doesn't idly wait for them to arrive. He is immediately dishing out orders to his squad to fortify its current location.

The east concourse is a raised circular platform at the stadium level, with the surrounding streets and buildings below. At each side of the nose of the platform, there are wide double flights of concrete stairs to bring fans up to the stadium. This is where Noble orders the majority of his troops to be positioned whilst they wait for the other squads to arrive.

Josh is ordered to take up a position at the centre of the platform, in-between the two staircases, and Alice quickly follows him before she is ordered elsewhere. They both find a position against the chest-high wall that is there to stop people from falling over the edge of the platform. Their rifles are quickly pointed over the wall, aiming into the streets beyond the stadium, as other troops take up positions at the top of the staircases on either side of them.

"That music is becoming quite annoying," Josh tells Alice, referring to the tunes from the stadium that are being carried on the breeze.

"I think it's relaxing," a male voice says. Josh turns to see that Carter has wound up next to him on the opposite side of him to Alice. *Just my luck*, Josh thinks, as he refocuses on looking out for the enemy.

"I know what you mean. We won't hear them coming, that's for sure," Alice replies to Josh.

"We have a good vantage point though," Josh offers. "We could see for miles if it wasn't for the tall buildings blocking our view."

"Keep your eyes peeled," Turner's voice shouts from behind them.

"The fun will start when we move out into the streets," Alice says.

"That won't be long. The other squads can't be far behind us," Josh tells anyone who is listening.

"No," Alice agrees.

"If it goes to shit, and we get separated," Josh tells Alice, "we meet back at this position."

"Okay," Alice agrees.

"Look out for me too," Carter insists, and both Josh and Alice turn to look at him.

"We will, Carter. Don't worry," Alice assures him.

"I'm getting a bit nervous now," Carter tells them.

"You should be, mate. This is going to be horrific. Just don't panic and lose your shit. Breathe and choose your targets, okay?" Josh says, trying to prepare him for something it is impossible to be prepared for.

"Okay, yes. I'll aim for their heads," Carter replies.

"If you can. If not, go for their legs. That will slow them down," Alice instructs.

This time, Carter just nods, the blood draining from his face. Josh and Alice look at each other with knowing expressions. They have seen the look on Carter's face before: he looks like he is going to freeze at the first sign of trouble. He could quickly become a liability, something they cannot afford to deal with. They both know it without having to say a word.

"Here they come," Alice announces, looking over her shoulder.

Josh turns his head to follow Alice's gaze. Two squads of troops are rounding either side of the stadium at speed and heading for their positions to fortify their ranks into one large unit. The new troops pile in behind squad B, breathing heavily, but if they thought they were going to rest before the next stage of the mission then they are sorely mistaken.

"Squad C, move out!" Sergeant Noble orders as the troops arrive.

Chapter 3

Pulling their rifles in, Josh and Alice turn to move out. Just as they turn, two helicopters suddenly appear in the sky above them, hovering out from over the roof of the stadium behind them.

"Apaches," Josh announces.

"Marvellous. Where was our air cover?" Alice shouts above the din of the aircraft.

"God knows," Josh replies, as he heads towards the steps down. "At least it's here now."

Josh estimates that there must be more than two hundred troops filtering down the staircases that lead down from the raised concourse. He and Alice are some of the first to reach the area at the bottom and they file forwards to allow the rest of the troops down.

Over two hundred soldiers might sound like a lot, but there is a massive area between Wembley and the quarantine zone. Two hundred troops will get swallowed up in the streets and open spaces between the two positions, and Josh knows it. They can only hope that the breakout from the quarantine zone is small or that more troops are inbound. The one thing that they do have going for them is that the area has been evacuated, meaning that the undead won't have humans to attack and swell their ranks with. No one but the men and women of the British Army moving forwards to meet them.

Sergeant Noble ensures that he is at the front of the throng of troops who are waiting for orders at the bottom of the staircases. He has been joined by the two other leaders of squads A and C, who are both also sergeants. The three men have a quick confab around a map that has appeared between them and then they turn.

"Squad B, on me!" Noble shouts over the din.

Noble's squad filters out of the gathered ranks and follow him as he turns to take the road directly in front of him, leading away from the stadium area. As Noble's squad move off, they see the other two squads begin to head towards another road that goes left, away from the stadium. Josh assumes that the two squads will separate as they move into the streets beyond.

Above squad B's heads, one of the Apache Attack helicopters hovers forwards to follow them. The pilot gains altitude to scan the surrounding area, his action decreasing the powerful noise of his aircraft at street level.

"At least one of them has stayed with us," Alice observes.

Gunfire sounds before Josh can reply. The multiple cracks of fire come from his right, south of their position, meaning they haven't come from any of the troops that have just left the stadium.

"We aren't the only ones on the merry-go-round," Josh tells Alice. "There must be other operations in this area."

"Let's hope so, because it's such a big area to cover," Alice replies.

"This is it, lads! They are close. I can feel it," Noble tells them.

Squad B, to a man, raise their rifles, ready to engage the enemy as they spread out and press forwards. Josh and Alice position themselves front and centre of squad B with Turner, and find Carter, Ant and Wrighty in close formation with them.

An ominous noise ricochets off the surrounding buildings, hitting Josh and Alice's ears, and they both glance at each other in fear. The unmistakable, deathly screech of the undead fills their stomachs with terror and their eyes dart to find the source of the sound.

"What was that?" Carter's nervous voice whispers.

"The infected," Alice replies. "They're here."

"Where? I can't see anything," Carter asks.

"You will, Carter. Be ready," Josh tells him.

"Contact left!" Alice shouts as her rifle explodes into action.

The muzzle of Josh's rifle cuts through the air as his body repositions. His aim instantly aligns with Alice's, and he sees the target shoot out of a side street on their left flank. The creature moves impossibly fast across the tarmac, aiming for the unsuspecting men on that side of the road.

Alice's volley of bullets misses its target, streaking past the fearsome creature and smashing into a building behind it. Glass shatters as the bullets explode into the building and the creature swerves, ready to attack its closest prey.

Bullets erupt from every direction as the squad finally reacts to the creature's attack. Josh holds his fire and watches as bullets rip into the beast only metres before it launches itself into the squad's left flank. Dozens of bullets slam into the creature, stopping it in its tracks and sending it flying backwards to crash into the road behind it.

Panicked members of the squad, terror etched into their faces, continue to spend ammunition even after the Rabid has been eliminated and lies bullet-ridden, dead in the road.

Josh leaves them to waste their ammunition as Sergeant Noble shouts, demanding them to "cease fire". Josh's concentration is elsewhere. The sights of his rifle point at the road from where the creature appeared as he waits for the next attack.

Eventually, Noble manages to regain control and the last bullet is wasted. Another attack doesn't come, yet Josh keeps his aim fixed and ready while he waits for Noble's next order.

"Where are they?" Noble eventually asks.

"They could be anywhere, Sarge. They could be holding back and waiting," Josh tells his superior.

"Really? I thought the fuckers would attack as one mindless pack," Noble says.

"Not necessarily. They are unpredictable and not always mindless, Sarge," Josh points out.

"You have experience of them?" Noble asks.

"Yes, Sarge, you could say that," Josh answers, from behind his rifle.

"What's your name, soldier?" Noble asks.

"Josh, Sarge. Josh Richards," Josh answers, wondering if the name Richards might be familiar to the sergeant.

"Good to have you with us, Richards," Noble says, with no recognition of Josh's surname.

"Thanks, Sarge," Josh replies.

"Corporal Turner, we need to clear that area. You and Richards take a team in that direction but keep heading east. The rest of us will continue on this road. We must push them back to the quarantine zone, understood?" Noble orders.

"Yes, Sarge," Turner agrees, nervously.

Noble allows Turner to pick ten troops for his mission. It is no surprise who makes up the majority of his team, with everyone from the back of the van chosen. Josh and Alice are at the forefront as they peel off from the main squad in the direction of the side road.

"How should we do this?" Turner asks, as they move off, not afraid to ask for advice.

"Carefully," Alice answers. "They could be anywhere."

"They will come to us. We just need to be ready and hope we aren't overrun," Josh adds.

"There could be hundreds of them," Carter says.

"There could be," Alice agrees.

"And the helicopter seems to have fucked off," Ant points out.

"Guess we're on our own then, Private," Turner tells him.

"Happy days," Ant says under his breath.

Squad B splits into two, with Noble leading his squad to continue east on the main road. Turner gives them one last look as he takes his squad off to the left and onto the side road. Turner wonders if the squad will be reunited when they begin to press east as they pass the mutilated body of the zombie in the middle of the street. He hopes so; there is safety in numbers and he feels extremely exposed in this small group of squaddies. Something tells him this is wishful thinking on his part, however. He has a funny feeling he may not see Sergeant Noble again.

"It's deserted," one of the newcomers to their group observes.

"Don't let your guard down. If there is one, there will be more," Josh tells the baby-faced soldier on his left.

"I don't plan to," the youngster replies, confidently.

Turner takes them past the first building, which stands at the corner of the road. The once smart-looking warehouse structure is now riddled with stray bullets and they step around the shards of glass scattered on the roadside.

"How far are we supposed to go before we turn back east?" Ant wonders out loud.

"Until I'm satisfied that there aren't any infected this way," Turner answers. "Or we meet up with one of the other squads that are clearing the area."

Josh sees movement off to the right and drops to his knee, his rifle primed and ready to fire. Around him, he is aware of the rest of the squad following his lead and dropping into shooting positions, but his focus is on his target.

"Hold your fire," Josh orders, as a scruffy, medium-sized black dog trots out into the road from behind some bushes. The dog freezes for a moment when it sees Josh and his surrounding comrades training their rifles on it. The poor mutt is unsure what to do.

Only after the squad gets back to its feet does the dog's tail begin to wag and then, after a couple of seconds, it makes its decision and runs towards them. Before Josh can shoo the dog away, Carter is calling to the mutt and rummaging in his pocket.

"Leave it," Josh tells Carter, not looking at either him or the dog but staying behind his rifle and searching for the enemy.

"Look at the poor bugger," Carter replies. "It's starving."

Exasperated, Josh glances to see Carter bending down to give the dog a piece of what looks like biscuit.

"Carter, leave the fucking dog alone and concentrate," Josh tells him, annoyed.

"Leave the dog alone, Carter. That is an order," Turner backs Josh up.

"Alright, alright. I was only giving it a nibble of food," Carter replies.

"Heaven help us!" Josh says, as Carter relents and tries to move the dog on.

The dog doesn't respond to Carter telling it to go. Instead, it sits down in the road and looks up at him, begging for more food. "It won't go," Carter tells them, as if this is a surprise.

"That's because you fed it, you idiot," Josh tells him in frustration.

"Let's move," Turner orders, completely ignoring Carter.

The squad begins to move forwards, finally making it past the bullet-ridden warehouse. Inevitably, the black dog decides to tag along for the ride, despite Carter telling it to "get lost". Josh feels sorry for the mutt; he isn't completely heartless. The poor animal probably is starving, but they can't afford the distraction. Even now, it is distracting Carter whilst Rabids are probably lying in wait at the very next blind spot. Josh puts it out of his mind, leaving Carter to deal with the mutt as, thankfully, the rest of the squad do too.

Adjacent to the first bullet-ridden warehouse is another smaller one, and the squad moves deliberately to clear the blind spots and shadows that fill the void between the two buildings. All of them are jumpy as they do their work, expecting an attack to come at any moment from one of the multiple nooks and crannies. Eventually, Turner announces that the area is clear and they move away, back towards the road. Josh is pleasantly surprised by the members of his squad: none of them lost their cool or panicked. *Perhaps there is some hope*, he tells himself as they rejoin the road.

Sporadic gunfire sounds over their heads, just as Josh's confidence was beginning to rise. Alice hears it too and she swings around through a hundred and eighty degrees to where the cracks sounded from, her rifle leading the way.

"That's close," Alice says. "I bet it's coming from our squad."

"Yes, I think you're right," Josh agrees.

"Should we go back and see if they need help?" Turner asks.

"That's your call, buddy. But we were ordered to clear this area, so I would suggest we get on with it. If we don't, we could be outflanked," Alice advises the corporal.

"She's right," Josh agrees.

"Let's get it done then," Turner orders.

"Contact," Ant shouts.

Josh sees a dark figure land in the road past the warehouses in front of them before he is back in a firing position. Ant releases a volley of fire at the creature, which has flown over the wall on their right. The creature is too fast though and darts to avoid the shower of bullets that slams uselessly into the wall behind it.

Alice takes up the challenge and fires a short burst from her rifle, whilst stepping forwards to meet the fearsome beast. Her first bullets miss the fast-moving Rabid, but she doesn't relent. Alice moves again, pressing forwards towards her enemy, whose evil eyes are fixed on her as she closes in on the danger.

Josh moves to back Alice up, but he is lagging behind her, terrified that Alice has overextended herself.

The creature is upon Alice and launches itself at her, its mouth widening, ready to feed. Josh's rifle is out of position. He has no shot as the beast flies through the air directly at Alice.

Alice suddenly halts her stride forwards, her rifle exploding into action, her aim fixed. Bullets rip into the creature, its head receiving the brunt of Alice's volley. Bullets slam through the beast's face and into the top of its skull, blood and brain matter erupting into the air. Alice steps aside as the creature's head is demolished, ripped apart by the swarm of bullets.

The Rabid's limp carcass lands exactly where Alice had stopped to fire, the body now at her feet. She fires another bullet into the back of the beast's head for good measure and then coolly steps around the body. Her rifle is already raised again and aimed towards the concrete wall, ready to engage any more of the undead that cares to challenge her.

Josh has finally regained a decent position and steps up to Alice's side, ready to take up the fight with her. His admiration for Alice bubbles inside him, filling him with the courage to meet the next wave of the undead, a wave that comes instantly.

Another Rabid lands in the road, but this time they are closer to the threat and despatch the beast immediately. Bullets from Alice and Josh rip into the creature as it lands, vital ones filling its head. More shadows fly over the wall and gunfire blasts out from behind Alice and Josh as the other members of their squad take up the fight with them. Rapid gunfire explodes on either side of them as yet more creatures come over the wall.

"Watch the right flank!" Josh shouts. He sees the weakness in their lines too late. The squad has got caught up with the obvious threat in front of them and has left the right side of the wall unguarded.

Josh attempts to swivel to meet the Rabid he sees flying over the wall, on their right flank. Forced to pull away from the main fight in front of him, he brings his rifle to bear on the large male Rabid in tattered clothes with a blood-spattered vicious face.

Bullets thunder out of Josh's rifle but the creature soars through the air impossibly fast. To no effect, the bullets slam into the Rabid's body, not even knocking the beast off its course, a course that will bring it down on the closest member of the squad to the wall, Wrighty.

Wrighty's head turns sharply towards the object he sees above him out of the corner of his eye. His mouth opens to scream in terror as he sees the beast's attack, an attack it is too late to stop.

The flying creature crashes into Wrighty with horrific force, knocking the panicked soldier sideways and off his feet. Any scream is whacked out of Wrighty when he is hit, his arms flailing backwards in a reflex motion to try to cushion his impact with the ground. The rifle, still in his clutches, bursts with bullets as he falls, the muzzle waving in Josh's direction.

Frozen in panic as he sees the rifle's muzzle spitting bullets in his direction, Josh scrunches his eyes closed to wait for the inevitable to happen. He feels the first bullet whizz past his head and his body tenses, retracting in on itself to receive the impact of the next one. More bullets speed past Josh but he doesn't feel them rip into his tender flesh and eventually he forces his eyes open.

On the ground in front of him is Wrighty, with the Rabid squirming on top of him. Wrighty stares at Josh in terror as the beast bites down into the side of his neck, pleading for Josh to help him. Josh's focus is taken by the rifle lying inactive on the ground next to the hideous scene. Wrighty has dropped the weapon and, somehow, every bullet it fired has miraculously missed Josh. *Impossible*, Josh thinks, as he raises his rifle and fires it into the beast's head.

Blood sprays across the road and the creature's squirming body goes limp, but Josh isn't finished. He takes a breath and then must sadly fire again. This time he aims lower and puts two rounds into the side of Wrighty's head.

Josh has barely noticed that the shooting around him has ceased and the attack from over the wall has been defeated, at least for now. He lowers his rifle slowly, guilt-ridden at having had to shoot his comrade.

"Oh, no," Josh hears from behind him, and the words come from Alice.

Turning around slowly, Josh dreads what is waiting. Initially, he sees the dark-red blood soaking into the road and only then does he see the unmoving body from which the blood is pouring.

"Who is it?" Josh asks Alice, who is standing over the body.

"I don't know his name. He was one of the new ones in the squad. The bullets came from Wrighty's rifle," Alice tells him.

Shit, Josh thinks. The bullets somehow missed me but not this poor lad. Josh feels yet more guilt for him to deal with. Will this nightmare never end?

"This is bad," Carter says. "What do we do now?"

"We press on," Corporal Turner tells Carter and the rest of the squad.

"We need to deal with him. I don't think I can do it again," Josh says, looking at Turner.

It takes a second for Josh's words to register with the corporal and then a few more seconds for him to act. Turner reluctantly aims his rifle and shoots once into the lad's head. His entire body jerks morbidly as the bullet hits home and then it goes completely still.

"Come on, lads, let's move," Turner orders, turning away from the hideous scene.

"We can't go on. It's too dangerous. We already have two dead, including our mate Wrighty, for God's sake!" Carter protests, not moving from where he stands.

"We can and we will, Private. There is no going back. We have orders to follow, vital orders, and if we aren't going to do this, then who is?" Turner shouts at his subordinate.

"We need more men, that's all I'm saying," Carter continues.

"There are no more. We are the last line of defence to stop this infection from spreading throughout the whole country. Now move it, soldier. That is an order!" Carter insists.

"We can get this done, Carter," Alice assures the petrified young private. "We'll clear this area and then join back up with the rest of the squad. Are you with us?"

"Yes, he is," Turner answers for Carter.

"Our squad is probably dead already. Or worse, turned into those horrible things," Carter says to the ground. "What we supposed to do, kill them all?"

"If we must, then yes," Alice tells him. "We must do anything we have to do to stop the virus spreading. The country needs us. Every family in the land is depending on us."

Alice's words strike a chord with Carter, her use of the word family is a masterstroke. Slowly, Carter's head comes up and he repositions his rifle into a position across his chest. Corporal Turner doesn't stand on ceremony when he sees Carter relent, he simply turns to lead the squad onwards.

Josh, standing next to Turner, feels drained already as the adrenaline filters out of his bloodstream. He wearily lifts his rifle up from where it hangs next to his leg and forces a foot forwards to fall into position behind Turner. He knows the adrenaline lag will subside, but right now he could curl up into a ball and shut his eyes. *Sleep is for the dead*, Josh tells himself. *What would Dad say if he saw how drained I am after one small engagement?* He would rip the piss, that is for sure, and tell him that there is still plenty more fighting to be had, that this is just the beginning. *And he'd be right,*

43

Josh reminds himself, *another attack is imminent so pull yourself together.*

Josh feels his strength build as he practises a few breathing exercises and mind tricks that his dad has taught him over the years. The exercises also sharpen his concentration and his eyes revert to darting around, searching for the next attack, one that will inevitably come. In the back of his mind, he wonders where his dad is right now. Is he still in the military's custody or has he managed to get himself back in the game? One thing that Josh is certain about is that there is going to be hell to pay when his dad discovers that Emily and Catherine are no longer secluded in Devon. Someone will regret making that move. There is no way Andy Richards will let that stand, no way in hell.

Alice remains close to Carter as they move off. She sees that he is struggling and continues to offer words of encouragement to the young lad. She also makes small talk with him, in-between moving her rifle from one place to the next out in front of her. Carter's mood seems to lift as he tells Alice about his family. Perhaps it reminds him of the importance of what they are doing.

Alice wonders where Carter's adopted dog has disappeared to. She doesn't mention it to Carter; she is just glad that the mutt has stopped distracting him.

Turner carefully approaches the wall from where the Rabids had attacked. Josh covers him as he nears the chest-high wall to take a look over it. Josh doesn't volunteer to take Turner's position, not this time at any rate.

"Anything?" Josh asks, as Turner's eyes reluctantly peer over the top.

"No, it's empty. It's just an empty concrete plot," Turner answers. "There is an opening on the opposite side: they must have come through that."

"Let's hope that's the last of them then," Ant offers.

"There'll be more, you can count on it," Alice tells Ant and the rest of the squad.

"Guaranteed to be," Josh agrees.

Turner doesn't hang around once he has seen what's over the wall. He moves back, giving himself plenty of distance from the blind spot of the threatening wall. More Rabids could move into the empty plot at any time.

The wall doesn't last: it soon gives way to a menacing steel-strutted fence with spikes crowning the top. The fence might not be inviting but at least the squad can see through it. Heavy machinery for hire, such as cranes, diggers and other plant, stands idly in the yard beyond the fence, painted in a multitude of colours. Each strut that the squad walks past changes their view of the yard. A large digger might block the view for several struts in distance but then daylight and the yard beyond will be revealed at the next strut. Turner slows when the yard is revealed, his rifle aimed into the gap between the metal struts, searching for movement, but nothing shifts.

"No chance that they could get in there," a voice sounds from the squad behind Turner. "Those spikes are enough to put anybody off trying to get in."

"Don't take anything for granted with these fuckers," Josh says in response to whoever made the comment.

"Watch your areas," Turner orders. "They could still come over that wall behind us."

The yard is big, stacked with expensive equipment and plant. Whoever owns the business didn't scrimp on its perimeter fence, which not only keeps out thieves but now also the undead. Nothing moves on the other side of the fence.

Turner relaxes somewhat and picks up some speed. He doesn't rush but the squad is soon approaching the end of the yard and a junction in the road. The squad spreads out to cover the roads to the junction, moving slowly and deliberately.

"Which way now?" Josh questions. "Do we continue north or circle round and head back to meet up with the rest of the squad?"

Turner surveys the options. Off the junction is a road that would continue to take them north or, on the right, the road skirts around the yard and heads east. "Contact, twelve o'clock!" a voice shouts, before Turner can make his decision.

Adrenaline and fear rush back into Josh's body as he automatically drops to his knee, raising his rifle ready to fire. He trains it on the road opposite at twelve o'clock but, just as he focuses on the movement, another shot rings out.

"Hold your fire! Friendlies inbound," Alice shouts.

"I see them," Turner confirms, his arm raised in the air to signal to the troops on the road opposite.

Turner's signal is seen and the troops approach to take up covering positions on the other side of the road, meaning that the whole junction is covered.

"Cover me," Turner orders as he rises. He steps out into the road to go and meet the leader of the other squad, which is made up of about the same number of troops as his.

Turner's squad waits patiently while the two men have a confab in the middle of the junction. The conversation doesn't last long and, after some pointing and a handshake, Turner turns to return to his squad.

"Okay, we circle back to our squad. They are continuing east in this area to rendezvous with the rest of their squad," Turner tells his men.

"Have they had contact?" Alice asks.

"No, they haven't seen anything," Turner answers.

"Lucky them," Carter pipes up.

"Yes, thank you, Carter," Turner replies, rolling his eyes as gunfire sounds again from the direction of their squad. "Come on, let's move," Turner orders.

On the opposite side of the road, the men from the other squad begin to move in the same direction in which Turner leads his troops. Whilst he follows the road round, next to the yard, the other squad filters onto another road that leads off into the surrounding area.

The formidable fence guarding the yard continues around its entire perimeter. This gives Turner and his men some comfort, at least on their right flank, as they turn the corner. Their left flank has large warehouses and businesses set back from the roadside and Turner slows as they move into this new area, which must be where the undead that attacked them sprang from.

"What do you think?" Turner says, directing his question towards Josh. "Any one of those buildings could have infected inside."

"We can't clear every building and I would imagine they are all locked up tight. If one of them was my building I would have made sure it was secure before I left it," Josh answers.

"True, but what about their grounds? This road looks deserted, but those things that attacked us must at least have crossed over it," Turner says.

"Definitely. And there's another road there that we should check out," Josh says, pointing left.

"The area is too big," Alice adds, from Josh's side. "Should we split up into two? One squad to carry on this road and one to check out that other one."

"I don't want us to split up, but I think we'll have to," Turner replies, thinking.

"You carry on down this road and me and Alice will take a couple of men and check out that one," Josh volunteers, reluctantly.

"Okay. If either of us hears gunfire we double-time it to its location," Turner suggests.

"How will we know it's us?" Josh questions.

"It will be closer. We should be able to tell," Alice says.

"What else can we do? It's useless really. There's no way we can properly clear this whole area with just us few," Turner says in frustration.

"We need a whole battalion," Alice points out.

"If only. We'll just have to do our best with what we've got," Josh says.

"Right. You take two men and do that road and we'll do this one. Don't wander onto other roads. Concentrate on that one and we'll have to double back if there are more once we join back up. We'll meet on the main road where we left the main squad, okay?" Turner informs them.

"Understood," Josh says. "We'll take Ant and..."

"I'll come with you," Carter volunteers, before Josh can finish.

"Carter," Josh says, despite his uneasiness at having the man tag along.

"Okay. But behave yourself, Carter. Josh is in charge, understood?" Turner says.

"Understood, Corporal," Carter replies, with a mischievous grin.

"See you on the main road then," Josh tells Turner.

Chapter 4

"Check your ammo," Josh tells the members of his tiny squad as they peel off from the others.

"Yes, Sir," Alice teases.

"Ha, ha," Josh replies slowly. "You'd better not be questioning my authority," he smiles at Alice.

"I'd question the idiot who put you in charge," Alice replies.

"Yeah, me too," Carter joins in.

"Shut it, Carter, and do as you're told," Ant scolds. "We need your total concentration."

"I was only carrying on the joke," says Carter, defending himself.

"You just need to worry about doing your job, mate," Ant tells Carter.

"Okay, that's enough. Let's get our heads in the game," Josh orders, as they close in on their road, his rifle already in position at his shoulder.

The side road is jam-packed with business units on either side, offering an array of services and manufactured products. An attack could come from anywhere and Josh takes them down the centre of the road in the hope that it will give them a chance to react. Gunfire continues to sound, but it is coming from a different direction to the one in which Turner took his men.

"Which way now?" Alice asks, as they reach the end of the first section of road. Another road goes off to the left and the road that they are on continues winding round to the right, which is the direction they need to go in.

"We stick to this road. That one is in the other squad's area," Josh says, nodding at the road going off to the left.

"But what about that?" Alice says, pointing to a footpath on the right that leads down the side of the end unit. "What's down there?"

"It goes into a small, wooded area and joins back onto the main road," Ant tells them.

"How do you know?" Josh asks, but then sees Ant looking down at his phone.

"I think we're going to have to check it out," Ant says.

"Let me see," Josh says, stepping towards Ant.

Josh sees from Ant's phone that, in the midst of all the industrial units, there is a hidden patch of green trees. "You wouldn't believe that was here," he says, surprised, as he swipes around the area and zooms in and out on the phone.

"See what I mean? We can't ignore it," Ant tells them.

"We were told to stick to this road," Carter says.

"Corporal Turner didn't know about it. Anything could be hiding in it," Ant replies.

"Okay. We clear the wood, meet up with Corporal Turner and then finish the road," Josh says.

"Wouldn't we be better meeting up with Turner first? The wood is going to have a lot of blind spots," Alice suggests.

"Yes, but that area is next in line," Josh replies.

"If you're sure," Alice says.

"I am. Let's go," Josh tells Alice, in spite of his misgivings.

Josh is moving to the entrance to the footpath before anyone can say anything else. As soon as he reaches it he can see the start of the wood only metres away. A narrow gravel path will take them between the businesses on either side and to the wood.

To begin with, the path is bright, well lit by daylight. The wood is on the right of the path whilst, on the left, the path is skirted by a corrugated iron fence. Machinery pokes over the top of the fence from what must be an industrial site on the other side.

"I don't like this," Carter says quietly, as the trees begin to take over and cast the path into shadow.

Josh doesn't like it either and wonders if he has made the right call. He presses on nevertheless, taking his team further into the dimness of the wood. Shadows, tree trunks and bushes are everywhere on the right of the path and then suddenly the sound of running water filters into his ears.

"There's a river down there. Look," Ant says, looking in-between the trees.

"They're hidden all over London," Carter tells them.

"Never mind the river. Watch out for Rabids," Josh orders.

"Why do you call them that?" Carter asks.

"It's a term my dad coined and it stuck," Josh tells him.

"Your dad?" Carter asks.

"Yes, but that's a story for another time. Concentrate on the enemy," Josh says, sternly.

Carter shuts up and does as he is told for once as Josh turns back to the path, his rifle darting from one tree to the next. He takes them forwards slowly and, as a team, they check blind spots through the eerily quiet wood. Reaching up above them, the treetops dampen the sounds of the outside world, including the gunfire.

Although it is not the end of the wood, Josh is relieved when he sees the path brighten ahead of them. As they approach the clearing, the sound of running water increases and, when Josh steps back out into the light, he sees why. Another river joins the first from under a small bridge they find themselves on top of.

"Lovely artwork," Alice says from beside Josh.

"Lovely," Josh replies, not sure if Alice is joking about the bright graffiti daubed on the barrier at the back of the bridge. He sees the 'art' carry on along the next stretch of pathway. It looks totally alien compared with the quaint wood they are in.

"What was that?" Ant says, suddenly.

Josh heard the noise too and is immediately on tenterhooks, his rifle searching. There is no mistaking the groan of the undead, but he can't see where it came from, he can't find a target.

"Down there," Alice says, pointing into some brambles at the edge of the water.

"I'll shoot it," Carter announces, aiming his weapon.

"Hold your fire, Carter," Josh orders.

"Why?" Carter moans.

"Because it will give away our position, dickhead," Ant tells him.

"Wait here, Carter, and shoot when I give you the signal. Make sure you shoot it in the head, first time, to keep the noise to a minimum," Josh orders.

"I'm a crack shot," Carter tells Josh, smiling proudly.

"Congratulations," Josh says, as he leads Alice and Ant over the bridge to take up covering positions for when the gunshot sounds.

A short distance over the bridge, the path snakes right, away from the fence and around a clump of trees. The three of them fan out across the path and a grass verge next to it, where they all take up firing positions. Satisfied that they have the area covered as well as they can, Josh gives Carter the signal to kill the Rabid.

After an inordinate amount of time, Josh begins to wonder what the hell Carter is doing and is forced to turn his head away from his position to see. Just as his eyes leave his area a shot finally rings out. So much for Carter being a crack shot. Josh's head quickly reverts to its original position and he waits to see if the shot has brought on an attack.

A small number of birds suddenly take flight out of the treetops, startling them all. They all manage to keep their cool and stay in position without accidentally firing at the sudden movement. None of them moves. Their rifles are poised, trained on the foliage, and they wait.

A shadow moves over Josh as Carter arrives behind him and proceeds to stand over him. Not bothering to tell him to get down and take up a firing position, Josh continues to look down the sights of his rifle.

"Shall we then?" Carter's voice sounds from above Josh, just to agitate him.

"Clear," Josh says, and rises to his feet.

"You are a plonker aren't you?" Josh tells Carter in annoyance.

"What?" he replies.

"You should have come over and... Oh, I can't be bothered," Josh says in frustration.

"I should have what?" Carter persists.

"Contact!" Josh shouts, pushing Carter aside and raising his rifle.

Josh has begun firing before Carter has finished stumbling. Acid boils in his stomach as he watches two Rabids dart across the bridge behind them. His first volley of bullets rips into the lead Rabid, slamming into the top of its chest before the last bullet smashes into the creature's face. The dead Rabid falls over the side of the bridge and disappears into the river below.

Josh releases another volley at the second Rabid, which is almost across the bridge and upon them. Gunshots erupt from behind Josh as he sees his bullets miss their target and blow holes in the graffiti behind the beast. He fires again, the Rabid now so close that he can barely miss the evil creature. This time he hits the Rabid, spraying it with bullets. The top of the Rabid's head explodes in an eruption of red gore that even the funky paintings behind cannot hide.

His two targets down, Josh's rifle lowers an inch and he turns back to his team. He hopes that Carter managed not to fall after he had shoved the young squaddie out of his line of fire.

Why are they still shooting? Josh asks himself, as he turns. The enemy is dead.

"Carter, on the left!" Alice shouts with fierce eyes and a crimson face.

Time stands still for Josh as he surveys the scene in front of his comrades. Rabids are in the trees and dead ones strewn on the path, staining the gravel with black blood and littering it with putrid guts.

Carter fires at the left flank, where two Rabids have appeared out of the clump of trees, next to the fence. His bullets hit the first, ripping into the creature's stomach, slashing its belly open to spill its guts. The injury is of little consequence to the fearsome beast, which continues to power relentlessly towards a panicked Carter.

Josh's second of paralysis is over, his terror causing a fresh dose of adrenaline to course through his body. He snaps the muzzle of his rifle up and, acting on pure instinct, depresses its trigger.

Bullets crash into the head of the Rabid with its guts hanging out, disintegrating its skull into a fountain of blood and brains. Josh doesn't see the beast drop, instead he instantly whips his aim over and fires again at the second creature. Bullets whizz past the second target, missing the creature's head by inches. Josh aims again but, before he can release another volley, the Rabid launches itself into the air, directly at Carter, who is down on a knee in front of him.

Carter freezes, his rifle a useless weight in his hands as he recoils from the attack, his eyes beginning to close to wait for the inevitable. Bullets pepper the side of the creature in mid-flight. Alice's determined expression is unwavering as she continues to fire, her rifle sideways on to Josh. The force of Alice's assault knocks the Rabid off its trajectory towards Carter and it lands on the grass beside the cowering squaddie.

Alice spins back to the front, to meet the continuing threat that is coming out of the trees head-on. Next to Carter, the Rabid she shot out of the air is down but not out, its arm carries its hand towards Carter's ankle. Josh taps two bullets into the creature's head before it can touch his comrade, spattering the gravel with yet more disgusting fluid to soak into it.

"Carter, open your eyes and fight!" Josh barks.

Carter's head spins as he opens his eyes and fumbles with his rifle. He is completely oblivious to what has happened to the fate he was sure was sealed for him. He manages to regain a modicum of composure and raises his weapon, aiming it towards the trees.

Only instinct tells Josh to check their back and he spins round to look behind him. What he sees fills him with dread: Rabids are speeding across the bridge in numbers.

The pin of the grenade is between Josh's teeth almost before he has registered that he has grabbed hold of one of his explosives. The pin falls out of his mouth in unison with his arm launching the grenade into the air. His arm circle through the air and pulls down onto the rifle in his other hand. Josh opens fire at the threat on the bridge, praying that his weapon has a few bullets remaining in its magazine to spend.

Bullets erupt out of his rifle's muzzle and he keeps the trigger held down until the rifle clicks empty. Just as it does so, the grenade explodes, right in the centre of the bridge.

The thunderous blast shocks Josh to his core, even though he knew it was coming. Flame and smoke envelop the top of the bridge, and expand into the surrounding area in a flash. Rabids' bodies fly into the air, their limbs separating from their torsos as they are ejected off the top of the bridge. The body parts tumble through the air before dropping into the surrounding trees and into the river below.

Smoke rises and billows out from the bridge, but Josh keeps his rifle aimed into the carnage, waiting for the area to clear. Something hits the ground in front of him and his eyes bulge when he sees a severed head roll around near his feet. Josh has to pull his eyes away from the mangled face that stares up at him from the ground. Impossibly, the jaw of the head still moves, the creature still not dead.

Josh doesn't divert his rifle to finish off the severed head. Not yet, as it doesn't pose a threat. He keeps it pointing at the bridge and, as the smoke begins to dissipate, he sees shadows squirming inside the cloud. Not waiting to see what will emerge from the thinning smoke he focuses his aim.

Shit, you fool, Josh suddenly thinks, *you're out of ammo!* He ejects the empty magazine out of the bottom of his rifle and reaches for a fresh one. A deathly screech from just in front of him forces his eyes up and he fumbles the magazine. It drops out of his grasp and hits the ground with a thud.

Alice! his mind cries, as the beast comes at him, out of the smoke. The Rabid is uninjured by the grenade's explosion and comes at Josh full tilt. Constant firing from behind him tells Josh that Alice is busy and won't be coming to his rescue, as she did for Carter. His rifle is empty and there is no time to fill it, not with the beast already reaching for him.

Josh swings the rifle through the air to smash it into his attacker. The creature sees Josh's attempt and easily avoids the blow, leaving Josh totally exposed. He feels stifling terror take hold of him. Nothing can stop the creature now: he is out of options.

The grey-skinned beast locks its black eyes on Josh. Knowing it has won and is going to fulfil its starving craving for flesh, it cranes its mouth open in anticipation.

Josh can only watch as the victorious beast prepares to take its prey down. *This is it,* Josh tells himself, *but at least you put up a fight!*

Just as Josh gives into his fate, he watches as the creature disintegrates in front of his eyes. Josh's confusion is total as he watches the creature's flesh ripped from its body and the bones beneath shatter and smash. An eye pops out of the Rabid's eye socket and explodes in mid-air as the side of its head collapses in on itself.

The Rabid collapses in a pile of flesh and crumpled bones just to the side of Josh and, for a moment, Josh thinks he is imagining the creature's destruction. He stares over at the pile of rot next to him, transfixed for a moment, wondering if he is dreaming.

A voice from his left disturbs him from his daydream and he looks over to where it came from. All at once, Josh returns to reality and sees the cause of his salvation. Turner and his men are in amongst the trees on the other side of the river, opposite the bridge. Turner looks over his rifle, which has just shot to pieces the Rabid that had attacked Josh. The corporal gives Josh a nod and a quick salute before he gets back behind his weapon and starts firing again.

By the time Josh has recomposed himself and retrieved the magazine he dropped, the fight is all but done. Josh pushes the magazine into its home in the bottom of his rifle, reloads the weapon and then shoots a single bullet into the severed head that had landed at his feet.

"Thank Christ they arrived," Alice pants, as she gets up from her firing position.

"Holy shit," Josh blabbers, when he sees a mangle of bodies just to the right of their position.

"I didn't see it before it was too late," Alice says sombrely. "I couldn't stop it, I had to shoot them both."

"You did him a favour then," Josh tells Alice, as he looks down at the petrified expression fixed on Ant's dead face.

That was nearly me, Josh thinks, as he watches Corporal Turner leap across a narrow section of the river to get onto their side. His men follow him across and he orders them into a defensive perimeter in front of Josh and Alice.

"I thought I told you to stick to that road," Turner says, as he joins Josh and Alice.

"You did. But we came across this area and didn't think we could go past it without clearing it," Josh replies, guiltily.

"Well, it would have had to be cleared, one way or the other," Turner concedes. "We came running as soon as we heard the first shot. We were in the grounds of one of the factories just over the fence from the woods."

"Thanks. It's lucky you arrived when you did," Alice says.

"Yes, it looked like Josh was about to get it." Turner looks over at Josh.

"I thought that was it for me, I must admit. Thanks, I owe you one," Josh tells Turner.

"Don't be ridiculous. We are all in this together, we gotta have each other's backs," Turner replies.

"Just a shame I couldn't have saved Ant," Alice says, sadly.

"You would have if you could have, Alice. I've seen you do it. You can't blame yourself. Okay?" Josh insists.

"I know. It doesn't make it any easier though," Alice replies.

"No, it doesn't. But we move on. What else can we do?" Turner adds.

"You saved Carter, Alice," Josh points out.

"Was it Alice that stopped that monster?" Carter asks.

"Yes. She blasted it right out of the air," Josh tells Carter.

"Bloody hell. Thanks Alice," Carter says, sincerely.

"There's no need to thank me," Alice responds.

"Well, I just have," Carter tells her.

A gunshot snaps from the defensive perimeter Turner has set up, making them all flinch and raise their rifles. Turner immediately stalks forwards to see what is going on, bringing the rest of the squad with him.

"What are you shooting at?" Turner asks his men.

"One of them was still twitching," the guilty party replies.

"Hold your fire unless absolutely necessary," Turner orders in frustration.

"Yes, Corporal," his young squaddie replies.

"Let's get this wood cleared and get out of here," Turner says. "It's beginning to give me the creeps," he adds.

"Me, too. But I suggest we use our knives if any of them are still... twitching," Josh offers.

"Roger that," Turner agrees, as he steps over the first corpse on the pathway.

Mutilated Rabids' bodies are strewn over the path and in the treeline. Each one must be checked to ensure it is dead. The squad begins the grim task of dealing with the carcasses littering the path. Despite the severity of the injuries inflicted on the infected creatures, some do still show signs of clinging onto their reanimated state and must be dealt with.

"Josh, Alice and Carter, cover us while we check the treeline," Corporal Turner orders.

Josh and the other two take up positions and watch nervously as Turner leads the three other men towards the shadows and the bodies lying there. Turner takes the responsibility of sticking his knife into the first head, but he is joined by the three others without having to ask.

Once Turner is satisfied, he peers into the woods beyond the treeline. Josh knows what his next move will be before he gives the order for Josh and the other two to move their covering positions up to him.

"Be careful in there," Josh advises, as Turner steps forwards. The woods must be cleared as well, so nobody questions Turner's decision. Even if one infected creature remains in the woods or in the undergrowth it must be found and eliminated.

As Turner and the other men move deeper into the wood, Josh, Alice and Carter move behind them to back them up. With every step, the wood gets dimmer due to the increasing tree cover but also because the day is drawing to a close. Evening will soon be upon them, something that does not fill any of them with confidence.

Turner decides not to recross the river. He makes the assumption that the infected won't have crossed it. Josh thinks it's a fair shout and the decision speeds up the process of clearing the area. The sound of running water fills their ears as they turn left and back towards the path, without finding any dregs of the undead.

There is still foliage to clear once they arrive back on the gravelled pathway, but with daylight above their heads again it doesn't seem so threatening. Turner uses his knife once as they inch towards the exit out of the greenery, but they aren't attacked. The undead that did attack them must have done it as a pack, all in one go, and, this time, they were no match for the squad's firepower.

At last, the squad reaches the edge of the wooded area and approach the exit with caution. Turner stoops down low and takes a glance behind before he makes his final approach to the exit.

In silence, every member of the squad steps out of the green oasis that manages to cling on in the industrial landscape. Josh and Alice look at each other with dread, disbelief and shock when they pull their eyes away from the scene on the road in the near distance. Each of them feels naive for not having understood the full implications of the gunfire that has been cracking over their heads while they have been separated from the main squad.

Ahead of them, where the main road is intersected by another road, carnage is scattered across the junction. Bodies pepper the roadside as well as the pavement beside it. There is no mistaking the camouflaged military uniforms that clad many of the fallen.

"Where is the rest of our squad?" Carter asks.

"Quiet, Carter," Turner orders under his breath, as he looks down the sights of his rifle.

Unable to help himself, Carter goes to speak again. Only Alice stops him from breaking Turner's concentration again. She slaps his chest with the back of her hand whilst putting her finger to her lips and giving Carter an angry look. He soon shuts up, displaying a wounded expression.

"Most, if not all are down," Turner tells them, lowering his rifle.

"We should recce the area," Josh suggests.

"I'm not sure. There is movement on the ground," Ant informs Josh from behind his rifle. "They're not dead."

"We must press on. Those are our orders. Plus, we can't leave our comrades like that," Josh insists.

"Quiet. Let me think!" Turner snaps.

"Where have the undead gone?" Carter wonders out loud, never doing what he is told.

"Same teams as before," Turner says, with a look of annoyance aimed at Carter. "Josh, you take the right flank and we'll take the left. We need to check the area out and find the rest of our squad."

"If there are any left to find," Carter points out.

"Let's just hope there are," Alice interjects. She pulls Carter's arm to get him into position before Turner completely loses his rag with him.

The two teams move down either side of the road in unison. There isn't much distance to cover but both teams take their time, expecting an attack from the undead at any moment. Gradually, they draw closer to the carnage and Turner signals for both teams to stop so that he can survey the bloodbath.

Josh takes the opportunity to take a closer look at the horror spread out on the road in front of them. He tells Alice and Carter to provide cover as he focuses the scope of his rifle.

"How many of our men are down?" Alice asks from behind Josh, but he doesn't answer immediately.

"It's worse than we thought," is all that Josh says after a long pause.

"What did I say?" Carter asks, from Josh's other side.

Josh ignores Carter's flippant comment, barely hearing it. The thud of his racing heart bangs against his eardrums as the muzzle of his rifle moves through the air to scan the entire scene. He can't find the words to describe what he is seeing to Alice. He loses count of how many camouflaged bodies lie in the road, but that isn't the worst of it. Only a minority of the bodies are motionless and Josh can only pray that these poor souls are dead because they will be the lucky ones.

Josh's rifle comes to a grinding halt when it picks out a familiar face in amongst the horror, next to the roadside. Sergeant Noble's open eyes are black pools, his head at right-angles to his body, which is flat on its back. Josh stares back at Noble through his rifle's sights and is powerless to move. Josh is conscious of the Rabid stooped over the sergeant, its head buried in his belly, feeding, but it is Noble's face that has him paralysed with terror. Noble's eyelids don't blink but the sergeant's chilling eyeballs move around in their sockets, searching for something while his innards are fed upon. In an instant, the eyeballs fix, finding what they are looking for, and, when they do, Noble's face morphs, his expression evil and sinister.

Noble stares straight back through the sights of Josh's rifle, seeing the shock and fear that Josh cannot control. Noble keeps Josh fixed in his glare while his body begins to move. The disgusting creature feeding upon him suddenly loses interest in Noble's bloody guts. At first, the movement is slow and awkward, as if his body's joints have seized up and must now grind against themselves to work again. But with each movement, Noble's body frees itself from its rigor mortis and rises from the roadside.

Josh's fear is stifling. He cannot wrench his eyes away from the beast as if it were an apparition, the image evil personified. Alice's voice next to Josh is distant, a dream, her words not registering.

"Josh!" Alice shouts and, finally, Josh hears her. Gunfire erupts from the opposite side of the road. Turner and his team have grabbed the initiative and now, finally, Josh sees the full extent of the threat that is facing them.

Noble, still in Josh's sights, is surrounded by creatures that have followed the sergeant's movement and have risen to stand in the road, eyeing their newfound prey. Josh's head clears and he refocuses his aim instantly, ready to join the fight. He depresses his rifle's trigger and a bullet spits out, directly at Noble, but Josh's delay has given the beast a chance. Noble bursts forwards in the same instant that Josh fires, the bullet vanishing, hitting nothing.

Suddenly, all that Josh sees through his rifle's sights is a blur of movement: there is no target to pick out. He fires anyway, into the mass of targets that is surging forwards to attack the squad. He keeps firing in the hope of regaining the advantage that he lost in his shocked paralysis, but his actions are futile.

"Fall back!" Alice shouts, grabbing hold of Josh's shoulder.

Josh's head spins, his trigger locked down, firing indiscriminately. His shoulder is pulled again, his head begging him to trust Alice. Her voice shouts again, "Run, Josh, run!"

Alice drags him to his feet and he is running, his boots hitting the ground hard. He concentrates on Alice in front of him and powers after her. He is totally unaware of what direction they are going in, not knowing where she is leading him to escape. He glances left and sees Carter's panicked face next to him, his eyes bulging in fear and exertion.

The pack of Rabid creatures is close behind him. Josh can feel it. On the opposite side of the road, Turner strides to outrun the pack, his men close behind him, but some are struggling to keep up.

"Keep going," Josh shouts to Carter beside him, "don't give up."

Something flies over Josh's head, an object released from Alice's hand. The grenade clatters into the road behind Josh and he reaches for his last remaining grenade as he increases the power to his legs. Any thoughts of saving the last of his explosives are gone and he pulls the pin just as Alice's grenade explodes.

Carter ducks as the explosion hits, but Josh barely flinches as the blast rips into the undead horde behind. Josh's hand opens and drops the grenade into the road, his stride widening yet further.

"Grenade!" Josh shouts to warn his squad, moments before the device explodes. The blast is muffled compared with the first, which can mean only one thing. Josh risks a look over his right shoulder for a second. In front of the black cloud of smoke rising into the air, the Rabid horde chase, the twisted figures closing the gap behind. Josh sees that Turner and his men are closer as both teams converge on the centre of the road, but one of the other team is being sucked back into the pack of death only feet behind him.

Alice carries them on, still taking the lead, unrelenting. She is heading towards the gigantic stadium from where they launched the second part of their mission. She must be taking them towards the high ground, the concourse at the top of the steps. Josh agrees with her strategy, but the road is long. Even the bulk of the stadium still looks tiny, and there seems to be no hope of them reaching it.

A scream shrills out from Josh's right. In the periphery of his vision, he sees a man struggling to keep up with Turner fall. The squaddie is hit from behind, the Rabid taking the poor bugger down hard. Josh flinches as the man slams into the roadside, his head cracking into the tarmac, where he is swallowed up by the ferocious horde.

Josh knows that it is only a matter of time before the same fate befalls them all. Any salvation they might find at the top of the steps is nothing but wishful thinking. The horde will strike before they have made it another ten metres, never mind reaching even the first step up.

A shadow above them gives Josh a glimmer of hope. The sound of an engine and a rotor cutting through the air brings more. Bullets rip into the ground directly behind them before the blast of the chain gun positioned beneath the Apache helicopter reaches their ears. Shards of tarmac erupt into the air and rain down over the squad as they run. No one breaks their stride to see the stream of thirty-millimetre bullets rip into the roadside and into the horde of undead. A second passes before the first Hellfire missile streaks through the sky, the pilot at least giving the squad a chance to clear the area.

A flash of brilliant white light bursts past them the instant the missile explodes, the squad hoping they have made it out of the missile's blast area. The explosion is massive: it erupts with unimaginable force. Supersonic hot gas billows against their backs, threatening to singe their skin, but it forces the squad on, pushing them further and faster.

"Fucking hell!" Carter cries in astonishment, as the explosion washes over him.

Carter's profanity tells Josh that they are still alive, that neither the horde nor the Hellfire has taken them down. He sees that the stadium is closer now and begins to hang over them, its arch cutting into the sky. Perhaps their last stand will be on the raised concourse after all, but there is still some distance to go.

The Apache's chain gun bursts out again, sending bullets strafing into the thinner pack of creatures, the bullets now finding it harder to locate their targets. Rabids that haven't been cut down or incinerated still hunt but the main pack has gone.

Suddenly, Alice changes direction. She has done it: she has managed to reach the bottom of the steps up to the concourse. Josh's tiring legs find energy when he sees Alice begin the climb. His amazement that they have reached the steps is quickly forgotten as his energy is sapped as rapidly as it arrived, each step upwards draining him further. The steps become a mountain, its peak lost in the clouds, and he feels himself falter, his legs giving up.

Someone grabs his arm to pull him along. "Only a few more," Carter shouts, his hand gripping Josh's wrist to force him on.

Gunfire erupts and bullets whizz past Josh's head from above. The firing continues as Josh finally reaches his peak, where he sees Alice taking cover behind the wall of the concourse, the muzzle of her rifle flashing.

Turner and his men follow Josh and Carter up the steps, but Rabids are almost upon them. Josh turns to lay down covering fire with Alice as Turner speeds past him. On the steps, Rabids launch themselves at two of the squaddies who have dropped behind Turner. Screams of terror do nothing to save them from their fate as Rabids hit them, knocking them down onto the concrete steps. Their bodies are lost as they are enveloped by the undead as they roll, falling back down the steps, where more Rabids pounce into the melee of death.

"We cannot stay here!" Turner shouts over the gunfire as the Apache overhead ceases its fire and flies off, the pilot evidently deciding that there are richer pickings elsewhere.

"No, there are too many of them," Josh shouts in agreement.

"The stadium!" Turner shouts, as he grabs a grenade from his combat vest.

The remaining four members of the squad are off and running before the grenade has bounced down the first step. Turner sprints across the concourse, right at the side of the stadium, aiming for a nondescript grey door. The grenade explodes as Turner clatters heavily into the door and grabs hold of the handle.

"It's locked!" Turner shouts, his words not surprising any of them.

"Move out of the way!" Alice demands, raising her rifle.

"They're coming!" Carter shouts, as Alice shoots out the lock next to the door handle.

Turner grabs the handle again and heaves. Wood splinters around the lock and suddenly the door pops open. Josh fires at the Rabids coming across the concourse as the other three rush through the door but, as soon as they are through, he ceases fire and follows them inside.

Chapter 5

"What do we do now?" Carter asks desperately, as Josh urgently pulls the door shut behind him.

No sooner has Josh pulled the door shut than a massive crash hits the outside of it, rattling it in its frame.

"At least the door opens outwards," Alice pants, waiting for the next crash.

"Who said luck isn't on our side?" Josh says, eyeing the door nervously, almost expecting it to disintegrate at any moment from the bombardment.

"We need to evacuate this area. That door isn't going to hold out," Turner says, looking around.

They find themselves in a confined area, with a door at the end of a short corridor with stairs off to the right next to it. Turner doesn't waste any time and heads down the corridor to check the door. Alice follows him whilst Josh and Carter step back and cover the door with their rifles.

"Thanks for that on the steps," Josh says to Carter.

"No thanks required," Carter replies. "It looked like you were spent."

"Think I'd run out of energy. It's been an extremely long couple of days," Josh tells him.

"Looks like it will be a long night too. It's getting dark already," Carter points out.

"Tell me about it," Josh replies, knowing Carter isn't wrong.

"It doesn't look like they're gonna give up," Carter observes, after another almighty crash against the door.

"Let's hope they don't figure out how to use a door handle," Josh jokes, but he doesn't crack a smile. He knows it's only a matter of time before the creatures do, or the door inches open by itself.

"Shit! I never thought of that," Carter says in shock.

"They aren't as mindless as you think," Josh tells him.

"Move, you two," Turner orders from behind.

Josh and Carter turn and leave their positions as the Rabids continue to attack the door. Turner and Alice are already on the stairs, their rifles jutting over the handrail to cover the retreat.

"The door is locked tight," Alice informs Josh and Carter.

"We don't want to make any more noise," Turner says. "Hopefully they will give up and fuck off shortly."

"I wouldn't count on it," Josh points out.

"At least we get the high ground that way," Carter says, as he turns for the stairs.

They reach the first level with the crashing against the door echoing up the stairs to them. There is a long corridor leading off the stairs with several doors joining it and Turner takes them down to the first door.

"This looks promising," Carter says, when he sees a sign reading 'KITCHEN 2B' mounted on the door.

Turner pushes the door and a wide smile spreads across Carter's face when a whoosh of air sounds and the door opens.

Darkness greets them as they step inside. "Hold the door," Turner says, as he looks for a light switch. An audible click is followed by a couple of flashes of light and then the light is constant. A jungle of stainless steel is spread out before them as, just as the sign suggested, they find themselves inside a large catering kitchen.

Before anyone has said a word, Carter is already opening one of the hulking refrigerators lined up against one of the walls.

"Bingo," he says with wide eyes, as he looks inside.

"We haven't time for that," Alice insists, despite the hunger pang she feels.

"Oh, come on. I know it's a bit early for dinner, but we might as well have a look while we're here. Who knows when we'll get another chance?" Carter protests.

"Okay, but let's make it quick," Turner says, looking at Alice and shrugging.

"If you can't beat them, join them, eh?" Josh smiles at Alice. He knows for sure that he could do with taking some new energy on-board. This time it is Alice's turn to shrug as she joins them. There are plenty of refrigerators for everyone.

There is plenty of produce stacked inside the oversized refrigerators. The problem is that most of it has spoiled, regardless of the cool temperatures the food has been kept at. Only the sealed packeted food is still fresh enough to consume and even some of that smells a bit ripe. Nevertheless, everyone has soon had their fill, aided by Carter finding stores of biscuits, crisps and such like stored away in other parts of the kitchen.

Carter is still filling his face while the others prepare to move out, and still chewing when a deathly screech echoes up the stairs and into the kitchen.

"They're inside the building," Josh says urgently, already moving across the kitchen.

The door out of the kitchen leads into an oversized banqueting room where guests with deep pockets are catered for before showtime. All the tables are set, and they wonder what event had to be cancelled on the day of the outbreak. The wondering is short-lived. Sound vibrations from beyond the kitchen draw closer. It is only a matter of time before their hunters find the kitchen. Nobody needs to be told that the undead won't be stopping to see what they can find to eat inside the kitchen. The only produce they are interested in requires a pulse.

The banqueting room is spanned by wall-to-ceiling windows that provide a fantastic view of the stadium. The hallowed turf, surrounded by some ninety thousand predominantly red seats, has become overgrown since the Wembley area was evacuated. Who's to say whether the grass will ever be cut again, never mind whether a football match will ever be played again in the famous stadium.

Josh tries the handle of one of the glass doors that are built into the wall of glass to see if they can escape that way into the stadium. The door is locked and, short of smashing the glass, there is no escape into the stadium that

74

way. He could easily shatter one of the panes of glass, but that would mean their position would be given away, and so he looks for a different option.

"This way," Alice shouts under her breath, as pans clatter in the kitchen.

Quietly and without question, the three men follow Alice through a door at the side of the long room. As they pass the bar, Turner eyes it longingly. What would he give for a stiff drink right now? The spirits-containing optics mounted at head height that are locked behind a mesh screen to keep them safe tease Turner as he passes.

"Keep going," Josh says, as he gets through the door. He knows it will only be a matter of seconds before Rabids emerge from the kitchen.

Alice hurries down the long corridor with Josh behind her and Turner bringing up the rear. They speed past various doors: some are entrances to toilets and others to what look like private boxes. All the doors are ignored in order to put as much distance as possible between themselves and the banqueting room while they can.

Alice stops when they arrive at the end of the corridor and find themselves at a junction. Stairs lead both up and down and there is a door on their right.

"The door must lead out into the stadium," Alice guesses, trying the handle but finding the door locked.

"That's where we need to get. This place is a rabbit warren," Josh says.

"We can't afford the noise of breaking the lock. Not here and now," Alice tells Josh.

"I know," he agrees.

"Let's try the stairs up," Turner says. "At least we'll be out of their direct line of sight then."

Carter turns and is the first to use the stairs. This time there is a fire door at the top and Carter pushes straight through it, only to find another long corridor.

"This is getting ridiculous," Carter says. "We'll be lost at this rate."

"I feel like the walls are closing in," Turner admits, looking at another door that must lead out into the stadium. "Try that door," he orders Carter, but it too is locked.

"Hold this," Turner tells Josh, handing him his rifle.

As soon as Josh has taken the weapon off Turner, Turner proceeds to rip his combat vest off and drop it onto the floor. He then takes off the sand-coloured light sweater he has on underneath the vest.

"Wrap it tight," Josh advises Turner, as he wraps the jumper around the muzzle of his rifle, which is still in Josh's hands.

"That'll do," Turner says, when he is satisfied with his makeshift silencer.

Turner's bullet smashes into the lock, disintegrating it. The blast from the rifle is dampened but a loud crack still rings out. Without much effort, Carter pulls the door open and, to everyone's relief, fresh air wafts into the corridor.

"Thank God for that," Turner says, filling his lungs as he unwraps his sweater from his rifle's muzzle.

"I can't believe how dark it is already," Carter says, looking out over the dim stadium.

"I've just thought: what happened to the music?" Alice asks. "It's stopped."

"Who knows, but it's another thing to be thankful for," Josh replies, as Turner pulls a now-singed sweater back on.

76

"Okay, let's move out," Turner orders, as he fastens the Velcro on his combat vest. "We'll take it easy. I'll lead. We don't know what's in this stadium," he adds.

"It's big enough to hide just about anything," Carter says, as Turner moves towards the door.

Outside the door and down a flight of steps is a concrete wall, designed to keep the riff-raff out of the VIP areas. Dusk has well and truly set in, especially inside the towering bowl of the stadium. Turner steps out and descends the steps to the wall to scope the full majesty of the stadium before him. Even in the fading light and with empty seats it is impressive. Turner can only imagine what it would be like at full tilt, after a goal has been scored or just as the band of the day walk out on stage.

"Look!" Alice says urgently, pulling Turner out of his daydreams of goals and rock concerts.

"What is it?" Turner almost snaps.

"That must be the large dining room we were in. I can see shadows moving behind the glass," Alice tells him, pointing.

Turner follows Alice's arm to where it is pointing, back around the curve of the stadium. His eyes focus on the wide expanse of glass and, sure enough, he sees movement in the darkness. He is sure that it's the undead he can see and he can only hope that is where they will stay.

"That's them alright," Carter says, never lost for words.

"What's the plan?" Josh asks, as if Turner knows what they are going to do next.

"Suggestions," Turner replies. "We are supposed to be pushing the infected back to the quarantine zone. Not hiding in here."

"We had no choice but to retreat," Alice insists.

"She's right," Josh confirms. "The rest of our squad were down and we were being overwhelmed. We had no choice."

"I agree, but what do we do now?" Turner replies.

"I suggest we get over to the back of the stadium and see what's happening there," Alice offers.

"Other troops were supposed to be arriving to reinforce us. Maybe they have arrived and we can join up with them. Surely they would come in from the back?" Josh adds.

"And hopefully in greater numbers, with more firepower!" Carter says.

"Okay. Agreed," Turner replies.

"Which way? Across the pitch or around the seats?" Josh questions.

"We go over this wall and around the seats: there's more cover that way. If we go pitch-side, we'll be completely exposed," Turner says, looking at the terrain.

"I agree. I'm not sure how we'd get down onto the pitch from here anyway. Let's move and see what we find," Josh encourages.

"Cover me," Turner orders, and looks over the wall.

There is only a small drop over the wall and all four are quickly down and in amongst the lower seating areas. Turner takes them right, through the narrow walkway in-between the seats. He ducks down occasionally, underneath railings, to take them into the next section. They are quickly approaching the long side of the stadium. Progress is good but, the further they move around, the more visible they will be to the undead that followed them into the stadium.

"Keep your heads down," Turner orders. "We are moving into their line of sight."

As soon as Turner speaks the words, a bang sounds behind them. The noise is coming from the same position where they climbed down the wall. Nobody needs to be told to take cover, and they all drop behind the seating in front of them.

"Have they have found the open door?" Alice asks, peeking over the top of a seat.

"They must have," Josh replies, doing the same.

"There's one," Carter announces quietly.

Sure enough, a figure moves in the darkness right behind the piece of wall where the door they came through is situated. If it wasn't for the few safety lights that are illuminated around the bowl of the stadium, they would never be able to see the threat. They watch as other shadows move to join the first figure and, within moments, a pack of undead have squeezed into the space, their faces looking out over the stadium.

"What do we do now?" Carter whispers. "If we move, they'll see us."

Suddenly, before anyone can offer a solution to their dilemma, and without warning, an ear-piercing screech reverberates in the void of the stadium. The incessant noise echoes in every crevice, drilling into their brains, making them cower lower behind the seating in front of them.

Finally, and thankfully, the chilling noise cuts off, leaving them all stunned, in no doubt of the danger that they find themselves in. None of them dare to move for fear of being seen by the bloodthirsty pack of undead creatures.

Josh tries to regain his composure, telling himself that he should be used to their deathly screams by now. His concentration almost makes him oblivious to the vibrating that has begun in his pocket, next to his thigh. All at once, the vibration registers with him and he dares to reach for his pocket to pull out his phone.

The word 'Dad' is illuminated on the phone's screen. Josh gasps in surprise, the word filling him with hope and optimism. Josh moves his thumb towards the screen to answer. He hadn't expected it to be his dad calling but there is no one in the world right now that he would prefer it to be.

"What the fuck?" Turner snaps under his breath from beside Josh, as Josh's thumb moves to answer the call. In the same instant, a hand moves across the light, slapping itself into place over his phone and cutting off the light. Josh's stomach drops horribly, as he looks timidly at Alice, the owner of the hand. He knows his mistake immediately, a mistake that could prove fatal for them all.

"They've seen it. They're coming over the wall. Fucking idiot." Turner spits, at the same time as another deathly screech shrills out into the air. "Run. We need to find a defensive position."

"Where? There are none that I can see," Carter blurts in fear.

Without warning, a deafening short volley of gunfire erupts from just over the top of the seats in front of them. Flashes of light burst into the darkness from the rifle's muzzle. The shots ring out in the empty stadium, ricocheting around the expanse before bouncing back off the overhanging roof to accost their ears again.

Alice isn't sure it is the right course of action, despite seeing her bullets hit their target. She has been trained to lay down covering fire before moving under enemy assault and she trusts in her training. Alice understands her training didn't account for undead zombies. The noise may attract more creatures, but their position is already compromised, and it might give them something else to think about.

As soon as she has released her burst of covering fire, Alice is up on her feet, ready to chase after Turner. Josh is in a daze next to her, mortified by his error, and she grabs hold of him to pull him into action. Thankfully, Josh moves, helped in no small part by Carter's eagerness to evacuate their position and by him pushing Josh from behind.

Ahead of them, Turner stops suddenly to turn and lay down some covering fire of his own. Automatically, he tries to zero in on the area of the wall from where the attack came. The darkness doesn't help him in finding his target, and neither does the increasing distance. He urgently looks for movement and quickly finds it, but not at the wall. Turner fires into the seats below the low wall where creatures are falling over the backs of seats, and over themselves, as they try to tackle the new, unfamiliar terrain they find themselves in.

Turner might laugh at the carry-on that is taking place as he fires another short volley. He might, if it wasn't for the constant movement of the creatures that are streaming down to join in the melee.

Alice is soon approaching Turner, but he doesn't turn to lead them on. He makes the others wait for a second while he unclips a grenade from his combat vest, with a glint in his eye.

The grenade's spring-loaded lever flicks into the air with a ping, separating itself from the body of the grenade. The lever tumbles through the air but, before it hits the ground, Turner has launched his fist-sized explosive into the air. Turner's throw is impressive, possibly up there with the best this sports stadium has ever seen. None of them can help but watch the grenade soar across the stadium, and all of them are in no doubt where it will land.

White and yellow light bursts out as soon as the grenade hits something solid. The bright flash illuminates Wembley Stadium in explosive light for an instant. The blast rips into the seating area at the perfect point, right in the centre of the infected horde. Pieces of plastic and flesh of the undead erupt into the air, the fireball taking the pieces high into the air. The explosion mushrooms in every direction, searing backwards to the wall, where it is forced upwards to obliterate even more of the creatures that are waiting to jump down.

"Bloody good shot," Carter congratulates. "Let me have a go," he insists.

"Negative, Private. Save them. We're gonna need them," Turner orders coolly, basking in his glory for a moment before he turns to press on.

Josh, who is equally impressed with Turner's throw, decides to take the initiative himself. He may have made a mistake earlier, but that mistake might just be their salvation. Without asking permission, Josh takes his phone out of his pocket while he follows Alice in front of him and proceeds to call his father.

Turner glances back towards his triumph but, as he does, he sees Josh looking at his phone. Turner sees red immediately, wondering what the fuck Josh thinks he is doing. Doesn't he know he's already put them all in imminent danger?

"Put that fucking phone away, you idiot. Are you trying to get us all killed?" Turner demands, almost going for Josh.

Josh sees the anger in Turner's eyes as he lifts the phone to his ear, unrelenting. *He looks about ready to rip my head off*, Josh thinks, as he sees Turner go for him.

"Alice, it's my dad trying to get hold of me," Josh says, putting his up arm to fend Turner off. "Tell him!"

Alice understands Josh's words immediately and places herself in-between Josh and the oncoming Turner.

"Your dad? Are you for real, fuckwit?" Turner seethes, whilst being held back by Alice.

Josh ignores Turner as the phone rings but, just as the ringing stops and the phone is answered, it is whipped out of Josh's hand. Josh spins around to see Carter grasping the phone in his sweaty hand, with a look of anger on his face to match Turner's.

"You really are a fuckwit," Carter says quite calmly, and he presses the phone's screen to end the call. "We haven't got time for you to speak to your dad. That grenade won't slow them down for long."

"I'm not an idiot, Carter. My dad is Captain Richards. He's SAS and he can help us. The only thing slowing us down is this discussion. Now give me the phone back," Josh demands.

"Yeah and my dad's Santa-fucking-Claus," Carter retorts, undeterred by Josh's information.

"He's telling the truth. His dad is SAS, and he can help us." Alice directs her statement to Turner.

Screeches from the undead stop the discussion in its tracks and all four of them turn back to the site of the grenade's explosion.

Through the remaining smoke haze, dark shadows move ominously. The threat appears distant and removed at first. Right up until the first shadow emerges out of the haze. The fearsome creature leaps forwards out of the carnage and lands astride the tops of two seats, balancing itself with ease, its eyes fixed on their position. More creatures become clearly visible behind the first, these ones lower down, standing in amongst the wreckage of the explosion. The numbers build and then, without warning, the beast up high on the seat leaps again, expertly landing astride two more seats. The distance it travels is astonishing, but this time it doesn't pause, it launches itself again even higher and further. As it takes its third leap, they all understand with dread that, within just a few more bounds, the terrifying creature will leave the seats behind and land on the green turf below. Once it does it will inevitably tear across the pitch until it is within striking distance of their position, its cohorts close behind.

"Carter, give him his phone back," Turner orders sternly, before turning to run.

Josh takes the phone from Carter, holds it in his grasp and takes off after Alice, who is close behind Turner. Carter chases after them all, all their arguments forgotten in the face of their fearsome new foe.

Chapter 6

Lieutenant Winters notices General Cox looking at him with suspicion. But as soon as their eyes meet across the hold of the helicopter, she diverts her gaze towards the window of the hold door. Winters keep his eyes on the general for a moment and he notices her eyeballs flick back in his direction to see if he is still looking at her.

Winters wonders what is going through Cox's mind. He knows all too well about her steely and unforgiving determination. He won't allow her striking good looks or flowing blonde hair to fool him although currently her hair looks as if it could hide a mouse in its midst. She has been burnt by Andy's outburst and her reaction to his rejection of her authority must not be underestimated. She will push back; Winters is sure of it. He can only hope that she doesn't decide that he is the easy target.

"Are you okay, Sam?" Winters asks into his headset. He sees that she is uneasy and unsure about what is in store for her.

"Yes, thank you, Lieutenant," Sam replies, keeping things formal.

"We won't be in the air for long," Winters tells her, quickly deciding that Sam's decision to keep things formal in their current situation is a good play on her part. "Have you been to Porton Down before?" he asks, playing along with her.

"Yes, Lieutenant, you know I have. I told you earlier, remember?" Sam answers, abruptly.

"Oh, yes. I'd forgotten you'd mentioned it," Winters replies, somewhat surprised by Sam's demeanour. *Perhaps she isn't acting with me?* Winters thinks. *Maybe she is biding her time to see which way things go when we land?*

To further confuse Winters, Sam cuts off their conversation by lifting her phone to look at it. He feels Cox's eye on him as he stares at Sam's face, which is illuminated by her phone's screen. After a moment's staring, Winters pulls out his own phone in an effort to appear unconcerned, even though he knows Cox has already dismissed him from her focus.

What is this effect Sam has on me? Winters ponders, as he continues to pretend that he is interested in the screen on his phone. *What do I expect her to do?* he asks himself, *bat her eyelids and blow kisses over to me, while we fly through the air?* He laughs at himself for acting so immaturely and he actually clicks his phone to find something of interest. Unfortunately, though, even the dire reading on the BBC News app doesn't stop the churning in his stomach or stop his eyes flicking up occasionally to look at Sam.

Winters has soon had enough depression and slips his phone away. Instead, after one last look round the hold, he puts his head back to rest his eyes and think. He won't get another opportunity to prepare himself for whatever scenario presents itself when they land. His thoughts are a jumbled mess, however, overridden by those for Andy and the plight of his family and, yes, Sam. His attempts to concentrate are further disturbed when General Cox's voice sounds through his headset, asking the pilot to put her onto a private channel.

Cox's request raises Winters' suspicions further. He opens his eyes to casually look at the time on his watch whilst also just happening to look over to Cox for a long moment. There is no deciphering what the general is discussing or with whom and he quickly gives up, closing his eyes again. *Cox didn't look at me once, so maybe I'm not the subject of her conversation*, Winters thinks, finally focusing on something useful. *Why would I be the subject? Andy's actions towards Cox weren't my fault. Am I just being paranoid? There may be nothing to worry about when we land. Cox knows what an asset I am so, sure, she will want me close at hand.*

Winters' thoughts quickly revert to Sam, his usual sharp concentration appearing to have deserted him.

He happened to notice, when he 'looked at his watch', that Sam was still frowning at her phone's screen. *Is there more going on with her than I have considered?* Winters thinks. He tells himself that he needs to remember that, whilst his crush on her may be growing uncontrollably, he hardly knows her. She might have family in harm's way that she hasn't mentioned to him. Or, worse, family that have been directly infected by the outbreak. She may have lost loved ones to the horror. All these things might be concerning her more than ensuring that she doesn't hurt his feelings or pay him insufficient attention.

He also must not forget that Sam is a spook working for the intelligence services. She claims that she was seconded from GCHQ but that could easily be a cover story. She could just as easily be an MI5 or MI6 agent, planted to spy on the military's response to the outbreak. If anyone should know the games the intelligence services like to play it should be me. I've had enough dealings with them in my time.

Winters fidgets in his seat, ordering himself to stop thinking about it. He is clouding his own mind with all this second guessing about one woman, when there are far bigger problems to think about. *Like helping to save the country for one!* he reminds himself.

Deciding to take his 'relationship' with Sam as it comes, Winters relaxes slightly and lets his mind wander onto other, more pressing, matters.

His mind hasn't wandered far before the pilot's voice sounds in his headset, informing his passengers that they are approaching Porton Down. His eyes creak open and he sees that he isn't the only one who has decided to take the opportunity to have a snooze. Both General Cox and Sam's heads lift wearily from the back of their seats at the sound of the updated information.

Sam gives Winters an enticing smile as she repositions herself in her seat and stretches her arms out. Her arms flop back down as she leans forwards to check that the cool box containing Andy's medical samples is still at her feet, which it is. Winters doesn't return Sam's smile, deciding instead to try to play it cool.

Sure enough, in no time at all, the pilot has landed the helicopter and killed its engines. Winters barely looked out of the window on their descent, already familiar with the terrain. He also adopts a nonplussed demeanour as they exit the helicopter into the security compound, which is watched over by machine gun placements. In fact, he passes through the security check with its cameras that scan them to see if they are infected, then travels out of the compound without muttering a word.

Once outside the gate, as they wait for the shuttle to transport them to Porton Down, Winters realises something.

He has arrived back completely empty-handed. They all have. Cox stands with only the clothes she has arrived in and Sam has nothing more than the cool box in her hand.

Winters can't help but think of his flight case, stranded back in the depths of Station Zero, surrounded by carnage and the undead. Basically, he has lived out of a flight case for longer than he cares to remember. All his essentials are contained in the undersized case, as well as the few meagre luxuries he could manage to fit inside it. Before he can even consider grabbing a shower, which he desperately needs, he needs to locate a change of clothes because the ones he is wearing are soiled, to say the least. He also needs a toothbrush, together with some toothpaste.

The shuttle ride is quiet: nobody says a word during it. Winters suspects that the two women riding with him are thinking about their own missing belongings, the same as he is. Or are they thinking that they are lucky to have made it back to Porton Down alive, as he should be?

As they leave the shuttle, two military personnel form the welcoming committee for their return. The first is a tall, haggard-looking man, who looks like he hasn't slept in a week. Winters watches as the man, his uniform displaying the insignia of a colonel, greets General Cox with a salute. The colonel pays Winters and Sam no attention, his eyes fixed instead on Cox. Beside the colonel, his accomplice is towered over by her much taller counterpart. A rather round woman who has gained the rank of captain follows the colonel's lead by saluting. General Cox returns the salutes, which Winters is also forced to perform to his superior officers.

"Thank God you've made it back safely, Ma'am. A shocking turn of events at the facility," the colonel says to Cox, in all sincerity.

"Thank you, Colonel Thomas. It was shocking, with some sad losses," Cox replies.

"Indeed, Ma'am. Colonel Taylor and Major Rees will be sorely missed. Both personally and professionally," Thomas insists.

"Yes, they will. But there will be time enough to remember them. Right now, we need to concentrate on our work. Thankfully we made it out with the patient's biopsies, which Sam here is kindly carrying," says Cox, looking down at the cool box that Sam is holding. "Please get them straight into storage."

"Of course, Ma'am," Colonel Thomas replies, but he doesn't make any attempt to take the cool box off Sam when she offers it up. Only after an awkward moment's pause does the captain beside Thomas suddenly jump into action and belatedly take the cool box in her hands, an embarrassed expression on her face.

"Thank you, Captain," Cox says, as the handover is made. "Prepare the lab, Colonel. I expect the work to begin as soon as possible. I will be overseeing proceedings after I have freshened up and had something to eat."

"Absolutely, Ma'am. However, I'm afraid that General Byron instructed me to inform you that he is expecting you to report to him as soon as you arrive, Ma'am. In person, Ma'am," Thomas tells Cox, nervously.

"I'm sure he did, Colonel. But I will be freshening up and eating before I do anything. Please inform him that I will report to him as soon as I have. Understood?" Cox replies, as a matter of fact.

"Of course, Ma'am. I will relay that to him as soon as I return," Taylor replies.

"Thank you, Colonel. Dismissed," Cox finishes.

Winters and Sam watch in silence as General Cox's welcoming committee do an about-turn and march off towards Porton Down's main square. Colonel Thomas leads the way, his captain struggling to keep up behind him. Not only is the poor woman considerably shorter than the lanky colonel, but she also has the cool box banging against her leg to contend with.

"Right, you two," General Cox says, turning towards Winters and Sam. "What am I going to do with you two?"

"Ma'am. I would like to assist you in any way I can. I think you will need all the help you can get, especially with Matt, your assistant, no longer being with us," Winters volunteers.

"I am sure you would, Lieutenant Winters. The question is, can you be trusted?" Cox questions.

"I don't know what gives you the impression I can't be, Ma'am? I have done everything you've asked and helped in any way I can. I don't control Captain Richards, Ma'am. He is his own man," Winters protests.

"But are you playing both sides, I wonder?" Cox presses.

"As far as I am concerned, there are no sides, Ma'am. The only side is fighting this infection. If my relationship with Captain Richards makes you doubt that then I apologise, Ma'am. I believe Captain Richards has a central role to play in our fightback. He is a loose cannon sometimes, yes, but vital nevertheless, Ma'am," Winters replies, sincerely.

"Indeed, Lieutenant. And what about you, Sam?" Cox asks, shifting her gaze.

"Same for me, General," Sam answers, after a moment's pause.

General Cox looks at Winters and Sam for an awkward amount of time in silence, considering. After switching her gaze from Winters to Sam and back again several times she finally speaks.

"Very well. Lieutenant Winters, you will take over Matt's duties, for the time being. I haven't the time or inclination to find another alternative right now. We have a lot of work to do, including welcoming Captain Richards' family here, by all accounts.

"Sam, I think I will keep you close at hand also, if you are willing to stick around? As I've said, we have a lot to do," Cox decides.

"Of course, General. I am more than willing to do what I can to help," Sam replies.

"Thank you, Ma'am," Winters responds.

"Good. Make yourselves presentable then and meet me in the square in one hour," Cox orders and, with that, she turns away to make her own way into Porton Down.

Winters and Sam remain motionless for a moment, simply watching Cox go, as they both try to work out their next move.

"Shall we get some food?" Winters finally asks.

"Lead the way, Lieutenant. I'm starving," Sam replies.

The mess hall is busy and it is a relief to go outside again after their food. They had spotted Cox sitting on the other side of the hall. The general didn't see them, however. She only had eyes for the meal in front of her.

"We'd better get a move on," Sam tells Winters, as they leave.

"I've got to get a new uniform before I can go back to my room," Winters tells Sam.

"Where are you going to get one of those now?" Sam asks.

"It won't be a problem. The army will provide," Winters replies, hoping.

"What block are you in?" Sam asks.

"Block A6. And you?" Winters asks.

"I'm in the same," Sam replies in surprise.

"That's handy," Winters says, smiling.

"Yes, isn't it? I'm in room 344," Sam says with what Winters thinks is a cheeky smile and he immediately makes a mental note of the number.

"You're on the floor below me then," Winters tells her, nervously.

"Am I? What's your number then?" Sam asks.

"Mine is 48... 7," Winters says falteringly, blushing.

"We are close then," Sam tells Winters.

"Yes, so you'd better keep your music down!" Winters says, immediately regretting his terrible joke.

"We had better get back to shower and change. We don't want to be late for General Cox," Sam suggests, still smiling at an awkward Winters.

"You carry on. I've got to go this way to get a uniform and some supplies," Winters tells Sam.

"I've only got a few things left in my room, but enough to get me by for now," Sam admits. "Did you really take everything to Station Zero with you?"

"Yes, I'm afraid so. Habit, I suppose. I'd only just managed to resupply after escaping London as well," Winters tells her.

"At least you're well practised at it then," Sam giggles.

"I am, but it's going to be a rush this time," Winters replies, checking his watch.

"You'd better jump to it then, Lieutenant."

"Yes, I had," Winters agrees. "I'll see you later."

"Not that much later," Sam giggles again, as she walks off in the direction of block A6.

Winters watches for a moment as Sam walks away before rolling his eyes, turning and heading off in the opposite direction.

Chapter 7

Even after rushing around, Winters admits to himself that he almost feels like a new man after finally having had a shower. Luckily, he knew exactly where to go to get his new uniform and his other bits and pieces. If he hadn't, he would have stood no chance of being on time. He realises he is cutting it fine now, despite restricting his allotted time in the shower. The last thing Winters wants is to be late for his first appointment in his new position working for Cox.

Moving at double time, Winters makes it to the rendezvous in the square with only seconds to spare. He sees that General Cox and Sam are chatting while they wait for him. Winters suspects that he could well be the subject of the two women's conversation, a suspicion that is reinforced when the chat stops as soon as he arrives.

"Cutting it fine aren't you, Lieutenant?" Cox says, while Winters pants for breath.

"Yes, Ma'am. Sorry, Ma'am, I had to locate some supplies," Winters replies.

"No need to explain, Lieutenant. Sam has filled me in while we waited," Cox tells him, confirming his suspicions.

"Very good, Ma'am," Winters says, wondering if his uniform is all that they had discussed.

"Right then, we'd better not keep General Byron waiting any longer," Cox says, and begins to walk towards the main building.

Cox is right, Winters thinks, as they walk. Byron is famous for his short temper: even Colonel Reed would have thought twice about making Byron wait. In fact, Byron is one of the only people that Winters ever saw Reed kowtow to.

Cox leads them into the building and takes them up to the floor where her office is. The last time Winters was here was with Major Rees, the night before they left for Station Zero, he remembers, as he and Sam wait outside while Cox goes into her office. Winters has a tinge of sadness when he thinks about Rees, even though they never really saw eye to eye.

Cox emerges from her office sporting a pair of spectacles and carrying an expensive-looking leather bag. Winters is sure she had an identical bag in her possession when they travelled to Station Zero. Winters wonders whether the general is so organised that she had a spare one stored in her office. She must have, he decides, and he wouldn't be surprised if the replacement contained an exact copy of whatever documents and personal belongings were in the other one.

I might need to up my game, Winters tells himself, as he follows General Cox, who is striding through the building. He suddenly feels totally unprepared: he hasn't even got a pen and paper with him to take notes, his satchel having been lost in the bowels of Station Zero.

After a short walk down a corridor they arrive at what Winters assumes must be General Byron's office area. There are two rooms, both with closed doors, and a waiting area complete with a youngish woman sitting behind a desk, who must be Byron's personal assistant.

"General Cox, how good it is to see you. We were so worried when we heard," Byron's assistant greets Cox, looking away from her computer screen with a smile.

"Thank you, Becky. We had a close call, a very close call," Cox replies.

"Apparently so. I've heard all about it. You must have been terrified," Becky observes.

"It wasn't pleasant," Cox tells her. "Is General Byron ready to see me?"

"I'll check," the receptionist says, reaching for a phone on the desk. "Please go right in," Cox is told after a moment.

"Sam, wait here please," Cox asks, before turning towards the widest door off the reception area.

Winters takes his cue and follows General Cox. It doesn't surprise him that Sam is asked to wait outside. She isn't military staff, after all.

"Ah, Jessica. Please take a seat," General Byron says, as they walk in. "I trust you are refreshed after your escapades in London?" he asks, barely looking up from the papers on the desk in front of him.

"Yes, thank you, Sir," Cox replies, whilst taking a seat in front of Byron's desk.

For a moment, Winters is unsure what to do with himself. He quickly forces himself to make a decision and takes one of the seats positioned at the back of the office, behind General Cox. Once settled, he has a quick look around the office, which is nothing special, before his eyes settle on General Byron.

General Sir Patrick Byron is an imposing figure, even in his position sat behind his desk. Winters knows for a fact that he is at least in his early sixties and his swept-back grey hair with matching long grey moustache do nothing to trim any years off his appearance. General Byron is the top-ranking general in the British Army. Although Cox is also referred to as a general, her official rank is major-general, two ranks below Byron's. In normal circumstances, his position would be considered honorary, he would just be someone to roll out on official occasions to meet dignitaries and sign 'important' papers. But these are not normal circumstances by any stretch of the imagination and Winters guesses he has been dragged back into the fray to actually make some meaningful decisions.

Winters has met General Byron before on a few occasions when he first became Colonel Reed's assistant, although he doubts whether Byron would remember their encounters. Back then, Byron was a major-general himself, and a formidable one at that. His résumé includes leading troops into the first Iraqi war as an officer and then commanding the second invasion of Iraq only thirteen years later.

"Would you like my report, Sir?" Cox questions.

"Not yet. We are waiting for the home secretary to join us. He is on his way down. The prime minister has asked him to report back," Byron informs Cox, who falls silent as she waits.

There is an awkward ten-minute wait for the home secretary's arrival. Byron continues working on the papers in front of him, without even offering his guests a drink. Cox sits patiently, as does Winters behind her, until General Byron's phone finally rings.

"He's here," Byron announces, with a hint of disdain, as he rises from his desk to greet the home secretary.

A second later the office door opens and a man who Winters has seen on television numerous times walks into Byron's office. Gerald Culvner is smaller than he appears when he is bullshitting the public on television. His tailored suit, immaculately brushed but thinning hair and pearly white smile do little to dispel Winters' notion of what an irritating man Culvner must be.

"Home Secretary, thank you for joining us," Byron says, coming around his desk to greet the politician.

"Good to see you again, General. I hope I'm not keeping you from anything," Culvner replies, shaking Byron's hand enthusiastically.

"Not at all. General Cox is ready to give us her report."

Nobody takes any notice of Winters as he stands at the back of the room, his arm extended just in case it is required to shake a hand. Culvner give Winters a cursory glance before taking a seat beside General Cox in front of Byron's desk.

"I hear that things didn't go to plan for you in London, General Cox," Culvner says, with a dose of fake sympathy.

"Not entirely, Home Secretary. I am pleased to report that the mission wasn't a complete loss, however..." Cox begins.

Winters sits and listens while General Cox gives a detailed report to her superiors. Impressively, she recounts the successes that her team had in the lab following the biopsies taken from the subject, Captain Richards. Winters is amazed when Cox produces a laptop from her leather bag and proceeds to play videos of the experiments carried out in the lab by Colonel Taylor and Major Rees. Videos that show mice being injected with a compound derived from

Andy's biopsies that were then introduced into a pen with other mice infected with the X5-1 virus.

To say that Cox is organised is an understatement, Winters decides. She arrived here barely an hour ago. Rescued by helicopter from the slaughter at Station Zero, with nothing but the clothes on her back. Yet here she is briefing the commander of the British Army and the home secretary in full detail, and with video evidence to boot. Winters definitely needs to up his game.

Following her description of the successes, Cox then recounts the mission's catastrophic demise in grizzly detail. She tells how Major Rees inexplicably became infected, turned into a raging monster and began the rampage that engulfed the entire Station Zero facility and, subsequently, the institute above it.

Cox doesn't whitewash over any details of the resulting carnage, no matter how savage. She describes their desperate escape to the helicopter and then Captain Richards' fury at her actions concerning his family, and his final ultimatum.

"So, despite your successes, Major-General, ultimately the mission was a failure and you allowed Richards to slip from your grasp," General Byron says harshly when Cox's report comes to an end.

"Sir, that is where we stand at this time, but..." Cox tries to speak but is cut off by Byron.

"Have you anything to add, Lieutenant Winters?" Byron asks, staring towards the back of the room.

Winters is taken aback when Byron addresses him directly. He hadn't realised that Byron even knew he was in the room, never mind the general recognising him and remembering his name. Winters is lost for words for a moment.

"Are you unable to speak without Colonel Reed's hand up your ass, Lieutenant?" Byron demands.

"Sir. Sorry, Sir. I was just surprised that you recognised me," Winters blurts in reply, conscious that both the home secretary and General Cox have turned to fix him in their gaze.

"Of course I recognise you. Do you take me for an idiot?" Byron barks.

"No, Sir, of course not," Winters answers, blood rushing to his face to make matters worse.

"Well, have you anything to add, Lieutenant?" Byron asks again.

"Sir, I think General Cox's report was accurate. The outbreak couldn't have been predicted and was unstoppable once it was under way. It was only by God's grace that any of us escaped the facility, Sir," Winters reports.

"I beg to differ, Lieutenant. An outbreak could have been predicted, should have been planned for and avoided at all costs," Byron retorts.

"Sir," Winters replies.

"And what about Captain Richards? I hear that you two are the best of buddies. Did you know what he was planning to do on the helicopter?" Byron asks bluntly.

"Sir, best of buddies is an overstatement. We have become familiar with each other since the outbreak happened and I think we have an understanding," Winters informs the general. "As to your question, no, I had no idea Captain Richards was going to do that on the helicopter. He didn't know himself until he found out about his daughter and he reacted to that information, Sir.

"As I believe General Cox was about to inform you, Sir," Winters continues, "all is not lost regarding Captain

CAPITAL FALLING 6 - BREAKOUT

Richards. His daughter and, er, his girlfriend are travelling to Porton Down as we speak. I believe that Captain Richards will arrive here under his own steam at some point to be with them, Sir."

"If he survives his latest escape into London, you mean?" Byron asks.

"Yes, Sir. That is an accurate assessment, Sir," Winters confirms.

"A complete balls-up from start to finish is my assessment," Byron barks.

"I might add, Sir, in his favour, Captain Richards does have another Special Forces' operator with him, that I know of," Winters says.

"One operator, Lieutenant. I don't think that will make much difference," Byron replies.

"If I may, General?" Culvner interrupts. "As the lieutenant said, all is not lost. As we speak, we have Captain Richards' samples available in the lab for further work. And it is entirely possible that Captain Richards will bring himself to Porton Down at some point. Do you agree, Lieutenant?"

"Yes, Home Secretary," Winters replies.

"Is there anything we can do to aid the captain's arrival, General?" Culver asks Byron.

"We can certainly try and locate him, Home Secretary, and insert more troops to bring him back," Byron answers.

"Well, let's do that," Culvner says, rising from his chair. "I will update the prime minister immediately. Thank you for your report, General Cox."

"Home Secretary," Cox replies, standing as Culvner turns to leave.

"I will speak to you shortly, General, for the latest," Culvner says to Byron, turning back. "Make sure you keep me abreast of any developments in the meantime."

"Of course, Home Secretary," Byron replies.

"Lieutenant," Culvner says, nodding his head at Winters as he leaves.

"Smarmy git!" Byron announces when Culvner has left and is well out of earshot.

"Sir," Cox replies, uncommittedly.

"General, continue your work on Captain Richards' samples. And no fuck-ups this time. Everyone gets scanned in and out of the laboratory, understood?" Byron orders.

"Understood, Sir," Cox replies.

"Make sure you have everything in place for when Richards arrives, if he arrives. We need to move quickly to gain any advantage. I will not have my grandchildren threatened by this outbreak. Is that clear?" Byron demands.

"Yes, Sir. Crystal clear," Cox assures.

"Make sure you are ready for Captain Richards' family to arrive. And treat them well. We don't want him pissed off when he sees them. I don't need to remind you how unpredictable he is when that happens, do I?" Byron asks.

"No, Sir," Cox responds.

"Carry on then," Byron tells Cox.

"Sir. What about locating Captain Richards and assisting him?" Cox asks.

"You leave that to me, General. You have your orders," Byron finishes.

Cox salutes Byron before she turns to leave but he is already sitting back behind his desk, fiddling with his moustache, looking down, concentrating on his papers.

Sam is bleary-eyed when Cox and Winters emerge from Byron's office. Winters suspects that Culvner leaving just before them has woken her up. Winters wouldn't mind a power nap himself; it has been a long and testing day. Something tells him that isn't going to happen, not any time soon.

Cox walks straight past the receptionist and Sam without saying a word. She keeps going until she arrives at her office and sits behind her desk, a look of annoyance on her face.

"How did it go?" Sam asks, as she and Winters follow Cox into her office.

"As well as can be expected," Cox replies, tempering her anger.

"That Culvner is a repulsive man, isn't he?" Sam says.

"Why do you say that?" Winters asks.

"He tried chatting me up on his way out," Sam informs them.

"I hope you gave him short shrift," Cox replies.

"I certainly did. I don't think he'll try it again," Sam tells Cox.

"I wouldn't count on it. He's tried it on with me more than once," Cox tells her, with a shiver of disgust.

"Politicians, eh?" Winters says.

"Indeed, Lieutenant," Cox agrees. "I'd also just like to thank you for backing me up in there. I don't think there was much more we could have done at Station Zero."

"Absolutely not, Ma'am. I agree, and there's no need to thank me," Winters replies.

"Okay, back to business," Cox says. "Lieutenant, we need to prepare for Captain Richards' family and I'm going to leave that task to you. I realise my mistake in taking them into custody and I think that it's best if I stay away from them. Wouldn't you agree?"

"It might be for the best, Ma'am. At least until they are settled in. I can make the arrangements and handle them if you wish," Winters agrees.

"I expect they will be arriving soon, so I will leave that to you, Lieutenant. I need to get over to the laboratory and oversee proceedings there. Sam, you will accompany me and help us process the data. Okay?" Cox says.

"Yes, General," Sam replies.

"Lieutenant, Matt's desk is the one outside this office. Please feel free to make use of it," Cox tells Winters, with a tinge of sadness.

"Thank you, Ma'am," Winters replies.

With that, General Cox makes sure she has everything she needs before getting up. She tells Winters to keep her informed of the expected arrival and then leads Sam out of the office and towards the exit off the floor.

Winters watches them leave before wandering over to his new desk. As would be expected, the desk is tidy and well organised. Winters pulls the chair out with a slight feeling of guilt.

Chapter 8

Winters makes himself busy, firstly registering his new position with the powers that be. He warns them of the pending arrival and wants to ensure he can be located when Catherine and the others do arrive. Next, he rings round to secure accommodation. Eventually, he is successful in securing two rooms in the same A6 block that he is staying in, one for Catherine and Emily and the other for Stacey and her mother, Karen. Winters wants them close at hand, just in case he is needed.

After contacting Sam to ask her to relay to General Cox that the arrangements have been made, Winters eases back in his seat. He takes the opportunity to survey his new surroundings properly, whilst beginning to think what is next in store for them all.

No sooner has he begun to think than the phone on his desk begins to ring. Upon picking up the phone, Winters is informed that his expected arrivals are at the main gate and passing through security. He is told that, once through security, they will be escorted to the carpark next to the main square and that he should be there to meet them.

Winters puts down the phone and sees, after checking his watch, that they have made good time. He then leaves his desk and makes his way out of the building and towards the main carpark.

The carpark is well lit but, unsurprisingly, very quiet. The Porton Down facility is in lockdown and nobody can arrive at the site or leave it without express permission. This makes it easy for Winters to see the car containing Catherine and the others as it pulls into the carpark, behind their escort. He sees them find a vacant space, which they pull into, and then rushes across to them.

After parking, the car's engine dies. Winters stands waiting at the back of the car, not wanting to crowd its occupants, who he knows will be exhausted and probably confused. He signals to the escort car that he will take over and it pulls away, soon disappearing out of sight and earshot.

Through the back window, Winters sees movement but none of the doors pop open. Understanding that Andy's daughter will need some reassurance, and possibly calming, after the security process, not to mention the ordeal she is living through, he continues to wait patiently.

Eventually, just as Winters begins to wonder whether everything is okay inside the car, the driver's door opens and Catherine appears.

Catherine sees Winters waiting for them and attempts a smile. Under normal circumstances, a smile from Catherine is enough to brighten anybody's mood. Sadly, Winters can't help but think how drained she looks in this instance, however. Her face barely lifts to follow her mouth's attempt at a greeting. Her radiance has deserted her. Winters completely understands why.

"Hello, Robert. It's good to see you," Catherine says, as Winters approaches to see if she needs any help.

"And you, Catherine. Sorry it's under such difficult circumstances again. How is everyone?"

"Tired and hungry," Catherine replies, unsurprisingly.

"I can imagine. It's been another testing day all round," Winters says.

"Yes, it has. I'm looking forward to thanking this General Cox in person for putting us through it. Didn't she have the guts to meet us herself?" Catherine scorns.

"I'm afraid that she is busy," Winters tells Catherine anxiously, wondering how she knows of General Cox.

"I'm sure she is. We will discuss her later. Right now, I think we just need to eat and get some rest. Is that on the itinerary?" Catherine asks, as she goes to open the back door of the car.

"Absolutely," Winters answers. "I have made arrangements for you to stay in two rooms in the same block I'm staying in. I can also arrange for some food to be delivered if you'd prefer?"

"That will be great, thank you. I don't think we've got the energy to eat out," Catherine replies.

"Hello, Lieutenant Winters," a young voice says from inside the car.

Winters looks down to see Emily emerging from the car. The poor girl's tired appearance is obvious as soon as he sees her. His heart goes out to her when he thinks about all that she has been through during the days since the outbreak began.

"Hello, Emily. How are you?" Winters replies.

"I'm okay, thanks. Have you heard from my dad or brother?" Emily asks, with a look of anticipation.

"I'm afraid not. But rest assured I will do all that I can to help them as soon as we do," Winters tells Emily, who is immediately disappointed by his answer.

"I know you will," Emily says, looking down at the ground.

On the other side of the car, Winters greets Stacey and introduces himself to her mother, Karen. Both say hello and move round to the back of the car, ready to depart. Catherine slams her door shut and follows Emily as she also leaves the car behind.

The walk to block A6 is a quiet one. Winters helps with their luggage. A few questions are asked about Porton Down and Winters tries to make them familiar with some of the site's layout. He makes sure they know where the convenience store and mess hall are in the main square. He doesn't fill their heads with too much information; he doubts they would absorb much detail in their tired state.

By the time they have entered the block and found their rooms on the third floor, Emily is walking like a zombie, as only tired children can. Winters wonders if she will even be awake by the time he has arranged for their food to be delivered.

"I've managed to get you two rooms together with an interconnecting door," Winters tells them, as he opens the first door and gives Catherine the key.

"We're allowed the key," Catherine says, with a look of surprise, as she takes it.

"You are free to move around the facility," Winters tells her. "Many places and areas will be off-limits, but that is the same for most of the people stationed here, including me. Everything you will need is based in the main square. I expect you need some supplies now. If you give me a list, I will make sure you get them. Toiletries, water, even clothes, just let me know. You haven't got to do it now. Text me and I will make arrangements."

"Thank you, Robert," Catherine says. "Can you arrange for the food right away, so that we can get some rest?"

"Of course," Winters replies.

As soon as they are settled in, and Winters has their meal orders, he leaves them to it. He sees that they are all shattered and the best thing they can do right now is rest. On the way back to his desk he stops by the mess hall and arranges for the food to be sent up to them. He also stops by the convenience store and arranges for some essentials to be delivered to the new arrivals.

Once he has taken care of everything, and has arrived back at his desk, he phones Sam to update her. She tells Winters that nothing is happening where she is. That she is just hanging around while General Cox goes about her business overseeing the work that is getting under way on Andy's biopsy samples. Sam tells him that she is worn out herself and can't wait to get into bed. Winters tells her the same before they say their goodbyes and the call is ended.

Winters must admit to himself that he is drained and is sorely tempted to take a snooze where he is sitting. He forces his eyes open and discounts any thoughts of sleeping at his desk. The area may be quiet now, but anyone can arrive while he is snoring and dribbling. He can imagine how General Byron would react if he found him sleeping on the job. It wouldn't be good.

Instead, after a time, Winters wearily pushes himself to his feet and goes off to find himself a coffee, in the hope that it will give him some energy. The building is quiet, with most staff having clocked off for the night, and Winters arrives back at his desk in no time, nursing his hot drink. He sits back down and wonders if there is anything he can do to keep his mind occupied and awake while he takes his first sips of the hot liquid.

He decides that his first task should be to see if he can get hold of Andy. *God only knows what situation Andy finds himself in now*, Winters thinks, as he taps his phone's screen. Andy's phone rings out but, just as Winters looks away in frustration, it begins to vibrate in his hand. His eyes dart back to the screen, but he sees that it isn't Andy ringing him.

"Hello, Catherine. How are you all settling in?" Winters asks, upon answering the call.

"Fine, thank you. We have eaten and the other three have gone virtually straight to sleep," Catherine tells him.

"I'm surprised that you haven't," Winters replies.

"Me too. But I can't sleep, I'm too worried about Andy. I can't get through to him on his phone," Catherine informs Winters.

"I've just this second tried calling him myself. His phone rang out with no answer," Winters says.

"I'm so worried," Catherine replies.

"I expect you are. I will contact you if I hear anything. I promise," Winters assures.

"I know you will, Robert," Catherine says. "Can you tell me what is expected of us while we're here? Have they any plans?"

"Not that I know of, Catherine. As far as I know, they are just accommodating you at Andy's request, and probably out of guilt," Winters replies.

"They should be guilty. A good man is dead because of their actions. General Cox has a lot to answer for," Catherine says angrily.

"So I've heard. A very unfortunate situation indeed," Winters concedes, flinching at Catherine's mention of General Cox again. He knows that trouble is brewing between Catherine and Cox. He also knows that he is likely to be caught up in the crossfire.

"An unfortunate situation?" Catherine says, forcefully. "I will make sure those two men are brought to justice, you can be sure of that. Wait until I see this Cox woman."

"Be careful there, Catherine. General Cox is in a powerful position, and this might not be the best time to butt heads with her. Especially with Andy in harm's way."

"I can't let this go, Robert. They shot a man who was only trying to protect us from being abducted and then they just left him there for his family to find," Catherine seethes.

"I'm not suggesting you let it go, Catherine. I'm just saying that think about how you go about bringing them to justice. Rather than antagonising General Cox right now, perhaps choose your moment and go through the proper channels," Winters suggests.

"You mean go to the police?" Catherine asks.

"That is certainly an option. But you may need General Cox on your side for the time being. If Andy needs our help, it will be on her say-so I'm afraid and, at the moment, you have the upper hand," Winters reasons.

"The upper hand? What do you mean?" Catherine questions.

"You have a card to play if you need to. Causing a stink with General Cox now could do more harm than good and weaken our position with Andy. I'm not telling you what to do, but perhaps it's better to think about it and bide your time," Winters replies.

The phone line goes silent for a minute, as Catherine thinks.

"Okay," Catherine finally says. "I won't report it now, but this isn't something I'm going to forget. I can't."

"And nor should you, but I think it's the right play for now," Winters says with some relief, as his phone begins to buzz again. "I've got to go, Catherine; I've got a call coming through."

"Okay. Please let me know if you hear anything about Andy, no matter what the time is," Catherine asks quickly.

"I will, and we'll speak tomorrow if I don't hear anything," Winters replies and he lowers his phone to see that it is Sam who is trying to reach him.

Winters isn't sure if he will cut Catherine off as she is still talking, but he switches calls in any case.

"Hi, Sam. What's happening?" Winters asks, urgently.

"Nothing much," Sam replies. "General Cox asked to tell you that we're finishing up here for the night and that you should also. She said to be back at your desk at 0700," Sam tells him.

"Oh, okay. Thanks for letting me know. What are your plans now?" Winters fishes.

"I know it's early, but I'm tired out, to be honest. I'm just going to go back to get some sleep," Sam replies, to the disappointment of Winters.

"I know what you mean. I might see you in the mess hall for breakfast then," Winters says, casually.

"Shall we meet outside our block at quarter past six and go together?" Sam suggests.

"Okay, great. See you then. Have a good night's rest," Winters replies.

"You too," Sam says, before she hangs up.

Thank God, Winters says to himself, *I can finally get some sleep.* He shuts down the computer in front of him and gathers together the few belongings he has. Still sitting on his desk is his coffee cup, which is three-quarters full. Winters picks it up, finding that there is still heat left in the liquid, and he debates whether to finish it off. *No*, he tells himself, you don't want to risk the caffeine keeping you awake, not tonight. Winters instead carries the cup out into the corridor, takes it into the toilets and pours the coffee away, with a tinge of regret, before relieving himself.

"Lieutenant Winters," an authoritative voice bellows from down the corridor as Winters emerges from the toilet, startling him.

"Yes, Sir," Winters replies, seeing General Byron standing holding his attaché case with his assistant, Becky, by his side.

"What are you doing?" Byron asks as Winters approaches.

"I'm just finishing up for the evening, Sir. General Cox has relieved me for the night, Sir," Winters responds, with a sinking feeling.

"I've just spoken to General Cox. We have a briefing in ten minutes and your attendance is required, Lieutenant. Follow me," Byron orders.

"Sir," Winters replies, suddenly regretting tipping away that caffeine hit. "I'll just grab a notepad and pen off my desk, Sir."

"Quickly then, Lieutenant," Byron answers.

As Winters moves, his phone vibrates in his pocket and he pulls it out while he walks, knowing who it will be before he answers.

"A change of plan, Lieutenant," Cox tells him. "We have been ordered to attend a briefing in approximately ten minutes. I'm on my way back over. Are you still there?" Cox asks, rapidly.

"Yes, Ma'am. General Byron caught me before I left and informed me. Shall I meet you there?" Winters answers.

"Yes. Meet me there and save me a seat, Lieutenant. My feet are killing me," Cox tells him.

"Yes, Ma'am. I will. See you shortly," Winters replies.

"And get me a coffee, white no sugar," Cox orders before she hangs up.

Chapter 9

Armed with nothing but his notepad and pen, Winters follows General Byron and Becky into the main foyer and then into one of the lifts.

"Colonel Reed, Lieutenant," Byron says, as the lift begins to take them up.

"Yes, Sir?" Winters replies.

"I will be interested in you telling me what happened to him, when we have the time," Byron says. "I've read the report but there's nothing like hearing it from the horse's mouth, Lieutenant."

"Yes, Sir. Let me know when you have the time, Sir," Winters replies.

"A terrible loss. Especially now," Byron adds, sincerely.

"Yes, Sir. Absolutely terrible," Winters responds.

Byron could well be the only person in the British Army who is mourning the loss of Reed, Winters decides. That is probably because Byron is one of the old school who was responsible for bringing Reed up through the ranks.

116

Byron is also a man who couldn't be bullied or manipulated by Colonel Reed. Reed wouldn't have dared. Byron has always outranked Reed by some margin and he can't have had any skeletons in his closet, not that Reed knew of anyway.

The lift doors open one floor up and Byron leads them out into the foyer before he turns right towards a set of double doors. The doors open out into a large space that is bustling with high-ranking military personnel and smartly dressed people in civilian clothing.

To a man and woman, everyone dressed in a military uniform stops whatever it is they are doing and cuts their conversations off dead when General Byron walks into the room. Each of them stands to attention and salutes the leader of the British Army as he walks past. Nobody is in any doubt who Byron is: his rank, and reputation, precede him.

Byron pauses to greet the admiral of the navy, who is chatting to the home secretary, Gerald Culvner, before he leads them towards another set of doors. Winters is unsure what to do for a moment. Should he follow Byron and the dignitaries, or wait outside with the lower-ranked officers who are accompanying their superiors?

"With me, Lieutenant," Byron orders, when he sees Winters wavering.

Byron takes them into a large conference room, where the briefing will take place. Tables and chairs have been hastily arranged in the centre of the room in a circular fashion, with other chairs around the outside providing extra seating.

On the far side of the room, a man and woman are already standing next to the tables, in deep conversation. Winters recognises both immediately although he takes a second look to check he isn't seeing things.

The woman is Angela Rainsford, the prime minister, and the middle-aged man she is talking to is Albert, Prince of Wales, next in line to the throne. Winters keeps following Byron around the tables, but he pauses as the general approaches the two people who are talking in order to join in their conversation.

"I bet you weren't expecting that, Lieutenant," says Becky quietly, as she stops beside Winters.

"No, I wasn't. That's for sure," Winters replies feebly.

"How long will General Cox be, do you know?" Becky asks.

"She is on her way. Not long I wouldn't think," Winters responds. "Where should I reserve a seat for her?"

"There's no need to worry. She has one reserved, the seat next to yours. Look," Becky says, pointing.

Winters sees that there are name cards that he hadn't previously noticed on the tables. He sees the one with General Cox's name printed on a piece of A4 paper and then, on the table beside hers, to his surprise he sees 'LIEUTENANT WINTERS' also emblazoned on a sheet of paper.

"It looks like you're sitting down with the big boys, Lieutenant," Becky whispers into Winters' ear.

"How did that happen?" Winters replies in surprise.

"Clearly, someone thinks you might be an asset to the briefing. Good luck," Becky tells him.

"Where are you sitting?" Winters asks quickly, as Becky moves away, like a child afraid of losing his new friend.

"I'm in the cheap seats back here," Becky tells him, taking a seat near the wall and behind General Byron, who is taking his seat next to the home secretary.

Winters hesitates before he places his meagre notebook and pen onto the table and pulls his chair out. The conference room is filling up but there is no sign of General Cox coming to join him. Winters looks nervously around the table, trying not to look out of place. He greets the man who takes his place next to him, unsure whether he should stand and salute the colonel. Winters stays seated as the colonel grunts at him in reply. He decides that he would be up and down like a yo-yo if he were to stand and salute every superior officer that takes a seat, which is everyone apart from him.

Realising that the colonel next to him appears to be offended that he is sitting further away from the centre of the room than a measly lieutenant, Winters leans forwards, away from the man. He takes a moment to appreciate what is happening. Not only is he sitting round the same table as the military's top brass, but he is also sitting down with the prime minister and the Prince of Wales. Surely someone has made a mistake.

"No coffee then, Lieutenant?" General Cox's voice sounds from behind Winters.

"Ma'am. No, Ma'am," Winters blurts, being too star-struck to see the general enter. "I'm afraid that I didn't get an opportunity," he adds, beginning to stand for the general.

"Stay seated, Lieutenant," Cox tells him, pulling out her chair.

"Thank you, Ma'am."

"What do you know about this briefing?" Cox asks once seated.

"Nothing, Ma'am. General Byron caught me unawares when I was about to leave for the night and he didn't elaborate," Winters replies. "Did you notice that the prime minister and Prince of Wales are in attendance, Ma'am?"

"Of course I did. I've met them both before. The Prince is very hands-on, he probably wants to know what the hell is going on," Cox suggests.

"Thank you, ladies and gentlemen. Let's bring this meeting to order," Gerald Culvner says to cut out what little chatter there is.

Winters listens intently as the prime minister; Angela Rainsford takes charge of the briefing and asks for updates on the current situation in London and beyond. Various high-ranking members of the military are directed to make their reports. As is the Metropolitan Police Chief, Anderson, who Winters hadn't noticed is sitting on the other side of the table from him.

Winters hears information that he is already aware of, like the breach of the perimeter of the quarantine zone near the suburb of Wembley. He also hears how the situation in Wembley is deteriorating, that the infected had begun to move out of the Wembley area, even making it as far as RAF Northolt. Pride is felt when the prime minister is informed that the infected in and around RAF Northolt have been eliminated and pushed back to the Wembley area.

Angela Rainsford, however, takes no pride in hearing that the infected have been pushed back. She demands to know what proposals there are to 'eradicate' the infected in Wembley and reinstate the quarantine zone. That is when General Byron stands to give the prime minister his proposal.

"If I may, Prime Minister, Your Highness," General Byron begins. "It pains me to say it, but Wembley is lost. Our troops in that area are fighting the infected with everything they've got, but there is no sign of them being pushed back to the quarantine zone. There are simply too many of the damn creatures and the area is too big.

"We do not have the numbers to extend the quarantine perimeter around Wembley without thinning the line still further. As we have seen by the current breakout, the line is already wafer-thin. We must make a stand and do it now before containment in Wembley is lost and the virus spreads."

"What are you suggesting, General?" the prime minister asks, impatiently.

"That we obliterate Wembley and then clean out the area," Byron says, bluntly.

"Are you suggesting another tactical nuclear strike, General?" the prime minister snaps. "Exploding a nuclear device at Heathrow, on the outskirts of the city, was one thing. Exploding another in central London is quite another, General. That is out of the question. We won't countenance it. Do you understand?"

"Yes, Prime Minister, but that is not what I'm suggesting. I'm suggesting using conventional ordnance. We obliterate the area. Exterminate the vast majority of the enemy. Plug the hole in the line and sweep through to eliminate any of the enemy remaining," Byron responds.

"Do we have the time to make those arrangements?" a new, well-spoken voice asks.

"I have already, Your Highness," Byron replies, bowing slightly in reflex. "We will be ready to execute in approximately thirty minutes. With the prime minister's say-so, of course."

Winters' head spins as he listens to Byron's plan. Conventional weapons can be just as destructive as nuclear ones if enough are used and he is in no doubt that Byron has more than enough at his disposal. Wembley and its surrounding area might have been evacuated, but what about the troops on the ground? What about Andy, Josh and Alice?

There is some toing and froing between the prime minister and General Byron. Angela Rainsford forces answers to some difficult questions out of the general, but she at no point dismisses the general's proposal. Byron admits that, even though the troops on the ground would be pulled back, inevitably there would be 'collateral damage'. Other participants in the briefing are questioned and required to give their opinions. Sitting on the fence is not tolerated by the prime minister. She expects frank answers to frank questions.

Prince Albert doesn't interfere with the debate. He simply sits listening with a regal air about him. But then, as the debate simmers down, he leans forwards.

"General Byron," Prince Albert says, cutting dead the remains of the debate. "Can you guarantee that the quarantine zone can be re-established if this operation is carried out? To give the scientists a chance to carry on with their work and come up with a viable solution, something that I hear is making progress."

General Byron, who is still standing, pauses for a moment before he answers. He looks over his shoulder towards General Cox to give himself time to continue his deliberations. Then his head slowly turns back towards Prince Albert, the room in total silence.

"I cannot guarantee that, Your Highness. There are no guarantees in any battlefield operation. I am open to other solutions, but we haven't come up with one and time is against us. If we don't act and act now Wembley will be the beginning of the end, if that hasn't begun already." Byron finishes and slowly retakes his seat.

Prince Albert leans back in his seat without saying a word, his hand rising to his mouth in consideration. The briefing continues in silences as everyone joins the Prince in considering the magnitude of Byron's plan.

Winters sits in turmoil because one thing hasn't been mentioned in this debate, and that is Captain Andy Richards. His turmoil is not because of his relationship with Andy, but because Andy is the only living person who has been infected but has not succumbed to the virus.

"If I may say something?" Winters hears the words coming out of his mouth and is as shocked as anyone that they have.

"Not now, Lieutenant," Byron scowls at Winters.

"And you are?" Angela Rainsford asks, leaning forwards to see who is talking.

"Please excuse Lieutenant Winters, Prime Minister. He doesn't know his place," Byron responds, before Winters can.

"General, Lieutenant Winters is sat at this table for a reason. Somebody in authority obviously thought that his input might have a bearing on this briefing. I would therefore like to hear what he has to say, before I authorise Wembley to be carpet-bombed into oblivion," Prime Minister Rainsford insists.

"I sat him at the table, Ma'am. Purely for assistance," Byron protests.

"Nevertheless, General, let's hear what the lieutenant has to add, if you don't mind?" Rainsford asks.

"No, Ma'am. By all means," Byron replies.

"Should I stand, Prime Minister?" Winters asks, suddenly feeling that he is in over his head.

"As you wish, Lieutenant," Rainsford says.

Winters gingerly rises to his feet and turns in the direction of the prime minister and Prince Albert. On his way up, he finds himself picking up his pen, as if it might give him some comfort.

"Ma'am, Your Highness," Winters begins awkwardly. "We may not have considered that a vital asset is currently somewhere in the Wembley area, Captain Andy Richards."

"Of course I've considered that," General Byron interrupts.

"Please let Lieutenant Winters finish, General," Rainsford insists.

"Ma'am," Byron agrees.

"I don't know if you are aware of Captain Richards, Ma'am. He is the only person that we know of who has managed to recover from the virus after being infected," Winters says.

"I am aware of him, Lieutenant. I am also aware that he is currently AWOL in the Wembley area," Rainsford confirms.

"I see, Ma'am. With all due respect to General Byron, and as much as I agree with his proposal, we absolutely must stop the infected here and now, before we lose complete control, Sir. Can we afford to risk Captain Richards becoming a casualty of the operation? He might be the only solution to the infection that we have, the only possible cure. The samples he has already provided might not be sufficient to do that, Ma'am.

"All I am saying is that it should be carefully considered before we continue, Ma'am," Winters finishes and quickly sits down.

"Thank you, Lieutenant. You have made a very good argument. Wouldn't you agree, General?" Rainsford says, by way of congratulating Winters.

"Yes, Ma'am, I would. Lieutenant Winters is quite right. Captain Richards may be the only solution to the virus, but Wembley is holding on by a thread. We cannot afford to wait on the off-chance that he might make it out of there, even if he is still alive. If we don't act now, we cannot contain the virus and I'm sure I don't need to remind you of the consequences of that, Ma'am," Byron responds.

"How can we get Captain Richards out of there before the operation? And tell me again, why is he even there?" Rainsford asks, and then waits for an answer which is not forthcoming. "Surely someone around this table can offer me an answer to my questions?"

"Prime Minister," Winters says, raising his hand in the air as if he were still at school.

"Yes, Lieutenant," Rainsford answers.

"I feel that we are responsible for Captain Richards being in Wembley," Winters says.

"How so, Lieutenant?" Rainsford asks.

"We placed his son in Wembley as part of the troop deployment. Captain Richards was promised by Colonel Reed that his son would be allowed to stay with him and be discharged from his duties if Captain Richards led the mission to recover the safe from the Orion building. We have reneged on that promise, and he has gone to get his son out of danger, Ma'am," Winters informs the prime minister.

"Not Colonel Reed again," Rainsford says, exasperatedly.

"I wasn't aware of any promise to release his son from the army," Byron announces.

"You wouldn't have been aware, Sir. The paperwork was never submitted. Colonel Reed met his demise before he could make it official," Winters says. He doesn't mention that Reed probably never intended to make Josh's discharge official.

"That doesn't answer my question about getting the captain out, Lieutenant," Rainsford points out.

"No, Ma'am, I was coming to that. I have built up a professional relationship with Captain Richards since the mission to Orion and I have his phone number. Let me try to contact him to convince him to evacuate before the bombers move in. I am positive I can reach him, but I can't guarantee he will listen to me, not if he hasn't found his son," Winters offers.

"That might make matters worse, Ma'am. If Richards becomes desperate when he learns what is about to happen to the area where his son is stationed," Byron points out.

"Surely we must try and do something, Ma'am? We can't just stand by while a vital asset is blown to smithereens," Winters pleads.

"Do we know where this boy is? Can we not extract him so that the captain follows?" Prince Albert suggests.

"I'm afraid that we have no way of pinpointing him, Your Highness. Our lines are scattered. The best we can do is to order a general retreat and get as many troops out of harm's way as possible," Byron says.

"Are we not tracking Captain Richards' phone? Surely he is being tracked if he is such an important asset?" Prince Albert demands.

General Byron doesn't answer for a moment. Instead, he turns to his PA, Becky, who is sitting behind him before answering. Becky doesn't speak, she simply waves her hand in a side-to-side motion.

"We are tracking Captain Richards' phone, Your Highness," Byron answers, turning back. "The phone infrastructure in the Wembley area is damaged, however, making the signal very patchy. We can confirm he's in Wembley, as expected, but we cannot pinpoint him, Your Highness."

"Thank you, General," Rainsford says, as Prince Albert sits back in his chair, deep in thought.

"Ma'am," Byron replies, sitting back down.

There is a long pause for consideration before the prime minister speaks again.

"Make your orders, General and proceed with the operation forthwith," Rainsford announces, giving Byron the green light to obliterate Wembley. "Lieutenant, get hold of Captain Richards and convince him to retreat together with the rest of the troops. His son might well be amongst those troops. Tell him that. You have approximately thirty minutes to get him out of there. Am I clear, gentlemen?"

Winters and General Byron confirm that they understand, at the same time rising from their chairs. The well-versed General Byron performs a quick and shallow bow to the Prince of Wales before he rushes to leave the briefing. Winters, however, doesn't give the Prince a second thought as he turns to rush out, his hand already in his pocket to retrieve his phone.

Chapter 10

"He isn't answering!" I tell Dixon and Simms as we speed through as many back roads as we can find to reach the Wembley area. Josh and Alice could have been taken anywhere but all three of us agree that the front line is the most likely place. From the little intelligence that Dixon was able to offer, and the view Simms and I had in the helicopter, Wembley is the new front line and the stadium area is as good a place as any to start.

"That doesn't mean anything, Andy," Simms tried to reassure me. "He might not have heard his phone, or he could be busy."

Simms is right on both counts, but neither fill me with confidence. If Josh hasn't heard his phone, it is probably because he is busy, but busy doing what? How much shit is he in?

"We'll find him," Dixon's gravelly voice announces confidently as he swings the car around another sharp bend.

I am glad that Dixon insisted on driving as we regrouped after Catherine had driven away with Emily. It took me some time to regather myself after they went, but I had to make sure my head was straight before rushing back into action. Heading back into battle in half-baked fashion would have put my comrades' lives in danger, not just mine.

Dixon and Simms left me to it and busied themselves on their phones, familiarising themselves with the terrain we would be heading into. When I finally joined them to do the same they were ready to walk me through the area and make suggestions as to where Josh was likely to be. There were many options but, after some debate, I decided that the best starting point would be Wembley Stadium, a focal point in the centre of the terrain. Once the decision was made, we carried out a weapons' check. Simms and I transferred some of our ammo to Dixon as we were weighed down with bullets. Then, after some coaching by each of us, we were ready to move out.

Dixon driving means that I can concentrate on trying to get hold of Josh or Alice. I'm not so pleased that I ended up on the back seat, however. Dixon isn't taking any prisoners with his driving and, each time the car's tyres screech, I'm either thrown against the door or straining against my seatbelt. In fact, if he takes the next corner much faster I wouldn't be surprised if the seatbelt was ripped from its anchors. *He must have been a fan of James Hunt in his youth,* I think, as I look at my phone again.

"Incoming!" Dixon shouts as a dark figure stumbles into the middle of the road.

The car swerves as Dixon takes evasive action so as not to hit the Rabid head-on. Whilst hitting the creature head-on could cause serious damage to the car or smash its windscreen, Dixon doesn't miss the opportunity to sideswipe the beast as he speeds past it.

The side of the car whacks into the Rabid, the hit happening right next to me on the car's back door. Suddenly I'm weightless for a second as the car's back wheel drives over something, probably the creature's foot, that lifts it in the air. As the wheel grips the road again, I turn to see the Rabid spinning into the middle of the road before it goes down. I would congratulate Dixon on taking another Rabid out, but I don't want to encourage him. He is already driving like a bloody maniac.

The authorities must be aware that the front line has moved on from Wembley. The Rabids are already in the streets around us and we are further out than Wembley. Where the front is now, I have no idea, and what the breakout means for the rest of London and beyond I dread to think.

Dixon made a good decision by taking the back roads. Rabids are in the streets, but they are few and far between. If past experience is anything to go by, you can bet that the main roads are either filled with the undead or clogged up with military transports.

"How much further?" I ask, having lost my bearings, what with all the commotion and concentrating on my phone.

"Not long," Simms replies from the passenger seat.

"Are we there yet?" Dixon says sarcastically, in a child's voice, from beside him. I let the jibe go, knowing it is only pre-battle banter.

"Just get there in one piece, old-timer," I reply, not completely joking as we swerve violently again.

"I'm like a fine wine," Dixon laughs.

"Corked and turned to vinegar?" Simms laughs but gets an elbow in his ribs for his trouble.

When Dixon finally completes his turn, which is close to happening on two wheels, we get our first glimpse of Wembley Stadium. Above the houses, further down the street, its massive arch cuts across the night sky. The arch is not fully lit, its lattice structure almost lost in the darkness and ominous smoke haze that hangs in the air over the stadium. The same haze drifts like fog down the road Dixon is speeding along. My eyes fix on the arch, which suddenly flashes brightly in the darkness, illuminated by a missile fired from an invisible aircraft. I panic. Is Josh in the target area of the missile, fighting the undead, unaware of his impending doom? The car goes completely silent, all of us lost in our own thoughts, contemplating the fight ahead.

I almost don't feel my phone begin to vibrate in my hand as I think, but the screen's bright light draws my eyes down. I snap back to reality when I see Josh's name displayed before me.

"Hello, Josh," I splutter urgently, putting the phone to my ear. "Hello. Hello!"

I panic as the phone line suddenly goes dead and I hear two beeps in my ear. *What the fuck's happening?* I think, as I look at the screen, which has gone blank. *Why did Josh hang up? What's happened?* I quickly fumble to find his number and press dial, but the line rings out.

"He was cut off and now he's not answering!" I say urgently to the two men upfront.

"It could be anything. He'll phone back," Simms tells me, unconvincingly.

I press dial again, desperate for Josh to answer, terrible thoughts popping into my head. The line rings before going dead and I pull the phone away from my ear, the connection not even forwarding to voicemail. *He must be in trouble*, I reason, *why else wouldn't he answer?*

Dixon crashes into another Rabid in the road but I hardly notice the bang against the side of the car. He is now having to constantly swerve right and then left to move forwards, his arms sawing at the steering wheel.

We near the end of the road and Dixon slows as much as he dares. Ahead is a junction that will take us onto the main road that leads to Wembley. The junction is clogged with dark shadows blocking our way forwards, but we have no choice: Dixon will have to plough into the melee of Rabids to get us closer.

Dixon accelerates but, just as the front of the car lifts, a hulking object suddenly appears across the junction, blocking it completely. Machine gun fire erupts immediately from the Challenger tank that has parked itself across the end of the road that we are speeding down. Bright-green tracer fire flashes towards us, threatening to obliterate the car's steel shell, and us along with it.

Dixon takes evasive action, swerving right, the tracer fire streaking across our left flank. All around, Rabids' bodies fall, ripped to shreds by the machine gun that blasts into the road.

"There!" Simms shouts, pointing right.

Dixon hits the brakes for a second, his hand wrenching at the steering wheel while his other hand rips up the car's handbrake. The tracer fire changes direction, coming straight at us, as Dixon takes us into a controlled spin.

Suddenly we are plunged into darkness, the car's headlights feeble after the flashes of green pyrotechnic flare. Dixon dabs the brakes again to slow us, his eyes struggling to adjust. I blink to clear my vision and gradually I see the rows of garage doors on either side of the car.

"Fuck me, that was close," Dixon gasps, as he takes us slowly down the path behind the surrounding houses. And he is right: if Simms hadn't seen the opening we'd be riddled with bullets and burning, ignited by the tracer fire.

We don't travel far before a tall, heavy, red wooden gate cuts off the path ahead and Dixon has to bring us to a stop, only feet away. Everyone is silent for a few seconds but then, without a word being said, we move.

I roll out of my door and straight into a covering position. My rifle points back down the overgrown path towards the green flashes that are still streaking from the machine gun. No shadows move against the flashes of green light but I stay in position, waiting for a signal.

"Clear," Dixon's voice sounds above the muffled clatter of the Challenger's machine guns.

I am up and turning instantly to make my way down the side of the car and past Dixon and Simms, who cover me as I move. I quickly reach the red gate, take up a position and signal for the next movement. Simms breaks his cover and scurries back to the gate, where he turns to cover Dixon with me.

Dixon picks up speed and plants his foot level with Simms and I to launch himself into the air. The gate bangs against itself as Dixon hits it and pulls himself up. A second later, Simms heaves against my foot to lift me up to where Dixon is balanced on top of the gate. Dixon and I lean down to grab Simms and he is the first to drop down to the ground on the other side of the gate.

None of us move when we hit the ground, where we find ourselves in near total darkness. We wait, hoping our eyes will make enough adjustments to allow us to move forwards. My eyes do little to allow me to see: all they can make out is the shadows of trees that spring up in every direction, blocking out what little night light there is.

"Follow me," Dixon says confidently from beside me.

"I can barely see a thing," I protest, looking in his direction.

"Me neither, but I ain't staying here. There's a crack of light at 10 o'clock," Dixon tells me.

I look in that direction and see the faintest slither of light, which is good enough for me too and I step after Dixon. All three of us tread carefully as we can't see the ground below our feet. Our arms are outstretched so that we don't walk face-first into a tree trunk and we head for the light.

The light gets brighter with each step, but we are totally exposed. Rabids could be close by, waiting in the undergrowth, ready to pounce and we wouldn't see them. Not wanting to risk switching on a torch, we can only hope that they can see as little as us if they are in here with us.

A few last stumbles bring us up to the light and, with it, the sound of heavy gunfire grows again. The break in the foliage is big enough for us to squeeze through one at a time, with Dixon leading the way.

With stars above our heads once more, Wembley Stadium fills our view ahead. Suddenly, a helicopter powers over our heads, from over the treetops behind, causing us to duck in reflex. We watch as it hovers across and towards Wembley's arch, the smoke haze spewing around it.

The mammoth stadium is close, but we still have obstacles to contend with before we can move closer. A wire fence is blocking our path. It reaches above our heads and cuts us off from the grass verge that slopes downwards. At the bottom of the steep verge are train tracks, at least three pairs of them, with another fence on the other side. In the darkness it is difficult to see what is beyond the opposite fence as the area is in almost complete darkness.

"Ready?" Simms asks, moving his rifle to his back and grabbing hold of the wire fence.

I nod, adjusting my rifle ready for the climb. The wire cuts into my fingers as I pull myself up the fence. Dixon and

Simms shimmy up the fence with ease, their well-versed technique making me look like a novice. I am too embarrassed to mention my stinging hands where the wire has pinched my skin as I drop down onto the grass on the other side of the fence. I don't mention the pain throbbing from the wound in my stomach either. I don't think traversing gates and fences was in my recovery plan after my recent 'operation'.

We slide down the grass verge with care. A sprained ankle or twisted knee could prove disastrous as we move into enemy territory. Care is also taken stepping over the train tracks in the darkness. Smacking your head on a railway line would be just as problematic.

My stomach protests as we reach the fence on the opposite side. I have to call a halt to proceedings for a minute while I pop three more paracetamol, hoping my kidneys can handle more pills.

"Got a headache, sweetie?" Dixon asks, grinning.

"You have no idea," I say to defend myself.

"What?" Dixon asks.

"I'll tell you another time, mate. It will give you a right laugh," I reply, and look nervously at the fence again.

"Over here," Simms shouts under his breath from our right.

I feel a large dose of relief as I see Simms pulling open a hole in the wire fence. I rush over to it, just in case it miraculously disappears before I can get through it. Simms holds it open for me as I duck through, my stomach giving thanks for this small modicum of luck.

As I rise on the other side of the fence, an explosion in the distance lights up the night sky for an instant. The light reveals that we have crossed into an allotment. Bamboo canes are stuck into the ground all around, with twines running up their length. The flash of light reflects off plastic sheeting that has been strategically stretched over areas of the ground to protect the grower's prized vegetables and fruit.

In that instant flash of light, I take a mental picture of the terrain, which could be described as an obstacle course. As my eyes adjust again to the darkness, I move left to where I saw a path cutting through the allotment. Dixon and Simms follow me without question, obviously having taken the same mental picture.

We quickly move to the other side of the allotment, following the path without incident. The gunfire cracking loudly all around tells us that we are closing in on our goal. We come to a stop next to a hedgerow that there is no way through.

"I saw a gate or something this way," Dixon tells us, and he takes us to the right.

Sure enough, we arrive at a slatted metal gate which must be the entry and exit for the allotment. Through the gate we see a wide main road and, towering above the road, Wembley Stadium, only a short distance away.

"So close and yet so far. What now?" Simms asks in a whisper, as he looks through the gate.

Just on the other side of the gate, the road is teeming with the undead. Creatures file past in their dozens, their stooped frames making them unmistakable. They are all moving from right to left, which will take them out of Wembley and further into the outskirts of London if their progress is allowed to continue.

"Why haven't they been taken out?" I wonder.

"They will be," Dixon assumes. "We've just gotta wait for the right moment to move."

"Look at the state of the road. Ordinance has already been dropped in this area, and it's peppered with bullet holes," Simms points out.

"And it will be again. It's only a matter of time," Dixon replies, confidently.

"And if it's not?" I ask.

"Then we find another way round," Dixon answers.

"There is no other way. If Josh is in this area he is somewhere on the other side of this gate," I say in frustration, taking my phone out of my pocket to try Josh again.

"Get back! Here it comes!" Dixon shouts suddenly, in a panic.

Luckily, the fast jet is moving relatively slowly, and Dixon hears the roar of its engine. I hear it too and am turning to get as far away from the road on the other side of the gate as I can before the bombs come down.

My mental picture of my surroundings is a blur of greenery, bamboo and plastic, and completely useless. I take my chances and run directly in the opposite direction to the gate and the road, lifting my feet up high in the hope that they won't get tangled up and trip me over. As soon as I leave the path, I feel vegetable stalks and other vegetation around my ankles, but I power forwards undeterred, as do the lads beside me.

Simms is the first to go down, his feet caught up in invisible twine or string. His mouth spews out every expletive under the sun as he scrambles back up to his feet.

Behind us, the roar of the fast jet reaches its crescendo. It is only a matter of seconds before the road behind us erupts. In my desperation to gain a few more feet before the inevitable occurs I snag my foot and feel myself falling forwards. I let the fall happen. Wherever I land is going to be where I try and ride the onslaught out.

My only cover is the soil and surrounding vegetable leaves that I land in. My hands move across my head to protect it, pushing my face deeper into the foliage and the soil beneath it.

My eyes are shut tight, preventing me from seeing the blinding flash as the bombs from above explode into the road. The ground shudders beneath me as multiple blasts erupt, my ears bearing the brunt. An instant later the debris begins to rain down on top of me as searing hot air billows across my entire body. My arms close tighter around my head as rubble peppers me. A larger piece whacks into the top of my right leg, making me wince in pain, but I don't move. I let the debris hit me. I can handle the pain just so long as I survive.

Eventually, the assault abates but I still stay in position with my face buried. I listen out for any sign of another jet engine approaching, but all I hear is the ringing in my ears.

"Is everyone okay?" Dixon's voice shouts over the ringing in my head.

I risk moving. Rubble and dust fall from my body as soil drops from my face and my eyes open. A dim glow illuminates the allotment. It sparkles off the shower of dust dropping through the air. The fires still burning in the adjacent road silhouette Dixon, who is a metre or two away from me. He is kneeling in the middle of the vegetable patch, his rifle trained on the road.

Next to Dixon, something moves as Simms peels himself off the ground. He rises from in amongst the bamboo canes and torn vegetable leaves. Gradually he rights himself, his aches and pains from the onslaught

138

unmentioned. Rubble and dust drop away from him. He too takes up a firing position.

"Fuck me, Richards. You know how to throw one hell of a party," Dixon announces, relishing every moment.

"I'm glad you're enjoying yourself, Sergeant," I respond, as I dust myself down before taking up a position.

"Something tells me this party is only just getting started," Simms adds to the banter.

"What, are there women on their way?" Dixon asks, his voice rising.

"I'm afraid I can't help you with that one, mate," I reply.

"Nobody can help him on that score!" Simms risks.

"Alright, Casanova, when was the last time you raised the Jolly Roger?" Dixon retorts but gets no answer.

"We'd better get moving while the going's good," I say to bring us back down to earth.

"Come on, Simms, don't let him become the party-pooper," Dixon says, as he gets to his feet, ready to move out.

Chapter 11

Dixon leads us out of the vegetable patch and towards a changed environment. Gone is the entrance gate, as well as much of the hedgerow. The allotment now opens straight onto the road, which is a scene of total devastation.

Nothing but dancing flames and swirling smoke move. Not even the undead stood a chance against the overwhelming force of the ordinance dropped from the sky. Every one of them in the immediate vicinity was either blown into a million pieces or incinerated, and probably both.

As I look upon the carnage, I realise that we have been lucky to escape with just a few bumps and bruises. Only the thick concrete pillars of the gate remain in place, and they are now battered and stand at odd angles. I dread to think where the rest of the gate has ended up. The metal struts could easily have come down on top of us, like javelins, to impale us. I count myself lucky to have escaped with a throbbing leg, instead of a severed one.

Across from us, the side façade of Wembley Stadium is in tatters and partly on fire. Every pane of glass in its towering walls is shattered and the steel is buckled and broken. Parts of its roof have melted or are fractured, the plastic no match for the blast or the ferocious heat.

"Do you still think that is where he will be?" Simms asks.

"Honestly? I don't know, but it's a good place to start. Let's get across the road while it's quiet and I'll try and phone him again," I reply.

Dixon nods in agreement and steps forwards. We fan out into the road, our rifles scanning for targets through the haze of smoke. The tarmac is still intact under our feet but, only a few metres away, the road is littered with smouldering craters sunk into the road. There are no prizes for guessing where the bombs struck but their devastation reaches much further than the roadside. Only the burning fires light our way. A couple of street lights still flicker, trying to cling onto life, but the rest are dead or completely demolished.

Debris pockmarks the road all around. Lumps of tarmac, soil and concrete are mixed in with shards of metal and glass, which crunch underfoot. Only remnants of the undead are visible. A shoe still filled with a severed foot here, a mutilated piece of flesh there. The bombs have done their job: they have made the road slick with sickening body matter.

Dixon leads us across the road in quick time, eager to leave the carnage behind. There is nowhere to hide from it though. As we leave the road, the going is just as tough. The blasts have ruined the wall that separated the grounds of the stadium from the road. Only the bottom few bricks remain and we step over them with ease, finally arriving at the stadium.

The concourse that circles the stadium has larger debris scattered over it. The pieces have either fallen out of the sky from the craters in the road or been blasted sideways from the wall. Along with the rubble are bigger body parts. We step around every type of limb that should be attached to a torso. Some have been ripped away at the joint, whilst others have parts of severed torso still attached. All of this is hideous enough but the few severed heads lying on the ground are the body parts we give the widest berth to. All of us are afraid that a jaw might snap shut onto our ankles, no matter how mutilated the head may be.

Any issues we may have had about entering the stadium are resolved. As we near the stadium, avoiding the parts of it that have fallen away from its side, we see multiple entry points have been carved open by the massive explosions. Doors have collapsed in on themselves under the force of the blasts, roller gates are buckled and some of the stadium's walls have been cracked open. Dixon is spoiled for choice about which one to use.

Suddenly, I am aware of my phone vibrating in my pocket and I reach for it, excitedly. Josh has beaten me to it, I think, as I pull the phone out, with my back against the stadium. My excitement is short-lived. It is not Josh trying to phone me. The phone's screen tells me that it is Winters.

"Winters, is everything okay? Have my family arrived safely?" I ask, suddenly worried that they haven't.

"They are here and settled in Andy, trust me. I'm not phoning about them. I've got an important update for you. Are you located in the Wembley area?" Winters asks, urgently.

"Yes," I reply. "We are next to the stadium. About to go in."

"Then listen very carefully," Winters says ominously, the phone line crackling.

"I'm all ears," I tell him, as the ringing in them from the explosions continues.

"In approximately thirty minutes, the military is going to bomb Wembley to kingdom come. I'm talking total obliteration. You must evacuate now!" Winters pleads.

"Don't worry, mate. It's just happened. It was close but we just managed to dodge it," I assure him.

"No, Andy! It hasn't happened yet. It has only this minute been given the go-ahead by the prime minister. I've just left the briefing when she green-lighted it," Winters informs me.

"Well somebody has jumped the gun, mate, because they just bombed the shit out of us," I say, confidently.

"Andy, you're not fucking listening to me!" Winters shouts down the phone and my confidence drains. It isn't like Winters to swear. "They are making their stand at Wembley. They are going to carpet-bomb the entire area to rubble. If they have just made a bombing run it has nothing to do with this operation. It's a sideshow. In about thirty minutes, that entire area will be obliterated. You need to evacuate immediately!" Winters demands.

"Not until I've found Josh," I reply feebly, my mind spinning with this new information.

"The brass is calling a general retreat. That includes Josh. He might already have evacuated. If you carry on, it will be a suicide mission. Think about your daughter. Retreat now, Andy, please, and look for Josh when you're out of the area. I will help you find him," Winters pleads.

"But what if he hasn't heard the order?" I ask.

"You will have to trust that he has. You stand no chance if you don't evac immediately. You have thirty minutes. Can you really find him that quickly and then escape if he is still there?" Winters counters.

CAPITAL FALLING 6 - BREAKOUT

I don't have an answer for him. I need to think, to talk to Dixon and Simms. Decide what we do. We are so bloody close to our objective.

"Thanks for the heads-up. I've got to go. Look after my family, mate." I pull the phone away from my ear even as I hear Winters begin to protest again.

"What is it?" Dixon asks, as Simms looks at me eagerly.

"In thirty minutes, they are going to obliterate the whole of Wembley. Winters said that bombing run was a sideshow. He said they are sounding a general retreat before the bombers move in, which should include Josh. He told me to evac immediately," I tell my comrades.

"We have no choice then. We have to retreat and pray that Josh gets out," Dixon says.

"I agree," Simms insists.

They are right, we have no choice. *Please God, let Josh make it out*, I think, as Dixon turns, ready to lead our retreat. I move to follow, but something holds me back. I look again at my phone. I can't leave without trying Josh one more time.

"What are you doing?" Dixon asks urgently, when he sees me stop.

"One minute," I reply, as I find Josh's number.

"Dad!" Josh answers almost immediately, in a panicked voice.

"Where are you?" I shout down the phone.

"We're hiding inside Wembley Sta..." The signal breaks up for a second. "...A pack of Rabids are hunting us, we're trapped! Where are you, can... help us?" Josh asks desperately, my stomach dropping as he explains.

144

"I'm just outside the stadium, but you've got to get out, Josh. They're going to bomb the entire area to smithereens," I tell him, urgently.

"We're pinned down, it's imposs… too many …em." Josh answers, his voice cracking, the signal intermittent.

"Where exactly are you?" I ask. Dixon steps closer to me, a determined expression on his face.

"We've barricaded ourselves in a… the lower part of the west stand of the stadi… came through…. access point just above and left of the Y in th… eats." Josh's voice breaks up, but I understand him.

"Okay, I'm coming. Be ready," I tell him, and hang up.

"Let's go. We've got about twenty-five minutes to find him and get out!" Dixon says, determinedly.

"Negative," I respond. "You two get to safety. This is too much to ask!"

"Nobody's asking and we ain't got time to debate the issue. Let's move," Dixon insists.

"He's right," Simms agrees, as the two men go past me and towards the stadium.

I am lost for words and stand motionless for a moment as Simms follows Dixon. Both men duck down low and step under a twisted roller gate and into the stadium.

"Come on, Captain, we ain't doing this by ourselves," Dixon smiles, when he sees me standing.

Immediately I move, ducking down low to join them. Inside, we find ourselves in a cavernous area with shuttered food and bar outlets. Flights of stairs are on either side of us but we look forwards, searching for a way to get out into the open area of the stadium.

"This way," Dixon says urgently, not stopping to take in his surroundings. He heads for a tunnel that leads into the bowels of the building. Simms and I rush behind him without question. The long tunnel must lead out onto the pitch but ahead of us are two large double doors that are shut tight.

Dixon doesn't wait to see if the doors are locked. His rifle is up and firing bullets into the wood around the locks as he approaches them. He doesn't hold back and, by the time he reaches the doors, any trace of the lock has disintegrated. Without breaking his stride, his shoulder slams into the middle of the doors as he arrives. With a crunch, the heavy doors spilt apart, creating a gap easily big enough for us to fit through.

Laid out before us, only a short distance away, is the hollowed green expanse of Wembley turf. Even now, with dark figures moving across the grass in the distance, Dixon doesn't pause. He knows there isn't time to fuck about. He presses home our advantage. Utilising the element of surprise, he steps onto the grass from behind his rifle.

"This way. He's in the west stand. That opening above the Y," I order, taking my turn to take the lead.

The three of us fan out onto the pitch at speed. Our objective is the opening above the blue seats in the form of the letter Y. Positioned in amongst the predominantly red seats, it is still some distance away. The dark Rabid figures that are also heading in that direction haven't seen us yet, but it is only a matter of time.

Simms is the first to choose a target and fire. I don't see his target, or if he hit it. I am too busy finding my own and there are plenty to choose from. My rifle crack rings out only seconds after Simms took his first shot. The creature turned to face me a second before I depressed the trigger, the beast alerted by Simms' shot. I don't miss the startled target and its brains are ejected from its head a moment before it drops onto the grass.

Our element of surprise is spent. Our enemy suddenly change direction and, with the sound of deathly screeches echoing, they attack. Beasts come at us across the grass, but none of us stops moving forwards. We move to meet them. Just as our Special Forces' training has taught us, in the face of overwhelming force, keep moving forwards and press home your advantage. We don't stutter.

Gunfire rings out into the chasm of the stadium. Each of us choose our targets and fire. Should we miss with our first shot we retarget and fire again. We find that we have another advantage. The flat surface of the pitch means there are no obstacles to overcome and nothing for the Rabids to use to hide from our onslaught.

Simms is on my left and Dixon on my right as we keep moving forwards, behind our rifles. Creatures drive at us low and fast, but they come head-on, directly into our line of fire. Multiple targets are eliminated. Dark-red blood spills onto the green grass. The thick goo splatters Wembley's turf, together with brain matter and pieces of bone.

We mercilessly thin out the undead horde until few targets remain. Away to our right, in the east stand, smoke rises from a smouldering fire, the remnants of an explosion. My guess is that is where the Rabids attacked Josh from, and that grenades were used to stem the flow of the undead. Hopefully, the ploy worked.

The only remaining undead come at us from the west stand, which is the same direction that we are heading in. These creatures are easy targets for our well-honed fighting skills. There are only a few in amongst the seating of the stand and they are quickly despatched. It doesn't go unnoticed by any of us that all the creatures are congregated near the large blue letter Y seating arrangement, which is exactly where Josh told me he went in.

As we reach the bottom of the stand, Simms shoots and kills the last Rabid that is still moving above us. We don't pause to scan the area in case any creatures have been missed, as we normally would. We cannot afford to stop. Time is against us. A far bigger threat will soon be looming in the sky above our heads. A threat that is totally out of our control.

Dixon is over the low wall separating the pitch from the stands even as Simms' shot still echoes around the stadium. I follow him without a second thought, as does Simms, as soon as he has pulled his rifle in. We rush up the steps in a controlled advance. Our three rifle muzzles swipe through the air, searching for targets.

Dixon nears the junction in the seating that will allow us to turn right and approach the opening that must be the one Josh used. The bodies of Rabids draped across the seating are barely noticed. Even the ones that are still twitching are ignored. When we are no more than three rows of seats short of the junction, an attack comes.

The Rabid bursts from the tunnel's opening and our rifles are on it immediately. I shoot first at the terrifying creature, its eyes ablaze, its bared teeth primed. My bullet misses, slamming into the wall behind the beast, concrete erupting into the air. At lightning speed, the Rabid darts forwards, its foot rising to plant itself on the back of the seat in front of it, from where it launches itself into the void between us.

Without any trace of fear, and with its arms outstretched in front of it, the creature flies towards the middle of our position, on a direct collision course with me. I flounder to bring my M4 into a shooting position. Fear courses through my entire body as the Rabid accelerates.

My rifle lags behind, not allowing me to take any kind of shot.

Gunshots ring out on either side of me. I am forced to take evasive action and drop down, hoping I can remove myself from its trajectory. Only the flimsy plastic seats in front of me offer any protection as Dixon and Simms continue firing. I cower behind them, waiting for the inevitable impact and pain.

A crunching noise sounds from directly behind me, the unmistakable and sickening sound of breaking bones and, with it, comes the crack of snapping plastic. Nothing crashes into me but, for a second, I daren't move. My head spins in terror, my ears ringing from the close-quarters gunfire.

"Clear! Move it, Andy!" Dixon's voice snarls, impatiently.

A hand grabs me from behind and I am dragged to my feet. Simms gives me a reassuring smile as he releases me, only to push me forwards. I risk a glance behind, in the direction of the sickening noise. A horrific face stares back at me, its skin in tatters, its neck twisted at an impossible angle. The Rabid is entwined with the seating. Shards of broken plastic stick into its body, which is a crumpled pile of shattered bones and torn flesh. There is another push in my back. I pull my eyes away from the hideous sight and look for Dixon.

Dixon has already moved up onto the narrow path that will take us along to the mouth of the opening. He stalks behind his rifle directly at the opening. Swiftly but deliberately, not wasting a moment. I move quickly to back him up, my head clearing somewhat. I ensure that I close the gap to him until I am on his shoulder.

Simms cleverly waits behind, just below our position, his rifle aimed directly at the opening. No other Rabids attack before Dixon has made it to the wall of the opening and, slowly, he turns the barrel of his rifle into the darkness beyond.

I wait patiently for Dixon to make his move, trusting his judgement. He takes as much time as he needs. His hand goes to a Velcro-fastened pocket on his left thigh and he pulls out two glowsticks. Expertly, while balancing his rifle in his right hand, finger still poised on the trigger, he cracks the glowsticks, bending them into his leg. Immediately, green light begins to form inside the plastic casing of the sticks. He helps the chemical reaction along by shaking his hand vigorously.

As soon as he is satisfied that the light is sufficient, he leans closer to the tunnel's opening and throws the glowsticks inside.

"Have you got any more glowsticks?" Dixon asks, quickly.

"Two," I reply. A quick shake of the head from Simms confirms he hasn't got any.

"I've got one more. Let's hope we have enough," Dixon says, before he steps forwards.

Dixon disappears from my view for a second as he turns into the opening. Cool green light silhouettes Dixon in front of me as I turn in to follow him. Steps lead down towards a concrete floor, where the glowsticks illuminate the surrounding area, which looks clear of any Rabids. Still conscious of time, Dixon moves quickly down the steps, coming to a halt three steps from the bottom. I draw level with him, moving to his right to cover that side of the staircase. As expected, the floor in front of us is wide, with shuttered-off food outlets and bars opposite our position. Signs above the shutters are mounted to inform customers of menus and prices.

I look right and into the dark void. The two glowsticks are not powerful enough to penetrate more than a few metres into the darkness. All I see is a foreboding blackness the further I try to see into the stadium.

"There," Dixon whispers from next to me.

I turn to peer into the darkness on his side, making sure I avoid looking directly at the glowsticks as my head turns. After a moment I begin to pick out shadows moving at the very edge of the glowsticks' range.

"How many do you reckon?" I whisper back.

"Christ knows. Could be five or twenty-five," he replies.

"Time to use another stick," I suggest, passing him one of mine.

"Get ready then," Dixon says, as he takes the stick from my hand.

My rifle is trained on the shadows as Dixon breaks his next glowstick, shakes it and tosses it into the darkness. Green light arcs into the darkness, illuminating more outlets on either side of the area as it flies. They are not where our concentration is fixed though. We look beyond them, waiting for the shadowy figures to reveal themselves.

Chilling green light is reflected back at us as the glowstick reaches its crest and begins to fall to the ground. Our focus doesn't waver from the pinpricks of light reflected from the eyes of the Rabid horde, even as the glowstick hits the ground and spins to a stop. Multiple pairs of eyes, too many to count, watched the glowstick's flight. Ominous and grizzly noises travel to us as the glowstick settles, its arrival alerting the creatures in the darkness to a new presence.

An ear-piercing screech hits us out of nowhere and suddenly a shadow moves in front of the glowstick that

Dixons has thrown. Instantly, I drop down, onto my haunches, resting my back against the wall behind me and flicking the M4 to automatic. Without invitation, I open fire, spraying bullets into the darkness. Muzzle flashes throw their light on the horde of undead and we finally see that there are at least two dozen creatures waiting in the darkness, more even.

The M4 clicks empty, and I eject the spent magazine out of it even as the shadows surge forwards. Within seconds I am firing again, not aiming at the almost invisible targets but filling the void with as many bullets as I can and keeping the barrage as close to head height as possible.

"Grenades," Dixon shouts from above me and I am conscious of ball-like objects following my bullets down into the void.

Another magazine empties its load and I eject it. At the same time, I move left, further into the staircase, hoping I will gain enough cover to protect myself from the oncoming explosions. This fight must end quickly. I throw caution to the wind and push another magazine into the M4 instead of worrying whether I am in the blast zone.

In unison, the explosions erupt and, in reflex, I duck further into the staircase, my eyes shut tight. My head turns away from the blinding light. Burning heat sears the side of my exposed face and hands but it is ignored. As soon as the heat dissipates, I force my eyes open again.

Gunfire erupts above me from Dixon's rifle. He is back in position an instant before me. My weapon lights up again to dispense its new magazine. Fire burns from the blasts, showing us our enemy, an enemy that was previously shrouded in darkness. Rabids surge at us through the carnage of the explosions that have devastated so many of their kin.

Dixon guessed between five and twenty-five creatures. That was an underestimate. At least ten Rabids are still on their feet, rushing to attack our position. They scramble through the fire and the smouldering pieces of torn-apart bodies of Rabids in their desperation to feed.

I aim more deliberately this time, the flickering light showing me my targets. The first creatures are taken out easily. These have been horrifically mutilated by the explosive force, and by the shrapnel from Dixon's grenades. Their catastrophically injured bodies have no right to be still functioning and our bullets put them out of their torment. The brains blown out of their heads add a new layer to the hideous carnage already surrounding them. Those creatures are the ones that bore the brunt of the grenade's power. They are leapt over by the beasts that they shielded.

The next wave is formidable. These creatures dart and swerve as they rush forwards, sometimes jumping to fly into the air. They bounce off walls and leap off any raised flat surface to avoid our bullets. They attack, their burnt, singed skin of no consequence to them.

As the creatures close in, Dixon and my angles improve and our targets get bigger. At this closer range, our bullets now seem to have more power to slow the wretches down and finally we begin to make our kills. Dixon's magazine empties and I increase my rate of fire to try and compensate, my rifle's muzzle zigzagging through the air.

In the instant that my rifle clicks empty, Dixon's is up and running again. He switches to automatic fire, spraying bullets at the last few Rabids that are almost upon us.

"Clear!" Dixon shouts, just as I take aim again with a full magazine.

I don't believe him for a moment. There must be more creatures to eliminate, and I search for my next. Slowly I realise that Dixon is right. All targets are down; there are no more Rabids to slaughter. I lower my rifle slightly, panting hard.

"That's where they must be hiding out," I announce anxiously, remembering our time limit.

"I fucking hope so!" Dixon snaps in reply.

"Move it then!" says Simms, urgently, who is still covering our rear above.

"Josh!" I shout, as Dixon and I move out of the stairwell and into the horror, both of us knowing that this is our last chance to find Josh and Alice. If they aren't here, then we have failed.

Josh doesn't answer and no door opens to bring my son out to me. I press forwards, stepping deeper into the blood and guts of the decimated Rabid horde to take one last look for him.

"Josh!" I shout, louder this time, as I look for a door that he might be hiding behind. But as my shout dies down my feet shake against the floor below. Only for a second do I think I am experiencing an earthquake. My reasoning quickly tells me that something much more sinister is happening.

"The bombing has started!" Dixon confirms at the same moment that my stomach drops. His voice is filled with a fear that I have not heard come out of his mouth before.

Chapter 12

"I'm sorry, mate, but they aren't here," Dixon insists. "We must evacuate. This place is about to go up."

"You go. I'll be right behind you. They've got to be here," I reply, desperately.

"We're out of time. Come on, Captain, think of your little girl," Dixon shouts, turning as the floor trembles again.

I am forced to concede that my comrade is right. It is time to evacuate. The bombing is some distance away now but that will change rapidly. We may already have left it too late to reach a safe distance. Reluctantly, I turn to follow Dixon, my emotions in turmoil.

"Dad!" a voice suddenly sounds from behind me. I turn back in disbelief and see Josh running towards me, Alice next to him.

"Josh!" I shout in reply. "The bombers are closing in. We've got to get out of here."

"This way, follow us!" Alice insists, as she draws level with Dixon and I, but then turns as if to go back the way she came.

"What do you mean, 'follow you'? We haven't got time to fuck about. We're going!" Dixon barks.

"It's too late to leave, Sergeant. The bombs are already dropping. We need to get underground. Trust us, please!" Alice pleads.

Dixon glares at me, blaming me for our peril but also leaving it to me to make the decision.

"Alice is right. It's too far to evacuate. We've only minutes before those bombers are overhead. We have to trust her," I tell Dixon, who looks back at me in surrender.

"Simms," Dixon bellows towards the stairwell. "Front and centre. Get your arse down here."

Simms rushes out of the stairwell, almost falling over himself. His look of terror is obvious as he runs towards us.

"What the hell! The bombing has started, in case you hadn't noticed. We've got to get out of here!" Simms demands as he arrives.

"Change of plan, sonny," Dixon tells Simms, as Alice and Josh take off back the way they came.

"Sergeant!" Simms protests urgently, but he follows reluctantly as Dixon and I move to follow Josh and Alice.

Following my son and Alice is a leap of faith for me but I trust Josh implicitly. Dixon and Simms hardly know him. God knows what they must be thinking as we follow them, moving deeper into the stadium. They are putting their lives in the hands of these two relative youngsters.

Josh and Alice tear into the stadium, following it as it curves round. I can barely see what's ahead of me in the darkness and wonder how they can see where they are going. Then I see a light shining ahead, directing them. The light gets brighter as we draw closer. Two silhouettes move behind it.

"Come on," an unfamiliar voice shouts from behind the light, the floor beneath our feet constantly rumbling.

"Go, go," Alice's voice urgently shouts in reply.

The beam of light sweeps right and then disappears. We rush to follow the glow that remains, turning into the stairwell, which only has one flight of stairs going down. I am the last through, just as the entire building shakes violently as sonic booms hit the outside walls. I know instinctively that we are running out of time. The bombers are closing in and the ordinance will soon be dropping right on top of us.

"Wherever we are going, we need to get there now!" I shout ahead, as I jump down the last steps before the first turn.

Nobody acknowledges me. Everyone is caught up in their own determination to scramble to safety. No caution is taken in case the undead have managed to find this stairwell and are waiting to pounce. That time has passed; all that matters now is getting as deep underground as possible before the building comes down on top of our heads.

We arrive at the bottom of the stairwell, but we aren't deep enough. We have only come down a few flights of stairs. At this depth, we will get no protection from the high explosives that will fall to vaporise us.

"Down here," the man holding the torch shouts, even as he has already broken into a run.

He heads right, down a narrow corridor, the torch in his hand the only source of light in our otherwise pitch-black surroundings. *How does this chap know where he is going?* I think, as I run after him, blindly. But run after him I do. My life depends on it. Any thoughts of us fleeing the blast zone have gone. I must trust in Josh's judgement, and in his faith in his brothers in arms.

"This is the door," he shouts, shining his torch onto a nondescript door as he skids to a halt.

Alice is filling the area around the door's lock with bullets as I come to a stop at the back of our group. Even while Alice is still firing, the man with the torch dangerously leans in and pulls on one of the door's handles. I don't blame him. If there was ever a time to be taking risks, this is it.

With a barely audible crunch, the door cracks open and Alice finally stops shooting. The man pulls at the door again and this time it bursts open. His efforts swing the door open violently and it travels out of his grasp to slam into the wall behind. The crash makes the whole wall shudder, as if it is about to collapse, the vibration travelling into the floor below. As one, we all chillingly realise that it wasn't the door that made the wall shudder. A massive crash above our heads confirms that the military's bombing run has reached Wembley Stadium.

"Get in, get in," I shout from behind, willing Josh to move inside.

Josh does bolt towards the door, but only after he has let Alice make her move towards it.

Dust sprinkles down from the ceiling above, wafting through the torchlight. We only have seconds before the ceiling collapses, and I push to make it through the door. I haven't a clue where it leads, but anywhere must be better than this.

I see another set of steps descending before me as I arrive at the threshold. I control my instinct to rush down them for a moment and instead grab hold of the door's handle to pull it closed behind me. My action might be a futile one against the high explosives falling from the sky, and the stadium about to collapse around us, but right now I will take any possible advantage.

Another colossal crash sounds from above as I descend the stairs, which vibrate and wobble beneath my feet. I keep going, trying to ignore the sound of the stadium above my head, and reach a turn in the stairwell. I don't pause to glance back at the door as I turn. At this stage, we are in the hands of the gods.

As we reach the next level, I am pleased to see that there is another turn that will take us even deeper underground. The deeper we can get, the better our chances of riding out the bombardment. Just as I turn, my legs are taken from underneath me as the ground moves impossibly far. I think my head is going to explode from the almighty boom that accompanies the ground shifting and I know instinctively that we are now directly below the bombs' trajectories.

I grab hold of the stairwell's banister, which shudders in my grasp, to stop myself from falling and hitting the steps. I see that below me the struggle is the same: shadows are grabbing onto anything they can find to keep themselves upright, any anchor that will stop them falling down the stairs.

I manage to right myself enough to stagger down a few more valuable steps before the next bomb explodes right on top of our position. This time I have hold of the banister as my legs shake and rubble begins to drop around me in the darkness. *Keep moving*, I tell myself, even as my legs begin to buckle under the vibrations.

In the darkness, I tread on something soft. Someone has gone down. I reach to try and help whoever it is but another earth-shattering blast hits just as I do. My hand loses its grasp on the banister and I feel myself falling uncontrollably.

Someone below me breaks my fall for a second as I bang into them, sending them flying down. The halt of my fall only lasts for that one second before I am tumbling again and, this time, I go down head over heels.

Luckily for me, I land on something soft at the bottom of the stairwell. My gratitude for my soft landing is quickly overridden by panic that I have hurt someone, possibly Josh, and possibly hurt them badly. I move in an attempt to see what damage I have caused, but another humongous blast shatters my attempt. Rubble falls on me, and dust clogs my lungs. I am forced to stay where I am, hoping that I am not too badly injured.

Dust continues to fall as the bombardment continues, but thankfully it begins to dissipate and move away from directly above us. All I can think is that I am still alive and that the stairwell is still standing. Air is still filling my lungs, although it is air full of dust and debris.

Eventually, the sound of coughing starts to overtake the sound of exploding bombs and the collapsing stadium. A chorus of coughing echoes in the confined space, together with moans of pain and suffering.

"Josh," I eventually splutter, when I manage to control my coughing. "Are you okay?"

"I'm okay," Josh coughs back at me after a long pause.

Suddenly, I remember that I am on top of someone and not on a sprung mattress. I move my weight gently, not wanting to hurt whoever is below me any more than I may have already. My hand finds solid ground and I carefully shift my weight onto it. With my weight shifted, I turn to look at who was below me, but I can't see them. Only a meagre amount of light is still being offered by the torch, wherever it is, and I turn again to try and find it.

Before I locate the torch, something shifts and the light suddenly brightens, enabling me to see the state of the stairwell. Of course, Dixon is standing over me. He might be covered in dust, but I see no other injuries on the body of the rugged sergeant, and I look away from him. Behind Dixon, I'm thankful to see Alice brushing herself down in amongst the lumps of brick and, next to her, thank God, is Josh. The dim light shows me two other men, one on his knees in front of Josh and the other sitting with his back to the wall on my right. I don't know either man, as far as I can tell, but their faces are in shadow and matted with dust. That just leaves Simms unaccounted for, and I get a feeling of dread when I realise where he must be.

"Simms, up on your feet!" Dixon orders, even as he pushes me aside to check on his buddy. "Simms, can you hear me?"

I don't want to look down and to my left but I force myself to turn my head around. I landed hard. I remember that much. I pray that Simms isn't hurt badly, but the feeling in the pit of my belly means that I fear otherwise.

"Simms, the bombing is over. Talk to me, mate," Dixon pleads, his body blocking my view. I move so that I can see, to check on the courageous young operator who jumped off the helicopter to back me up not more than a few hours ago.

Dixon goes deadly quiet, his hand reaching for the neck of Simms. My stomach sinks further when I peer around Dixon and see Simms' head against the base of the wall at a strange angle.

"He hasn't got a pulse," Dixon tells me sadly. "He's dead."

"No," I reply in desperation. "Are you sure? He could be knocked out."

"Yes, I'm fucking sure," Dixon confirms sombrely. "He's gone."

Why did it have to be me? I think remorsefully, selfishly. *He is only here because of me. He came along to help me. Why did it have to be me who killed him?* I suddenly go dizzy and weak, unable to hold my position. I fall away from my comrade, landing on my back in the dust. Sadness and guilt rise inside, threatening to overwhelm me.

"Dad," Josh says, moving to see if I am okay. "Dad," he says, leaning over me, "It was an accident, it's not your fault." But I don't want to hear his words, because at the end of the day it is my fault. Simms would be safely back at Porton Down if it wasn't for me. I roll away from Josh, from everyone, turning towards the wall. Lost in my guilt.

Minutes pass without me moving. I hear a commotion around me, but it becomes meaningless. I hear Josh's voice talking to me, feel his hand on my shoulder, but it is of little comfort. What is the point of any of this? Aren't we all destined to end up dead like Simms anyway, sooner or later?

Josh's hand leaves my shoulder and I'm glad he has given up. If he knew what was best for him, he would leave me here and let me rot. His mother left me; so why shouldn't he? My best friend Rick's head exploded all over me when he tried to pull me out of almost the exact same situation. And then there was Dan, happy-go-lucky Dan. My buddy would have followed me anywhere, and he did, right to his horrible death on the roof of the Orion building. They say that history repeats itself. Well, the proof is in the pudding and Simms is yet more proof. Proof that I'm no good and that if you stay around me too long, you'll end up just like him, with your neck snapped in a dark and dingy hole in the ground.

CAPITAL FALLING 6 - BREAKOUT

Chapter 13

A powerful hand takes hold of my shoulder, one that I am unable to resist. The hand pulls me over, against my will. I find myself on my back, looking up at the scarred face of Dixon.

"Come on, mate. This isn't the first time we've been through this, and it certainly won't be the last," Dixon tells me. "You know that we have to carry on regardless. They'll be a time to wallow, but this isn't it. So, get your shit together and get back on your feet."

Dixon rises and offers his hand to me. I know that he's right: what other choice is there? My head clears somewhat, and I grab hold of his hand. Dixon pulls me up onto my arse and then heaves to bring me up to my feet. Small chunks of rubble and a cloud of dust fall away from me. I rub the grit out of my eyes and sheepishly look over to Josh.

"No need to say anything, Dad. Just so long as you're okay," Josh says, before I can say anything.

"I will be, son. Thanks," I tell him, even though I still feel sick.

"It's completely blocked," a male voice says, as a figure comes down the stairs.

"Well, that's not a surprise," Alice counters. "We have a collapsed stadium above us."

My head continues to clear and I look up to the top of the stairs. Even through the darkness I can see rubble protruding that has fallen from the stairwell above. Without needing to take a closer look, I know it will be impossible for us to escape back the way we came. That rubble will be the tip of the iceberg, a berg constructed from tons of steel, brick and concrete, with a smattering of undead corpses in the mix.

"And you are, Corporal?" I ask the man who recced the rubble.

"Corporal Turner. And you?" he replies, offering his hand.

"I'm Josh's dad, Richards, and this is Sergeant Dixon," I tell him, shaking his hand.

"That's Captain Richards to you, Corporal," Dixon demands.

"Sir. Sorry, Sir," Turner blurts in surprise, snapping to attention to salute me.

"Captain, retired, Corporal. There is no need for saluting," I insist.

"Yes, Sir," Turner replies, lowering his hand.

I nearly tell him that there is no need to call me Sir either, but I don't want to countermand Dixon's instruction.

"This is Private Carter, Dad," Josh says, introducing the other member of his squad to me. "Be patient with him, he takes a bit of getting used to."

"That's not true, Sir. There's nothing wrong with me," Carter says, defending himself.

"Okay, Private. I believe you," I tell him.

"Shall we get on now that we have all been introduced?" Dixon growls.

"How did we end up down here?" I ask. "When we spoke, you were trapped in a room? How did you find this... bunker?"

"We can thank Carter for that," Alice responds. "Apparently, his best friend at school had an uncle who worked on the maintenance of the stadium. When he was young, the uncle took Carter and his friend round. Luckily, Carter remembered this subterranean part of the stadium. We just had to find the entrance."

"But what about being trapped?" I question.

"When Carter remembered, we broke through the wall into the adjoining area and sneaked out," Josh replies.

"How marvellous," Dixon says sarcastically. "Is there a way out of here, or shall we carry on shooting the breeze?"

"Calm down, mate," I smile. "We're just getting our breath back."

"In your own time then, Captain," Dixon replies, unhappily.

"We do need a way out though," Josh says.

"Haven't you got one?" I ask urgently, looking at Carter.

"Hopefully, there is one," Carter replies. "I can't remember."

"What do you mean, you can't remember?" Dixon says, exasperatedly. "Why did you drag us down here then? This could be our tomb."

"At least you're not blown to smithereens, are you, Sergeant? A little gratitude wouldn't go amiss," Carter retaliates.

"Okay, okay," I intervene, before Carter receives a bloody nose. Josh was right about him, that's for sure. "Carter does have a point. We would never have made it out of the blast zone," I concede.

"That'd be better than being buried alive down here," Dixon moans.

"Well, we're here now, so why don't we see if there's a way out?" Alice suggests.

"Agreed," I say.

Dixon is on it instantly. He is definitely a man who likes to keep busy. He orders Corporal Turner to cover the rear, even though there is no risk of attack from that direction. Then he conjures up a flashlight, clips it to the front of his rifle and takes charge of leading us off.

The stairwell winds down for two more flights. Rubble and dust are strewn across the steps as we descend. We hardly notice these trip hazards, however: we are too busy inspecting the rather worrying extensive cracks in the walls that follow us. We aren't out of danger, not yet. The whole place might still come crashing down at any moment. If the powers that be decide another bombing run is in order, there is a highly likely chance the whole place will be destroyed, and we will be crushed.

"What's all this?" Dixon asks, when we reach the bottom, sweeping his rifle from side to side. The beam of light reveals a selection of wide pipes and what look like large mechanical pumps, together with their control panels.

"This is the guts of the stadium," Carter informs us. "It's where water is pumped around the stadium and some of it is warmed to be pumped under the pitch to heat it when it freezes."

"You remembered something from your tour then," Dixon teases.

"Give me a break. I was only about thirteen," Carter replies.

"You mean a whole three years ago?" Dixon presses.

"Six years actually, Sergeant," Carter retorts, pushing his luck again.

"Shine your light over there," I tell Dixon, pointing, before the conversation gets out of hand.

Dixon shifts position and the beam of light falls directly on a door nestled in-between several pipes that disappear into the wall. As soon as the light hits the door, the tension in the room lifts slightly. The door offers us a glimmer of hope.

"Is that wall on the east side? Because if it is, it could lead under the pitch," Josh surmises.

"It's definitely on the east side and there's only one way to find out where it goes," I reply.

Dixon doesn't need a second invitation. He steps forwards to approach the door, his rifle ready to fire. The door has a sign stuck to its face stating, 'NO ENTRY', which tells Dixon that there's no point in trying to see if it's unlocked. And he doesn't. He begins to fire, filling the lock with bullets as he moves towards the door.

I don't get my hopes up. Even if the door does lead under the pitch, there would have to be a tunnel. A tunnel that has more than likely been destroyed and has collapsed as a result of the bombardment. I don't voice my concerns though. Everyone's nerves are on edge as it is. There is no point killing their hopes before we have looked. After all, I have been known to be wrong in the past.

"Hold on!" I bark at Dixon, as he lowers his rifle and goes to try the door.

"Why?" he asks, turning to me in confusion.

"Look," I tell him, pointing.

Dixon's eyes follow my finger to where a massive crack opens up directly above the door. It looks like the entire wall is unstable and is only being held by the door-frame and the door below it. The door-frame is bowing badly in the middle at the top. The wood is bent so far that it is touching the top of the door.

"If we open that door the whole place could come down," I insist.

"What other choice have we got?" Dixon replies, looking around at the other concrete walls.

"We haven't," Josh says from beside me. "That door is our only option. We've got to go for it."

"I agree," I tell him. "But let's get prepared. As soon as that door is opened, we may only have seconds for all of us to get through it. That's if there is anything on the other side."

"Okay. As soon as I open it, if we see that there's another room or hopefully a tunnel, then we go for it. If not, we're trapped here anyway. So better to get it over and done with. Let the roof come down!" Dixon insists flatly.

Everyone agrees with Dixon's assessment, and an orderly queue is formed near the door. I pull rank, positioning myself next to the door so that I can yank it open to let everyone through. Dixon argues that he should be the one to open it, but I won't entertain any arguments against me going last. I have enough on my conscience, and couldn't bear to go sooner and see the room collapse on those at the back. My only solace is that Josh ends up third in the queue. He is behind Alice and Dixon. Dixon is front and centre, and he will make the call on whether to go or not.

"Are you ready?" I ask Dixon, who is staring at the door that he has caught in his beam of light. He doesn't move, his face fixed in determination. After a second, he nods his head sharply and I pull at the door's handle with all my might.

At first, nothing happens. The door won't budge. I panic that the lock is still intact or that the weight of the wall above has jammed it shut, never to be opened again. Then I hear something, a creaking, scraping noise from above my head, and I feel the handle give a little. I release the pressure, move forwards slightly and then jolt backwards with all my strength.

Suddenly I am flying backwards, the door travelling with me. My feet rush to keep up, to stop me from falling arse over tit again. They somehow manage to control my fall, keeping me from staggering backwards until I slam into the wall adjacent to the door, the blow knocking the air out of my lungs.

Dazed and confused for a moment, I struggle to comprehend what is happening. Adrenaline rushes into my bloodstream to bring me back to my senses, allowing me to hear the violent cracking noises behind me. I look for my comrades, but they aren't there: they have disappeared. Something whacks me on the head as I realise that they have disappeared through the door. I look down in reflex to see what hit me, but the darkness hides the culprit. *It can only have been a piece of rubble. The wall is unstable. It's about to collapse*, I tell myself in a panic.

Josh's voice cries out, calling for me. It forces me into action, but I have dithered for too long. My arms push me off the wall just as another chilling crack crunches and something else hits the floor nearby. I twist my body left to where the opening is. I see light shining from beyond the door, marking my path, until a waterfall of dust pours over me. The dust covers my head, filling my eyes and blinding me and I suck it down into my lungs to choke on.

My beacon of light is extinguished by the dust. I can't see the opening; I can't see anything. I rush forwards to where I last saw the opening, putting my faith in my internal compass to get me through the door. Pain shoots down my back as something else falls and hits me, but I keep rushing forwards, hoping and praying that my aim is on target.

My foot bashes into an unseen obstacle and I trip forwards uncontrollably. Thankfully, I just manage to put my hands out to break my fall before I hit the ground. I feel the ground shudder beneath me and an almighty rumble erupts as mortar and steel begin to crash down. This is it, I tell myself. I'm about to be crushed beneath Wembley Stadium, buried here forever. All I can do is pray that Josh is safely clear. But that is a question that, hopelessly, I will never know the answer to.

Something touches my arm as the noise of the building's collapse escalates. A hand grabs my wrist, pulls at my arm, stretching it. I am aware of the ground moving beneath me, despite the chaos. Heavy pieces of rubble bash into my legs, but I don't care. *Pull me,* I scream in my head, *drag me clear before it's too late, before the rubble becomes bricks and boulders to crush me.*

My body scrapes along the ground. I have no idea how far I've been moved. I can only hope that it is far enough to save me from being flattened. The sound of collapsing intensifies. The earth shakes under me. My free arm involuntarily wraps around my head in a feeble effort to stop it from being crushed. I stop moving just as the calamity reaches its crescendo. Then, as quickly as the chaos started, one last massive crash brings silence.

Silence and darkness envelop me, forcing me to ask if I have been crushed, moved into the afterlife. A heavy cough bursts out of me, telling me different. Another cough follows the first, ejecting material out of my lungs, allowing them to work again. A voice talks over the uncontrollable coughing but all I can concentrate on is clearing my lungs. Tears stream down my face, attempting to wash my eyes out. Only when my fit passes can I hear what the voice is saying.

"Dad, talk to me. Are you okay?"

"I think... so," I splutter, in-between ever-decreasing coughs.

"We need to move, Dad," Josh insists. "Can you get up?"

"Water... has anyone got any... water?" I splutter.

A moment passes before my hand is taken hold of and I feel a bottle put into my clutches. Raising my head to meet the bottle, I pour water into my mouth. My lips close around the liquid to swirl it around my mouth. The bottle is raised to pour cool water into my eyes and I force them to stay open to receive it. I spit the water out anywhere. It doesn't matter, and my mouth feels better. The bottle returns to my mouth and this time I swallow some water before again pouring water into my eyes.

Grit and dust might remain to irritate but finally I see light, as well as Josh in the shadows watching over me.

"Get me up," I tell my son. "Where are we?"

"It's a tunnel but it's not stable and it looks like it's blocked just ahead," he tells me.

Aches and pains smart and my joints creak as Josh drags me to my feet. Shadows move as the light beams move around in the enclosed space. The tunnel is narrow and reaches to just above head height. I see the cracks in the surrounding wall immediately, wondering how it is still standing. Behind, no more than two metres away, is the doorway we escaped through. It has vanished, replaced by twisted steel and shattered masonry.

"Are we trapped?" I ask.

"I don't know. I haven't really looked. I was too busy dragging you. Sergeant Dixon is checking it out," Josh replies.

"Thanks, Champ. I thought I'd had it."

"It was close. I thought we both had for a second," he tells me.

"And we're still not out of the woods. Let's see what Dixon has found," I reply.

Dark figures are gathered round, a short distance away, blocking our view of the tunnel ahead. The rest of our crew are gathered at the other end of the tunnel, their heads bobbing about, trying to see what is going on. Alice is near the back and asks if I am okay as Josh makes a path through to get me to the front.

My heart sinks as I move towards the front and see Dixon standing next to another pile of rubble. I stop behind him to survey our next challenge, not saying a word for a moment.

"It's not as bad as it first appears," Dixon says, when he sees me.

"Really! How do you work that out?" I ask, confused.

"There's steel and concrete but look, there is also soil and grass," Dixon points. "We can get through this."

"We must get through. Suggestions?" I ask.

"I've tried to shift some but it's stuck pretty tight. So, you know what I'm going to say," Dixon says, raising his eyebrows.

"Great minds think alike. It's risky but let's do it," I reply, smiling.

"What are you two cooking up?" Alice asks from behind.

"Whatever it is, I wish they'd get on with it," Carter says.

"I would guess it involves a grenade," Josh adds, sarcastically.

"Unless anyone has got a better idea?" Dixon snarls over his shoulder. "No? Well, everyone back up then, as far as you can. I suggest you find whatever cover there is."

"The whole tunnel might come down," Turner questions.

"You're right, Corporal. It might. If you've got another suggestion then I'm all ears," Dixon answers.

"We could call for help. I've got a faint phone signal again," Carter suggests.

"The odds of the military sending a rescue party are about as slim as you doing what you're ordered first time, Private. Now move back!" Dixon barks, grabbing the torch off Turner at the same time.

"Kids, eh?" I say to Dixon, as the others shuffle backwards and we're left on our own.

"That one should have been left on the bedsheets," Dixon tells me, seriously.

"A bit harsh, mate," I reply.

"He's a bloody know-it-all," Dixon says, rolling his eyes.

"We were all young once," I tell him. "Anyway, we need to create a hole as close to the top and in the middle as we can. We want the blast to be focused upwards, to break through. The last thing we want is it directed inside here. Turner made a valid point just now."

"He did. Here, hold this," Dixon says, handing me his rifle.

As I take it, he pulls out his combat knife before approaching the pile of rubble. Taking care not to snag himself on any of the protruding metal bars that are entwined with the rubble, he finds some solid sections in the pile to plant his boots on. Once in position, he goes to work with the knife.

"There's a lot of soil up here," he tells me, as the knife sinks in and I begin to wonder if he might dig us out instead.

"Keep going," I encourage but, just as I say that, he hits something solid. "That's not deep enough. The blast will rip the tunnel to shreds."

"I know. Are any of those steel bars lose?" he replies.

After trying to pull a few bars out of the rubble, one does slide out, with a little persuasion. The bar is a good length and I pass it up to Dixon. It takes some time but, using the bar and his knife, Dixon manages to break through any solid parts to burrow a fairly deep hole in the top of the rubble.

"That should be deep enough," Dixon says, passing the bar down.

"How do you want to do this?" I ask.

"Once I pull the pin we'll have ten seconds," he tells me. "I'll push the grenade down with the bar, pack the hole with as much soil as I can and then make a run for it."

"If you're sure," I reply, after a moment's consideration.

"Not really, but what the fuck?" Dixon replies, grinning. "Are you ready?"

I make him wait for a second while I find something slightly smaller than the grenade that he can use to push it in. The end of the bar will probably slip to the side. Eventually, I find a piece of wood that looks ideal. I even manage to knock it onto the end of the bar to fix it in place. Dixon then has a test run, just pushing the bar and wood into the hole. The test goes well, so Dixon insists on getting on with it.

"Get ready," I shout over my shoulder in warning.

"Let's do this!" Dixon says, psyching himself up.

"Make sure you leave enough time to get to cover," I say, looking up.

"Don't worry about me. As soon as you hand me the bar, make a run for it," Dixon replies, with a mischievous smile.

"I'm serious," I insist. "You'll have ten seconds at the most."

"I know. I'll allow eight. Ready?" Dixon asks.

"Ready," I reply.

Dixon unclips a grenade from his body armour and gives me one last look as he pulls the pin. Then it happens: the lever springs away from the grenade, he stuffs it into the hole and grabs the bar from me. I don't see Dixon push the bar into the hole, or him pull it out, because I am running back towards the others.

In my head, I'm counting as I go. I make it back to the other end of the tunnel on the count of four and, by the time I've hunkered down tight with the others, I've reached six seconds. I don't have time to think about our peril as eight seconds pass without Dixon arriving and then, boom, the grenade explodes.

The ground shudders, the blast ripping into my ears. My body tenses, waiting for the hit, which comes quickly. Once again I am showered in rubble, which is accompanied by a searing wave of hot gas that billows against me, threatening to char my skin. I'm hit heavily by something big, big but soft. A body. *Dixon,* I announce to myself, as I cower for cover, *but is he alive or dead?*

Quickly, the energy of the explosion dissipates. My body begins to uncurl, thankful that the tunnel hasn't collapsed and nothing has injured it badly. My concerns rapidly switch to Dixon, who is flopped across me like a ragdoll.

"Dixon?" I ask urgently, praying for a response.

No response comes so I have to ease him off me. I try to do it as carefully as possible, taking hold of him as he slides off me as I move. Gently lowering him to the floor, I rest his head back. The darkness, together with the smoke and dust hanging in the air, makes it impossible to get a good look at him. He had held the torch between his teeth the moment before he went to work. It is only the one attached to his rifle, buried somewhere beneath us, that is supplying the meagre light we have remaining.

"Dixon! Talk to me, mate!" I demand.

"Is he okay?" Alice asks in a concerned tone from over my shoulder.

"He isn't responding. I can't see properly," I quickly reply.

"Here, use this," Alice says, as a light suddenly blinds me.

I take the phone off Alice urgently and shine it down towards Dixon with a terrible feeling of foreboding. The light illuminates Dixon's face, which is matted with dust, debris and patches of blood. His eyes are shut and I can see no signs of him breathing.

"Dixon!" I say again anxiously, reaching for the side of his neck to see if there's a pulse.

"Woo-hoo! Well, that was a rush," Dixon suddenly exclaims, his eyes snapping open to nearly give me a cardiac arrest.

"Are you hurt?" I ask, still getting over the shock, as I hear giggles coming from behind me.

"I don't think so. Help me up so that we can find out," he replies.

"Are you sure? Why don't you stay there for a minute?" I suggest.

"Fuck that. I want to see my handiwork." Dixon dismisses my suggestion, already beginning to pull himself up off his back.

Alice and I help him to his feet and he stretches his back out, accompanied by a long groan. He doesn't delay for long, however, keen to see if his efforts have borne fruit. Dixon leads us through the debris, the torch on Alice's phone lighting our way. Wafting his hand through the air to try and help clear the remaining smoke and dust, he comes to a stop next to the pile of rubble. Alice's light reflects off the smoke haze blocking our view, but then something happens to raise our hopes. A breeze blows through the smoke, parting it, clearing our view and showing us a small gap in the top of the pile, next to the roof of the tunnel.

Chapter 14

Winters lowers his phone, knowing that he shouldn't be surprised by the way the conversation went. He should have known Andy wouldn't give up on his son so easily, despite the warning about the impending catastrophe that has just made very clear to him. Deciding to give himself a break, Winters puts his phone away. He has tried his best. At the end of the day, Andy is his own man and will make his own decisions. Winters suddenly remembers Catherine and Emily's arrival with a sinking feeling. What is he going to tell them?

While Winters is still deep in thought, people in uniform start to stream past him. The meeting has obviously come to an end and Winters moves to the side, standing to attention as the top brass file past. Anderson strides by, the police chief even lowering himself to nod at Winters as he goes.

"Well, Lieutenant, you certainly made an impression," General Cox says, as she appears at Winters' side. "Follow me."

Cox does an about-turn to take Winters back the way she came, back towards the briefing room. Winters follows, confused, and wondering if he has got himself into trouble.

Winters is presented with an empty briefing room save for three people, the prime minister, the home secretary and Prince Albert. All three of the dignitaries watch Winters intently as he enters. His palms begin to sweat as Cox leads him through a gap in the tables to stand directly in front of the prime minister. She then steps back, giving him the floor.

"Report, Lieutenant. Have you spoken to Captain Richards?" Rainsford asks.

"I have just got off the phone to him, Ma'am," Winters replies.

"And?" Rainsford presses.

"Captain Richards was noncommittal, Ma'am. He thanked me for informing him of the impending operation and then hung up. He was right outside the stadium when I spoke to him. In my opinion, he won't leave unless it's with his son. He even asked me to look after his family before the call ended," Winters tells the three officials in front of him.

"So, we are no further forward," Rainsford observes.

"Can we delay General Byron's mission to give Captain Richards more time?" Prince Albert wonders.

"I'm afraid not, Your Highness. Changing the schedule could have unforeseen consequences. The general has already made it very clear that Wembley is on a knife edge. Any delay could be disastrous."

"We could give Richards all the time in the world and he still might not find his son. The boy could already be dead, or worse, infected," Gerald Culvner, the home secretary, scoffs.

"We might regret it if we lose Captain Richards. That's all I'm saying," Prince Albert adds.

"I agree, Your Highness. We are going to have to let this one play out. The ball is already in play," Rainsford replies.

"If I may, Ma'am?" Winters says.

"Of course, Lieutenant," Rainsford replies, holding out her hand.

"I've only known Captain Richards for a short time. But the one thing I've learnt is that he is very resourceful, especially where his family is concerned. His daughter is now on site here at the facility and my money would be on him finding a way back to her, Ma'am," Winters offers.

"Well, let's hope you're right, Lieutenant," Rainsford responds. "Now, if there isn't any other business, I must leave. I have a video call with the American president scheduled in ten minutes."

"I think that's everything," Culvner says.

"Very good then. Dismissed, Lieutenant. Be sure I receive an update if you have any news on Captain Richards, won't you?" Rainsford asks.

"Absolutely, Ma'am," Winters replies, unsure if there is any formality he should carry out before he turns to leave.

"And good luck with your continued work, General," Rainsford adds.

General Cox thanks the prime minister as she stands to attention and salutes her. Winters mirrors Cox: he follows her lead and performs a bow to Prince Albert before he trails behind Cox as she leaves.

"Was that okay, Ma'am?" Winters asks, after they have left the briefing room.

"You did well, Lieutenant," Cox replies.

"I hope that I didn't offend General Byron when I spoke earlier," Winters enquires.

"I don't think so. You spoke your mind, which he would have appreciated. In fact, he has ordered me to report back to him about how you get on with Richards. He is in agreement on how important he may be," Cox replies.

"I thought I may have pissed him off, Ma'am," Winters says.

"It would take a lot more than that to piss him off, Lieutenant. The general has seen it all, and then some," Cox tells him.

"I can imagine, Ma'am," Winters replies.

"I'd better get back to the lab, Lieutenant. I think it is only fair that you should update Captain Richards' partner with the current situation. She may know already, but she might not. She might even be able to talk some sense into him," Cox orders.

"Yes, Ma'am," Winters replies, reluctantly.

"After that, you are dismissed for the evening. Be at your desk at 0600 but keep your phone on in case you're needed. And update me immediately if you have contact with or receive an update from Captain Richards. Update me before anyone else, no matter what the time. Understood?" Cox insists.

"Understood, Ma'am," Winters confirms.

With that, General Cox makes her way to the exit. Winters doesn't move, waiting for her to go. A moment later, the prime minister and Prince Albert, along with the home secretary, leave the briefing room, heading in the same direction as General Cox. Winters stands to attention until they are out of sight, when he slouches back into a normal stance.

There is no putting it off, Winters thinks, as he retrieves his phone. There is no way he would have given Catherine this news, not now. He would have waited until he knew one way or the other about Andy, and Josh for that matter. Instinctively he knows that Andy has withheld the information from Catherine. He wouldn't have worried her with it. She may even panic, and who could blame her?

But it isn't up to him. Cox has given the order and Winters has no choice but to carry it out. Cox is playing another angle to draw Andy out of Wembley, Winters does not doubt that. She is hoping that Catherine will do what Winters failed to do.

The exercise is not only pointless, however, it is also cruel. Catherine won't be able to convince Andy to evacuate without Josh, it is too late for that. Andy probably won't even answer her call, even if he can. All that telling Catherine will do is worry her to death. Nonetheless, with a deep sigh, Winters phones Catherine.

"Is everything okay?" Catherine answers, already sounding fraught.

"I need to talk to you. Can you leave Emily and meet me?" Winters asks.

"What is it? Tell me," Catherine insists.

"Not over the phone, Catherine. Can you meet me in the main square in ten minutes? Do you know where that is?" Winters replies.

"Yes. I'll be there," Catherine says and hangs up.

Winters doesn't hang about. He doesn't want Catherine arriving and wondering where he is. She will be worried and in unfamiliar surroundings. Plus, he thinks that a coffee will be in order so he will have to make a pit stop at the convenience store.

Winters sees Catherine standing impatiently in the middle of the square when he emerges from the store with two coffees. Her arms are wrapped around her midriff and her head turns continuously, looking for him. She sees Winters almost immediately as he exits and rushes across the square to meet him.

"What is it? What's happened?" Catherine asks urgently the moment they meet.

"Let's sit down. I've got you a coffee," Winters replies, motioning towards an empty bench.

"It must be bad if you've got me a coffee," Catherine replies but takes the coffee.

"Was Emily okay with you leaving?" Winters asks, buying time on the way to the bench.

"She was asleep," Catherine utters.

"Good. And the others?"

"Everyone is fine. Now, what's wrong? Is it Andy?" Catherine asks again as soon as they sit.

"I spoke to Andy about ten minutes ago and he was okay," Winters informs her.

"He isn't answering my calls!" Catherine replies, just as Winters suspected.

"I've been ordered to update you with his situation," Winters says reluctantly, to get the ball rolling. "If it was up to me, I wouldn't be telling you this until we know more, because it will worry you. I was…"

"Just tell me, Robert," Catherine cuts Winters off in desperation.

"Okay. As you know, Andy is in the Wembley area searching for Josh," Winters says.

"Yes," Catherine confirms.

"Well, Wembley is being overrun with the infected and the authorities have decided that can't continue. So, in about fifteen or twenty minutes they are going to completely bomb the whole area," Winters says, as Catherine goes into shock.

"What does that mean for Andy and Josh?" Catherine asks.

"That's the point. We don't know for sure. The military are retreating from the area and Josh could already be out," Winters says.

"But Andy won't leave until he's found him," Catherine cuts across him again.

"I'm afraid I don't think so. As I said, I spoke to him to try and convince him to evacuate, but he cut me off without telling me what he was going to do. I got the impression he was going to continue to look for Josh," Winters confirms.

"He's been in areas that have been bombed before," Catherine says in hope.

"Not like this. They are going to totally obliterate the area. If he has stayed, his chances aren't good," Winters tells her, but immediately wishes he hadn't.

"Oh, my God." Catherine goes white. "What can we do to stop them bombing?"

"I've spoken to the prime minister twice. I've just left a meeting with her. There is no stopping it. I tried to plead Andy's case, but they can't risk the infection spreading further," Winters says, sorrowfully.

"Maybe he will listen to me!" Catherine says, urgently looking for her phone, tears starting to flow down her cheeks.

Winters watches as Catherine finds her phone and desperately dials Andy. The phone rings but Catherine receives no answer, as she hadn't before and as Winters knew she wouldn't. She brings the phone down urgently to redial, but Winters puts his hand over hers to stop her.

"He won't answer you. He's in the field and it would be too much of a distraction for him," Winters gently tells Catherine.

"But I've got to try!" Catherine replies, her eyes now streaming.

"Please, Catherine. All we can do is wait and see. And hope that he will phone us when he can," Winters says.

"I can't lose him, Robert," Catherine weeps. "Emily can't. It would destroy her."

"I know. We've thought we had lost him before, more than once, and he's turned up like a bad penny. So, let's wait and see," Winters reminds Catherine, trying to keep his own emotions in check.

Catherine leans into Winters for comfort and he pulls her into his side. Her body shakes with emotion and all Winters can do is hold her and wait for her upset to die down.

Minutes pass and gradually Catherine's sobbing calms. Winters is patient: he sits and waits for Catherine to pull away from him, back into a sitting position. He passes her a tissue out of the packet that he thankfully also picked up in the store.

"What now?" Catherine asks, as she dries her eyes.

"We wait and hope," Winters replies.

"Will you come and wait with me, so that I will know immediately if he tries to contact you?" Catherine asks. "I don't want to leave Emily for too long."

"But we don't want to worry Emily unnecessarily either. She will wonder why I'm there," Winters replies, after a moment's consideration.

"She is asleep," Catherine points out.

"But if she wakes to find me there it will disturb her," Winters counters.

"Yes. You're right, of course," Catherine agrees.

"I'm going back to my room now anyway. I'll walk back with you and I'll phone you if I hear anything. Okay?" Winters says.

"Thank you, Robert. You have been a good friend through this," Catherine tells him, trying to smile.

"I'm just trying to do the right thing for everyone," Winters replies.

"It's not always easy, is it?" Catherine says.

"You can say that again," Winters agrees.

"The bombing will probably have started now, won't it?" Catherine asks.

"It won't be long. There's nothing we can do about that. We've just got to wait to hear. Come on, I'll walk you back," Winters says, getting up from the bench.

Catherine takes another tissue to dry her face before getting up to join Winters. They walk back to their block in silence. Both watch other personnel going about their business whilst lost in their own dark thoughts.

"Promise me you'll tell me if you hear anything, Robert," Catherine pleads, when the lift doors close to take them up to their floor.

"You know I will. I promise," Winters replies.

"Even if it's bad news. I need to know. But then I suppose if we don't hear anything it means the worst," Catherine surmises.

"Not necessarily. Not immediately anyway. We need to give it time, Catherine, and be patient. I know it won't be easy," Winters replies.

"It's awful," Catherine says.

"Yes, it is," Winters agrees, as the lift door opens.

"There's no need to get out, Robert. Thanks for telling me and being there for us. I don't know where we'd be without you," Catherine says, before she gets out of the lift.

"There's no need to thank me," Winters insists.

"Well, I just did," Catherine replies, seriously.

Winters reminds Catherine of his room number and that he is only one floor above her as the lift doors close and she disappears. He presses the button for his floor with a heavy heart. God knows what Catherine is going to do now. Probably sit in the dark in silence and wait for news, Winters decides.

Chapter 15

Thinking about news, and despite his tiredness, the first thing Winters does when he enters his room is to switch on the television. Even though it appears that he is now a part of the military's inner sanctum once more, he is only on the periphery. He hasn't been invited to observe the operation in Wembley from the tactical command centre. So, like everyone else, he will have to see what coverage the television can offer. The only difference being that he won't be flabbergasted when the bombs start dropping.

Almost as soon as the television comes on, the newsreader, who is herself in a state of total shock about what she is being told into her earpiece, cuts off her report. The picture immediately switches from the newsroom and the screen goes dark. The newsreader carries on commentating as the camera providing the picture tries to focus in on a distant object. The newsreader struggles to keep up with events, finding it hard to believe what she is saying. She reports on a major military operation about to be carried out in the London suburb of Wembley. Just as she mentions Wembley, a bright flash illuminates part of the television's screen, but the picture is still blurred. Once more the camera adjusts as another flash erupts onto the screen.

189

The light assists the camera operator, who zooms in on it, and, finally, the picture focuses.

A fireball rolling into the night sky fills the television screen. The newsreader keeps jabbering but Winters doesn't hear a word she says. His concentration is on the visuals assaulting his eyes.

The camera pans out to give some perspective and to show that the fireball is only one of many reaching into the sky. With every passing second, another fireball bursts onto the screen, filling it, and forcing the camera to zoom out further.

To begin with, the awesome display of explosive power is nondescript. The destruction could be taking place anywhere, but then the camera finds its perspective.

On the right of the screen, directly in the path of the advancing bombardment, is the unmistakable outline of Wembley Stadium. The famous stadium flashes brightly with each explosion and the resulting fireball. Its white lattice arch, which reaches over the stadium's entire expanse, is illuminated by a different kind of light on this night.

Winters finds himself shaking with disbelieving nervous energy, his stomach in knots. He would be feeling gutted watching the pictures in any event, even if he didn't know that the stadium is where Andy was when he last spoke to him. That Josh, Alice and countless other troops are in the vicinity adds to his feeling of dread, and he begins to feel queasy.

The devastating bombardment advances towards the stadium relentlessly. The famous structure is now unwaveringly the focal point of the camera's shot. Occasionally, the newsreader attempts a stuttering commentary, but she has been shocked into an almost stunned silence.

Is Catherine watching these pictures? Winters asks himself, the sickness in his stomach growing. He can only hope that she isn't, that she is attending to Emily instead of looking at her phone. That she is doing anything other than watching these horrendous images. He can only imagine what she is going through if she is watching in silence, with Emily asleep nearby.

Hopelessly, the bombardment closes in on the stadium. The camera operator mercilessly zooms in closer until the stadium fills the right side of the viewfinder, the explosions advancing on the left.

The picture shudders, vibrating violently. Winters scolds the camera operator until, in horror, he realises that it is not the picture shuddering but the stadium itself. The structure of Wembley Stadium, its very foundations, is succumbing to the shockwaves of the ferocious bombardment. And then, with a flash of light, the first bomb hits the west side of the stadium. Explosions overpower the entire television screen until they meld into one complete fireball and Wembley Stadium completely vanishes from view.

Winters' stomach convulses and bile bitterly fizzes into his mouth. Grabbing the nearby waste bin, he wretches into it uncontrollably, tears streaming down his face. He becomes distraught, unable to stop himself. His thoughts are overridden by thoughts of the destruction of Wembley and of his friends, who cannot have survived its obliteration.

A moment passes. His head is still over the bin, his mind spinning. Winters wonders how he can come back from this trauma, this feeling of hopelessness. He then feels something else, his phone vibrating.

Somehow, he manages to compose himself enough to fumble for his phone. Through bleary eyes, he sees that it is Catherine who has messaged him and the message simply reads "Robert!" *I must pull myself together*, Winters orders himself, *Catherine needs me.*

Winters discards the waste bin, determined that he won't need it again. He switches off the devastation on the television and goes into the bathroom to recompose himself and freshen up.

Within minutes, Winters leaves his room behind, rushes down to Catherine's and taps on her door. For a moment he thinks he has tapped too quietly, not wanting to disturb Emily if she is asleep. Raising his hand to tap again, he stops himself when he hears the door's handle click.

Catherine emerges from her room in a terrible state. Her face is glistening with tears as she slides out of a narrow gap before gently pulling the door to. Winters is unsure what to do as Catherine steps out of immediate earshot of the door before collapsing on the floor, distraught.

Winters doesn't need to ask if she has been watching the events unfolding in Wembley and the obliteration of the area, including the stadium. Catherine curls up into a ball right there on the floor, sobbing uncontrollably.

There is nothing that Winters can say to ease Catherine's pain. Instead, he sits down, right next to her, lifts her head, shuffles in and places it on his legs. His own concerns and grief are forgotten. He is here for Catherine. He must be the strong one.

Catherine sobs and Winters strokes her head in a caring manner. Time passes and Winters is unable to stop himself from replaying the television images over and over in his head. Just as Catherine must be doing. He tries to imagine a way that Andy, Josh and Alice could have survived such a catastrophic annihilation, but he fails. The destruction of the stadium was total: it will now be no more than a pile of burning rubble and twisted steel, together with the rest of the area.

Gradually, Catherine's sobbing abates. She becomes still on Winters' legs. He feels sure that she has drifted off to sleep. His own eyes are heavy, becoming impossible to keep open, and his head relaxes forwards into a position that is uncomfortable but not uncomfortable enough to stop him drifting off to sleep.

Winters' dreams are filled with death and destruction. Every one of the people he has known during the infection visits him in one form or another. Not all the images are tortured but it is hard to see the ones that aren't through the horror. Andy's daughter, Emily, so cute and yet so strong, visits him. She calls for him through his nightmares, her voice soothing and reassuring.

"Lieutenant Winters," Emily's soothing voice calls, "Lieutenant Winters."

Winters jolts out of his fraught slumber, his neck stiff, and can still hear Emily's voice in his head. His eyes prise open to see a figure standing in front of him. He wonders if he is still dreaming.

"Lieutenant Winters, why are you out here with Catherine?" Emily asks.

Winters is not dreaming. Emily has woken up and found him and Catherine here in the hallway, outside her room. How did she know we were here? Winters wonders. Was I snoring?

"Hi, Emily. Did we wake you? Catherine and I were talking and we didn't want to wake you, so we came out here," Winters says, thinking quickly, having no idea how long he nodded off for.

"No, you didn't wake me. I just woke up and Catherine had gone. Stacey and Karen are still asleep and so I thought I'd look out here and I found you," Emily says, stretching.

Catherine stirs on Winters' lap at the sound of voices. She will get a shock when she finds Emily looking over her.

"Catherine, Emily is awake. She is here," Winters says to Catherine, trying to prepare her.

"Hello, Emily," Catherine says, pushing herself up. "I must have fallen asleep, while we were talking."

"Is everything okay?" Emily asks, with a puzzled expression. "It looks like you've both been crying. Has something happened? Is Dad okay?"

Catherine's head drops as she sits up as Emily asks her question. She doesn't answer Emily. Winters knows that she is struggling. He should be the one to tell Emily, Winters decides. It is too much for Catherine right now and Emily may possibly hold it against her. That is the last thing either of them needs. Winters steels himself to tell poor Emily what has happened but, before he can, his phone vibrates.

Winters feels guilty when he reaches for his phone. This is no time to use a message as an excuse to delay, but he doesn't stop himself. His phone's screen illuminates and a rush of adrenaline pumps into him when he sees who the message is from. The message is from Andy and Winters, with a trembling hand, clicks onto it.

We are alive, the message reads. *Tell Catherine, and I'll phone as soon as I can.*

"Emily," Catherine begins to say, her voice cracked and upset.

"Your dad is okay, Emily," Winters interrupts, excitedly. "He has just messaged me."

Winters places his phone in Catherine's hand. She lapses into a stunned silence, staring at the screen for the longest of times. Winters feels her shaking beside him. He knows that she is desperately trying to bring her emotions

194

under control in front of Emily and decides to give her some time to do so.

"What's going on?" Emily asks, as Winters pushes himself up to his feet.

"Nothing to worry about, Emily," Winters deflects. "Just the usual dramas. Can you help me get a drink, please? I could kill a cup of tea and I'm sure Catherine could also. Come and show me where everything is, will you?"

"Okay," Emily replies, suspiciously.

Winters takes hold of Emily's hand to make sure she doesn't delay and takes her back into her room, giving Catherine time to gather herself.

A couple of minutes later the hot drinks are made and Catherine comes back into her room. She gives Winters one of her broad smiles and whisks Emily into her arms to squeeze her tightly.

"You two are up to something," Emily insists, as the wind is squeezed out of her.

"No, we're not. We just couldn't sleep and so went out there to talk," Catherine answers, her voice almost back to normal.

"Can I have my phone back, please? I need to make a call," Winters asks.

Winters retrieves his phone from Catherine, telling her that he will be just outside. As soon as he is out of earshot, he dials General Cox's number.

"Hello, Lieutenant," Cox answers.

"Ma'am. I have just received a message from Captain Richards. He is alive!" Winters replies.

"Are you sure, Lieutenant?" Cox questions. "I find that difficult to believe."

"Nobody is more surprised than me, Ma'am. But yes, I'm sure. I have just this minute received it. He said he will phone as soon as he can," Winters confirms.

"This is excellent news, Lieutenant. We need to move on this immediately. I will inform General Byron," Cox says.

"And the prime minister, Ma'am," Winters asks.

"Yes, don't worry, Lieutenant. I will inform the general of her order," Cox replies.

"Thank you, Ma'am."

"Report to the general command centre. We will need you there. It is on the floor above my office, Lieutenant," Cox orders.

"Understood, Ma'am," Winters replies, and hears the line go dead.

Nearly forgetting to, Winters clicks back onto Andy's message to reply to it. He tells Andy that he has received it and that he will tell Catherine, even though he already has. That Andy should phone him ASAP so that he can plan to extract them. Winters know that Andy will update him as soon as he is in a position to do so. Andy won't want to be in harm's way any longer than he has to be. Winters then goes back to see Catherine.

"I have been ordered back on duty, I'm afraid," Winters tells Catherine, as he goes back into her room.

"I thought as much," Catherine replies and approaches Winters, her arms outstretched. She whispers "Thank you" into his ear as she hugs him goodbye.

After saying goodbye to Emily, Catherine shows Winters to the door.

CAPITAL FALLING 6 - BREAKOUT

"I know you will tell me when you know more. I will also phone you when I have spoken to Andy to tell you what he says," Catherine says quietly, after pulling the door to behind her.

"I will and, yes, phone me as soon as you hear from him. Any intel could be vital if we are going to launch a rescue mission," Winters replies.

"Thank you again, Robert. I won't forget all that you've done," Catherine smiles.

"There's no need for that, Catherine. I'm just glad he's still alive. He's like a bad penny, just as I said," Winters smiles back.

"A bad penny indeed," Catherine agrees.

Winters says goodbye and turns to leave, hearing Catherine gently close the door behind him. *There is no rest for the wicked*, Winters thinks, as he makes his way out of the building to report to the general command centre. Something tells him that his night has only just begun. *I must remember to thank Andy when I see him,* Winters smiles to himself.

Chapter 16

I click send on my message to Winters, hoping the one bar of signal my phone has will be sufficient to carry the message. It should be. I imagine Winters will be astonished to receive it, just as I am astonished to still be alive to send it. I hope that Catherine won't be too aggrieved that I haven't messaged her directly. I am not entirely sure of her situation and how much she knows about what is happening with us. Winters is the best person to relay an update to her.

"When you've finished checking your Facebook," Dixon says to me sarcastically, as I put my phone away.

"Sorry, just updating Lieutenant Winters while I had a signal. We need him to be ready to help," I tell Dixon.

"I'll let you off then," Dixon replies, as he passes another piece of rubble down to Josh.

Dixon is proud of his handiwork and insists on finishing the work himself. With each piece of rubble that he carefully removes, the gap between the top of the pile and the roof increases. He scoops away the smaller pieces and the soil with his bare hands, which rain down around his feet. There is nothing I can do to help, so I am not sure what he is moaning about.

"You'll fit through there if you pull that stomach in," I tease the sergeant, even though he has no sign of an oversized belly.

"I will but I'm not sure you'll get yours through... Sir," Dixon quips back.

"Fair point. Maybe a bit more work is required," I concede.

Dixon rolls his eyes as he turns to unearth another piece of rubble. A few minutes later, whilst slapping his hands together to clean them, he decides that he is happy. Josh offers to be the first one through, but Dixon refuses his offer, instead telling Josh to pass him his rifle.

After heaving Dixon up by his boot, Turner moves in to help Josh up, even as Dixon's feet search for an anchoring point to push himself off from. Josh waits eagerly for Dixon to disappear and make room for him to go. Josh goes, followed by Alice and Carter and then Turner lifts me up. The gap is narrow, but Josh is waiting to help pull me through the dirt and into the night. Before I have the chance to survey our surroundings, Josh scurries back into the hole headfirst, like a rabbit, to help Turner lift out.

I follow Josh down to take hold of his ankles, which poke out of the hole. He will need securing when he takes Turner's weight. I'm afraid to lose him again as he goes in. I hear a shout of "Pull" and I take the strain, gradually pulling Josh back out. Turner finally emerges, looking relieved to have got out of the tunnel and back with his buddies.

Picking up my rifle, I turn to find Dixon. I find myself rooted to the spot, flabbergasted, as my head turns to take in our surroundings. *Have I been transported to an alternate reality?* I wonder. I can't stop my body inching round to take in the full three-hundred-and-sixty-degree view of devastation that threatens to close in on me.

Less than an hour ago we entered one of the most awe-inspiring stadiums anywhere in the world. Ninety thousand seats looked down on us from the towering stands that reached up to the sky. Those stands have now totally collapsed, obliterated by the ferocity of the bombardment. Their buried plastic seats are burning, pouring noxious smoke into the air. The smoke cuts into my lungs, forcing me to cough, which only irritates my lungs still further.

We have emerged closest to the pile of twisted metal and concrete that was once the west stand. I cannot identify a single blade of grass on the pitch that stretches out before me. Deep craters have been sunk into the pitch and the ejected matter from those craters covers everything, along with rubble and shards of steel from the annihilated stands that surrounded the pitch. The arch that towered above the stadium has completely vanished from the sky above. Whether it crashed to the ground outside the stadium or exploded into fragments I don't know, but my guess would be the latter.

"It's devastating, isn't it?" Josh says from my side, with a cough.

"Totally," I reply, struggling to get my head around the devastation.

"It's a miracle we survived," Josh adds.

"An absolute miracle," I confirm, struggling to breathe.

"What now?" Josh asks, wheezing.

"We need to get away from this smoke before it does real damage," I tell him, whilst wondering how we are going to achieve that.

"Tell Winters to send in a helicopter," Josh suggests, dropping to his knee to try to find some cleaner air.

"We can't wait that long. We'll have suffocated from this smoke," I reply.

"And a helicopter won't risk coming down into this," Alice points out.

"Dixon," I shout, lowering to take a knee with Josh, where the air is a bit better.

"There, at ten o'clock," Dixon replies, pointing, without me having to ask the question.

I follow where Dixon is pointing and see the gap in the rubble he has spotted. The stand there must have taken a direct hit, splitting the structure in two. There is still a sizeable pile of rubble that we will have to traverse, but it is a good deal lower than the other options we are surrounded by.

"Shall we?" Dixon asks, when I move forwards to his position.

"This isn't going to be easy," I tell him. "We must move cautiously. The ground will be unstable. There might be other underground structures that have been damaged and could collapse underneath us."

"Does the Tube pass under the stadium?" Dixon asks.

"I hadn't even thought of that. I was talking about other tunnels like the one we've just come out of. I don't know if it does," I reply, my concern increased.

"Well, we can't stay here, we will choke to death. Ready for an evening stroll?" Dixon grins.

"Lead on. But carefully, my friend. Understand?" I reply.

"I'm always careful," Dixon replies, as I raise my eyebrows at him.

I tell everyone of my concerns and watch where they are treading. I discreetly position Josh in front of me when Dixon moves off. With him in front of me, I can see him if the ground does give way and may have a chance of grabbing him. Alice is at Dixon's shoulder, with Josh behind her. Perhaps Josh is thinking the same as me because he has Alice in front of him. Carter is behind me, moaning and chuntering, with Turner bringing up the rear.

The flashlight fixed to Dixon's rifle helps him pick a path in-between the wide deep craters that loom like black holes, ready to swallow us whole. The burning fires throw a dull glow over us, but their light has no power as the thick smoke eats it up.

Dixon warns us of numerous hazards as we move and his warnings are passed down the line. Shards of metal that have fallen from the sky are embedded in the ground, threatening to cut through our boots and rip into our feet. Separate craters overlap each other, the debris between them unstable, and areas of the ground smoulder with burning material.

Gradually we inch forwards, Dixon taking my advice for once and taking it steadily. Each of us overbalances at some stage but all of us manage to catch ourselves. We close in on the north stand and the path that we hope will take us out of the stadium. As we move closer though, our doubts increase. Compared with our other options on the perimeter of the stadium, the gap in the north stand is far lower than the massive piles of debris surrounding it. Even at the lowest point in the gap, worryingly, the smouldering debris is substantial and fraught with danger.

"Can anyone see another option?" I ask, when Dixon comes to a stop a few metres away.

"There is no other option," Dixon replies, before coughing deeply.

"We've got to go for it," Alice wheezes.

"Can't we call in a helicopter?" Carter asks.

"No pilot is going to come down into this smog," I restate.

"Then we press on," Dixon insists, unclipping the light from his rifle before repositioning the weapon on his back.

Alice follows suit by putting her rifle onto her back. As she watches Dixon set off, a light suddenly appears in her hand also. It's her phone's torch, ready to brighten her path.

Debris crunches under Dixon's boots with every step that he takes towards the large, wide wreck we must cross. He pauses when he reaches the foot of our mountain to inspect the way forwards. His beam of light will only penetrate a short distance into the smoke that rises through every crack or hole in the wreckage ahead of him. The poor visibility will only allow him to pick his starting point and a metre or two into the remains of the north stand. Constant creaking noises and crackling sounds of burning cause him to think twice before mounting the fearsome obstacle.

From where I am standing the whole structure looks unstable, as if it might collapse further in on itself at any moment. It is impossible to know what lies beneath the outer crust of smashed concrete, steel and plastic. Each step could cause the ground to cave in and take us down with it, to fall into the void and be swallowed by the abyss.

Dixon only pauses for a moment though; he won't let the danger defeat him. He puts a boot forwards to test his first step. Invisible debris shifts under his weight and falls into the pile of rubble beneath but, after taking hold of a steel strut poking up through the debris for balance, his other foot leaves the ground. After a quick glance behind him for moral support, he takes his next tentative step.

Alice delays before following Dixon's path. She waits until Dixon has moved off onto another part of the wreckage. Her delay is wise: one piece of wreckage may take the weight of one person but not necessarily two. As soon as she is satisfied, Alice goes, stepping exactly where Dixon did.

"It seems quite stable," Dixon shouts over his shoulder.

"You're doing well, but one step at a time," I shout back to temper his confidence.

As Alice clears her first hurdle, Josh begins his journey, and then it is my turn. My heart is in my mouth as I take my first step and feel the wreckage shift as my weight is applied to it. Sharp creaking noises accompany my weight transfer and I shine my phone's light around to double-check my footing and the wreckage around me. Light is reflected off blocks of concrete and steel beams in places but, in others, it disappears into black voids. My mind insists that we are crazy to put even one foot on this wreckage, but my sore lungs remind me that we have no choice.

A crash behind me causes me to spin my head around. I find Carter too close for comfort behind me, with an overconfident expression fixed to his face. *The idiot looks like he's out for a walk in the park*, I think angrily.

"Keep back. Stay on your section," I bark at him, shining my light at him.

"I am on my section," he quips back at me.

"I'm not fucking arguing with you. Stay back. That is an order," I shout at the idiot, fixing him in my glare.

"Yes, Sir," he calmly replies, nonplussed.

I resist the compulsion to whip out my Sig and put a bullet in his forehead to solve the problem. I don't discount that course of action completely, however, if he doesn't do as he is ordered. I am not going to end up at the bottom of this pile of rubble because of his impatience. I have a little girl waiting for me and I've come too far and gone through too much to be kept from her because of this idiot.

Corporal Turner gives Carter an earful to add to mine and thankfully he slows his progress. In fact, the further we progress into the danger, the further he falls behind me. I expect that he has had a near miss and nearly tumbled into a hole that I didn't see. It's a shame I missed seeing his frightened little face but at least it keeps him away from me.

"Watch it, Dad. There's a mutilated Rabid on the right here," Josh warns from just ahead.

I heed his warning as I take my next step, prepared for the horror. How the creature's head became crushed between a hulking piece of masonry and a wide steel beam I cannot fathom. Was the beast fleeing to escape the wave of bombs raining down? Or was its body blown high into the air to become entwined in the collapsing stand? I don't know and it doesn't matter. The only thing that matters is that it's dead.

The Rabid's skull has split, oozing the contents of its head onto the masonry below. My foot tries to avoid stepping on its brains, which already have a boot print pressed into them. As grim as the scene may be it is a chilling reminder that the risk of collapsing wreckage isn't the only threat we face.

Step by precarious step Dixon finds a route over the twisted wreckage and begins to close in on the end of his life-or-death challenge. As I reach the peak of the mound, I feel that I'm in the middle of an ocean, with waves of rubble towering over me on each side. On relatively solid ground, and whilst waiting for Josh to move on, I take a moment to survey the entire scene of the destruction of Wembley Stadium.

The holed and churned-up pitch, whilst visible through the thick fog of smoke, is unrecognisable as a football pitch. Images of a World War One battlefield spring to mind as I look along its length. Haunting, smouldering shadows come in and out of view through the swirling acrid smoke. They are all that remain of the towering stands that once stood in praise of the pitch below.

"Dad," Josh calls from behind me, his voice pulling me out of the shocked stupor that has taken hold of me.

I turn away from the heart-wrenching scene to see that my son has moved off, and that it's time for me to move again. Carter is also getting too close for comfort and I try to increase the gap to him with my next step on the debris.

Halfway across the gap, a noise suddenly thunders overhead. Smoke billows down on top of me, assaulting my eyes and lungs. The rotors of the incoming helicopter swirl the thick toxic smoke in every direction, making it unavoidable. My eyes begin to stream, blurring my vision as I move. I reach out to grab the piece of metal that I was aiming for. Relief washes over me when my hand grabs onto the cold steel and my feet plant themselves on the rubble below.

"Josh," I shout, as my arm wipes across my eyes to soak up the tears blurring my vision.

"I'm okay," I hear Josh's voice come through the smoke.

"Is Alice?" I shout back.

"Yes, I can see her," Josh confirms.

"Turner!" another voice desperately calls behind me.

I swivel to see Carter struggling to anchor his feet. His arms are outstretched in front of him like a mummy in an old black and white film. The lad is blind and dangerously close to stepping off the rubble and into one of the black voids that offer only one fate. *Why is he still moving?* I panic. *He is on firm ground so why doesn't he just stop moving?*

"Don't move! Stay where you are!" I shout back at Carter.

"I can't see," Carter cries back.

I go to shout at the fool again, but I am too late. All I can do is watch in stunned silence as Carter's foot steps onto nothing but thin air. A shrill, child-like scream escapes his lips, and he begins to topple forwards. There is nothing in front of him but blackness with shards of twisted steel protruding from it. *Carter is doomed*, my mind races. *If the fall doesn't kill him, his landing will. He is sure to be impaled on the jagged steel.*

Appearing out of the billowing smoke like an apparition, Turner suddenly springs forwards. Just as Carter begins to fall, Turner grabs the back of Carter's combat vest and yanks him backwards. Carter stumbles backwards on the concrete block below his feet until he hits a steel girder pointing up vertically behind him and comes to a whimpering stop.

Turner's heroics come at a catastrophic cost for him. Pulling Carter back has left him overbalanced on the edge of the precipice. His arms wave frantically into the air to try to correct his balance, but he is too far gone. There is nothing that can save him.

I cannot avert my eyes as I watch Corporal Turner fall over the edge. His head spins, his eyes, bulging in sheer terror, look straight at me, desperately, calling to me to help him. His mouth gapes open to release a chilling high-pitched scream as he disappears from my view into the black hole below. In an instant, Turner's scream is cut off. Not even the noise of the helicopter above can mask the sickening thud of his landing or the metallic ringing sound as he crashes into the steel shards below.

"What's going on? I hear Josh shout behind me. I cannot answer him though. I am too shocked and sickened by what I have just witnessed.

My eyes finally wander over to Carter. He is slumped next to the steel girder he bashed into, wiping his eyes in silence. My feelings of malice towards him become uncontrollable and I find myself leaping back from my perch to cross to the moron. I grab him by the scruff of the neck, meaning to throw him down into the abyss. To send him to follow his saviour, even as he screams in protest.

My eyes are full of water, whether from the smoke or the needless loss of Turner, I don't care to think. Carter moves easily under my power, and I drag him towards the edge of the block beneath us to receive his retribution.

"Dad!" Josh suddenly shouts at me, having doubled back to see what is going on. "What are you doing? Where is Corporal Turner?"

Nothing, son, I scream in my head. *Nothing that concerns you! Justice needs to be meted out and I am just the man to do it!* Carter screams desperately as his head and then shoulders move over the edge. In the shadows, far below and behind Carter's petrified face is the twisted figure of Turner's body.

"See what you've done, you total fucking moron?" I shout straight into Carter's face. But Carter's terrified eyes won't leave mine to look down at the result of his incompetence. My grip around his neck begins to relax. He will see what he's done soon enough.

"Dad! Whatever you are doing, stop it now!" Josh shouts earnestly at me. "He isn't worth it."

Josh's words strike a chord with me. Carter isn't worth having on my conscience for eternity. I have too many demons already residing inside to allow this streak of piss to join them. My grip tightens around Carter, and I reluctantly pull him back from the edge, leaving him in a whimpering pile at my feet.

I haven't heard the helicopter above move off. I only realise that the assault of its blades has ceased as I stand panting, looking down at Carter below. Tragically, I now find myself having to get Carter back onto his feet and moving, no matter how tempting it is to turn and leave him to wither and die.

"On your feet, soldier," I order, but he doesn't move. "Get on your feet or I leave you here. The decision is yours."

Slowly, Carter moves and gingerly pushes himself up and onto his feet. He looks at me with fear and guilt, guilt that he has brought upon himself. I don't feel one ounce of sympathy for him.

"Do you want me to go first, Sir?" Carter asks, timidly.

"Yes, but if you fuck up again, don't expect me to come and save you," I snarl in reply. "And don't go anywhere near any of the others. They don't need you pulling them down. Understood?"

"Yes, Sir," Carter confirms, wiping his puffy eyes again.

I find my anger lessening as Carter continues his crossing. He looks nervous and unsteady, frightened even, as he waits for Josh to move off again. Carter is obviously something of a dimwit. If he hadn't joined the army, he would have probably ended up stealing cars for a living or at best flipping burgers. I came across young lads such as Carter many times in my time in the services. Many of them didn't last long: they were either killed or relieved of duty for one reason or another.

"Watch your footing," I advise the young squaddie when he prepares to leap forwards. Carter makes his leap without incident and, as soon as possible, after a quick farewell to Turner, I follow him.

Without the helicopter churning up the smoke, pockets of relatively fresh air are once again available to breathe. Carter follows Josh on the trail laid out by Dixon, who stands watching, ahead of us. He peers behind me, searching for Turner, but, with a knowing look, turns to continue when I signal for him to do so.

From my vantage point above Dixon, I see him make one last leap. I can see the relief on Dixon's face when he turns to watch Alice hit solid ground next to him. Josh has fallen back because of the sickening drama but, as I progress, so does he. My relief is palpable when I see him land at Dixon and Alice's side.

Carter stumbles, nearly falling over when he lands on solid ground. He catches himself before sloping off behind the others where, to his credit, he takes up a covering position.

I thump to the ground with mixed emotions. Josh approaches me to see if am okay. I tell him I am. Dixon gives one last look back at the wreckage to see if Turner will appear. When the corporal doesn't, Dixon turns to join Carter in covering our position without saying a word, Turner's demise probably reminding him of the loss of Simms.

"What happened back there?" Alice asks, when I get my breath back. Josh, who is still unsure himself, also looks at me for an answer.

"It was an accident," I am forced to concede. "Carter lost his shit and Turner fell in saving him from falling."

"Come on Alice," Josh interrupts, as she starts to ask another question. "Best to leave it for now," he says, taking her to join Dixon and Carter.

Chapter 17

"Lieutenant Winters," Winters hears shouted across the square as he makes his way to the general command centre. For a second, he thinks that the female voice belongs to General Cox. He turns in the direction of the shout, ready to stop and salute, but sees straight away that it isn't Cox calling him.

"Good evening," Winters says to Sam in a suave manner, trying to impress. "I thought that you would be tucked up in bed."

"If only," Sam replies, rolling her eyes. "How could I sleep after watching the annihilation of Wembley? It made me sick to my stomach. All I could think about was your friend Andy and the other people there. I'm so sorry."

"Unbelievably, Andy survived the bombardment," Winters quickly informs Sam.

"Wow, that is unbelievable, but good news. I bet you were relieved," Sam says, surprised. "I'm surprised how anyone could have survived that."

"As was I. He messaged me to tell me only a short time ago. Catherine was beside herself until I gave her the good news," Winters admits.

"Catherine: that's his girlfriend, isn't it?" Sam asks.

"Yes, sorry, I forgot you haven't met her. She's lovely. You'd like her," Winters guesses.

"How do you know what I like?" Sam asks.

"I just meant…"

"I'm only teasing," Sam smiles. "I'm sure I would. Is she here?"

"Yes, she has arrived, with Andy's daughter and two others. They are in the same block as us. On the same floor as you actually," Winters informs Sam.

"Oh, then I will definitely have to meet her," Sam replies.

"I'm sure you will," Winters says. "What are you doing now?"

"Well, after watching the awful pictures on the television, I did go to bed, but I couldn't sleep. I was in shock I think, and then General Cox phoned me to see if I could go to command to meet her. It came as a relief, to be honest. Something to keep me busy and my mind off things," Sam tells him.

"Sometimes, it's best to keep busy," Winters agrees from long experience. "I'm on my way to command too. Shall we?" he asks, turning.

"We shall, Lieutenant," Sam replies, walking beside Winters.

"You can call me Robert, you know," Winters says.

"I know," Sam confirms. "But I prefer Lieutenant while we are here, if you don't mind?"

Winters doesn't mind in the slightest. Especially if there is a chance she might call him Robert when they're not here and, from what Sam has just said, there is definitely a chance of that.

Sam clears security and enters the command centre first while Winters' credentials are checked. She waits for Winters to catch up before carrying on into the large room.

Winters has seen enough of this type of room before to not take much notice of the set-up. Sam's head, however, turns this way and that so that she can get her bearings, and take in the scene.

Obligatory large screens have been hung on the wall to broadcast the latest news and operational information to the decision makers who are in attendance. In the past, Winters would simply have followed Colonel Reed as he scythed his way through such a room to reach the business end. Now though, Winters pauses to find General Cox, so that he can report to her, but she is nowhere to be seen.

"This way, Lieutenant Winters," General Byron orders, as he whisks past Winters' shoulder and into the command centre from out of nowhere.

"Yes, Sir," Winters replies, hiding his surprise, shrugging at Sam and moving to follow the general. He doesn't like to leave Sam behind, but he has little choice in this instance.

The room parts to allow General Byron through. He, of course, breezes along to the business end without a hitch. Winters guesses that the general had stepped out of the room for a moment and that Cox hasn't arrived from the lab yet.

Prime Minister Angela Rainsford is already in attendance, a stern expression fixed to her face. Winters doesn't need to wonder why she looks so serious. Not after the shock he felt watching the destruction of Wembley and he isn't the prime minister who gave the order and presided over its result.

Rainsford watches Winters following General Byron. Perhaps she is hoping he has some more positive news regarding Andy that can detract from her current woes, which can only be stifling for her.

"Hello again, Lieutenant Winters," Rainsford says, moving from one hip to the other as he approaches, ignoring General Byron.

"Prime Minister," Winters replies, standing to attention.

"At ease please, Lieutenant. Have you received any more communications from Captain Richards?" Rainsford asks.

"Not yet, Ma'am," Winters tells her, wishing he did have some positive news for her. "He messaged that he would phone as soon as he can, as I'm sure you are aware. I am still waiting on that call, Ma'am," Winters adds, holding up the phone in his hand.

"Exactly how long ago did you receive the message?" Rainsford asks.

"Fourteen minutes ago, Ma'am," Winters tells her after checking his call log.

"Do we know how he still has a phone signal, General?" Rainsford questions.

"No, Ma'am. I don't have that information. A cell tower must somehow still be in operation in that area, or he might be picking up a signal from outside the target zone," Byron guesses.

"Get me an answer, General. We cannot afford him to go 'offline'," Rainsford orders.

"Yes, Ma'am," Byron replies, looking at Becky to get that information for him.

"And see if we can track him," Rainsford adds.

"Ma'am." Byron again looks at Becky, who immediately takes a step back, her phone in her hand.

"I think it's time for you to try to phone him, don't you, Lieutenant? In case we lose all communications, if we haven't already," Rainsford says.

"Ma'am, I am sure he will phone me as soon as he can and it's safe to do so. He will want an evac as soon as possible," Winters replies.

"That wasn't a request, Lieutenant," Gerald Culvner pipes up from beside the prime minister.

"He could be in a compromising position, Home Secretary. Me calling him might be a distraction," Winters insists.

"Just phone him, Lieutenant. That is an order," General Byron interjects.

"Yes, Sir," Winters submits.

The line goes silent, trying to connect. Winters takes the opportunity to let his eyes wander as he waits. He sees that Sam has moved to watch proceedings from nearby. He also sees that General Cox has arrived. She is approaching Sam from behind and then the line clicks dead.

"No connection," Winters reports, uneasily.

"Try again, man!" Culvner demands, rudely.

Winters is already on it, but again there is no connection. He quickly tries for a third time, but the result is the same. Winters' concern grows, as he looks up, not having to say a word.

"Keep trying," Byron orders.

"Is there any more we can do, General?" Rainsford asks.

Becky returns, approaches the general and leans in to whisper in his ear.

"Ma'am," Byron says, leaning away from Becky. "We cannot say how Captain Richards managed to send a message, but we are still investigating. I can also confirm that we are unable to track his phone at this time," Byron reports. "I have, however, given the order to helicopter mobile field cell towers into the area. We will have some cell coverage restored in approximately..." Byron looks at Becky for a timing. Becky, who actually took it upon herself to make the arrangements on the general's behalf, mouths the word "Fifteen" at the general. "Fifteen minutes, Ma'am."

"What other preparations are in place, General?" Rainsford pushes.

"We have an evac team standing by, Ma'am. They can be over Wembley within ten minutes. We just need coordinates," Byron responds.

"Can we send in a reconnaissance flight? To search for Captain Richards?" Rainsford asks.

"Yes, Ma'am. A good idea. I will make that happen," Byron confirms.

Winters sees General Cox talking to Sam out of the corner of his eye as he continues to try and connect to Andy, without success. Sam's face is one of surprise and confusion and he wonders what information Cox is conveying to her.

"Okay, let's move on. I'm sure Lieutenant Winters will inform us as soon as he reaches Captain Richards," Rainsford says, looking at Winters.

Winters nods his confirmation to the prime minister, whose head drops in thought. Unsure if he should stay where he is or retreat towards Sam while he tries to reach Andy, Winters looks towards General Byron for direction. The general gives him none. So, without anyone dismissing him, Winters continues to stand awkwardly where he is, lifting his phone up and down to his ear.

"Have the troops moved in to clear the Wembley area?" Rainsford suddenly asks, her brain kicking back into gear.

"The troops are being deployed on the ground as we speak, Ma'am. First reports are that the terrain is, unsurprisingly, difficult, Ma'am," Byron responds.

"As expected, General," Rainsford replies. "And what of the work in the lab? How is that progressing?"

"General Cox has made herself available to report, Ma'am. If I may call upon her," Byron asks.

"Yes, of course, General," Rainsford confirms, waving her hand.

"Lieutenant, if you please," Byron says.

Winters does an about-turn and, with his phone clamped to his ear, goes to get General Cox. Cox starts to move as soon as she sees Winters approach her, having guessed that she is up. In fact, Winters has barely moved when Cox draws level with him and so he stops and stays in the background, keeping within earshot.

"How is your work progressing, General?" Rainsford asks, when Cox reaches Byron's side.

"It is early days, Prime Minister. The research is only in its infancy. We are, however, receiving some very encouraging results. The work done by my colleagues Colonel Taylor and Major Rees at Station Zero has given us a head start," Cox begins, giving well-deserved credit to her now-deceased colleagues.

"In layman's terms, we believe we have identified and isolated the specific enzyme from Captain Richards' biopsies that cause a reaction in the body. This reaction allows the body to produce a pheromone that, although undetectable to the human senses, is we think an indicator of those infected with the virus. The pheromone causes an infected creature to sense that another is carrying the virus. Or, in Captain Richards, case, masks the fact that he does not carry the virus.

"Simply put, Ma'am, Captain Richards has gained the ability to produce the pheromone when he is not infected with the virus. Hence he becomes masked to those who are infected because they sense the pheromone on him."

"I understand, General. Thank you. Can this enzyme be reproduced and is it safe for the human body?" Rainsford questions.

"This is where we are running into trouble, Ma'am," Cox admits. "We can reproduce the enzyme but in only very limited quantities. We have such a small amount of the enzyme from Captain Richards' biopsies to work with and the enzyme degrades rapidly. To successfully reproduce the enzyme, we need more of it, in its original form."

"I see," Rainsford says, putting her hand to her mouth.

"And in answer to your second question, is it safe for the human body?" Cox adds. "We don't know that as of yet. We have managed to administer the small amount of enzyme we do possess to lab rats without an adverse effect. The rats then showed signs of reproducing the pheromone and becoming masked to those infected with the virus. But is it safe for humans? More research is needed, Ma'am, and human trials."

"But you can't proceed with that until you have more of the enzyme?" Rainsford questions.

"Precisely, Ma'am. It is paramount that Captain Richards is retrieved," Cox confirms, and everyone looks around at Winters.

Winters shakes his head whilst holding up his phone to let everyone know that he hasn't managed to reach Andy. Heads turn and eyes move away from their interrogation of Winters to return to General Cox.

"General, what about a cure for the virus?" Rainsford asks. "Have Captain Richards' biopsies offered any solution for the long term?"

"Nothing has been identified so far, Ma'am. But, as I said previously, it is early days and we have limited samples to work with," Cox replies. "We need Captain Richards back!" she insists.

"General Byron, what does the evac team consist of?" Rainsford asks, changing direction.

"Two helicopters carrying eight men, Ma'am," Byron replies.

"Special Forces' men?" Rainsford questions.

"Er... no, Ma'am," Byron answers, awkwardly.

"General, I hope you understand the gravity of us retrieving Captain Richards?" Rainsford asks, forcefully.

"You have heard what General Cox has just said. I think you need to improve your plans, don't you? Use every asset at your disposal to get him back!"

"Yes, Ma'am. Of course, Ma'am," Byron responds, confidently.

Whilst Rainsford thanks General Cox for her update, Winters considers what Cox has just reported. *It is obvious that Andy is vital, not to finding a cure at this stage, but a means of fighting back against the infection. She also mentioned human trials. Winters is no scientific expert but surely it is premature to be considering human trials on a newly discovered enzyme? These things take years of research and development to advance towards human trials... don't they?*

Cox is dismissed to allow her to continue her work and turns away from the prime minister. She indicates to Winters to follow her as she passes him, heading back towards Sam.

"Lieutenant," Cox says, when they reach Sam. "Sam and I are returning to the lab. Hopefully, it is only a matter of time until you reach Richards and the extraction team go in. We need to prepare for his arrival. I expect you to tell me as soon as he is inbound. They won't let you out of their sight until he is secured.

"It is vital that we gain some control when he arrives. He needs to be treated properly, unlike before, which I take full responsibility for and regret. He is far more important than I ever expected or even considered. Mistakes were made and we don't want to repeat them. Understood, Lieutenant?"

"Yes, Ma'am. I will keep you front and centre with respect to what is going on," Winters agrees.

General Cox suddenly stands to attention and Winters looks round to see the prime minister approaching their position. He also stands to attention, waiting for her to pass. The prime minister smiles at Winters and Cox as she makes her way out of the command centre, saying something that takes Winters by surprise. She says "Hello, Sam" as she passes.

Both Winters and Cox look at Sam with confused expressions when the prime minister has left, both of them wondering who Sam actually is.

"You know the prime minister?" General Cox asks Sam, whilst Winters still stands in confusion.

"I do, General. She is a friend of my father's," Sam confesses.

"You never mentioned it," Cox says.

"It never came up, General. I have only met her a few times," Sam replies.

Winters isn't so sure that Sam is 'mentioning' the complete truth now. "A friend of my father's" seems very convenient, especially for a spook. Once again Winters is forced to wonder what Sam's job entails at GCHQ. Or should he be wondering what work she carries out for other, more clandestine, agencies?

Sam is still a mystery woman in Winters' eyes. She is beautiful, intelligent and he is forced to admit to himself that he is looking forward to unravelling her mysteries. Winters is so lost in his anticipation that it takes him more than a couple of seconds to feel his phone begin to vibrate in his hand.

Shit, Andy! Winters thinks, as he urgently looks at his phone. He has somehow found a signal. Winters' panic subsides when he sees that it is not Andy but Catherine phoning him. Winters shakes his head at General Cox and

Sam, who peer at him in anticipation, to let them know that it isn't Andy phoning.

"Hi, Catherine. Are you okay?" Winters asks.

"Not really, no. I'm going out of my mind. Is there any news?"

"Nothing yet, I'm afraid. We are trying to contact him, but the phone network is unstable. Helicopters are on standby to fly in and get him just as soon as we reach him, or when he reaches us. It's a waiting game at the moment. Try not to worry too much," Winters updates Catherine.

"That's easy to say. I can't handle being stuck in this room any more. Emily is asleep and Stacey has agreed to watch her. I'm coming to you. I need to be in the loop! Where are you?" Catherine insists.

"I'm in the command centre," Winters replies, taken aback. "You can't come here. You're not authorised. Please sit tight and I'll..."

"No, Robert," Catherine cuts Winters off. "I'm coming so you'd better get me clearance. I'm not willing to stand on the sidelines any longer. I need to be where Andy's fate is being decided," Catherine demands.

"I haven't got that authority, Catherine," Winters admits.

"Is General Cox there?" Catherine asks, surprising Winters again.

"Yes," Winters replies, awkwardly.

"Then put her on the phone, will you, please?" Catherine asks.

"Hold on," Winters replies.

"Ma'am," Winters says, holding his hand over his phone's microphone. "It's Catherine Hamilton. She is insisting on coming to the command centre so that she knows what is going on with Captain Richards. She wants to speak to you to get clearance."

General Cox looks uncertain for a moment, even scared of taking the phone. Winters understands why she would be doubtful about speaking to Catherine. He is sure that she will refuse to talk to her. After a moment's thought though, Cox puts out her hand to take the phone.

"Ms Hamilton. This is General Cox. How can I help you?"

"We speak at last, General," Catherine says, forcefully. "I am sure that you understand that I have my grievances with you and the actions you have taken, but that is for another time. I want to know what is happening with Andy at first hand. So I ask you to give me clearance to come to the command room. I won't interfere or make any trouble. I just need to be there. Will you do that?"

Winters looks at General Cox, trying to read her thoughts and decipher what Catherine is saying to her. Cox looks deep in thought, weighing up different scenarios, and then she speaks again.

"I can assure you, Ms Hamilton, that I know mistakes were made. Decisions were taken that I regret and that I can only apologise for. So, in the interest of goodwill, I will give you clearance to watch over the evacuation of Captain Richards. I must insist, however, that you always remain in the company of Lieutenant Winters and that you don't interfere or become a distraction to the operation. If that does happen, I'm afraid that I will be forced to revoke your clearance. Is that acceptable?" Cox asks.

"Yes, General. That is acceptable. Thank you," Catherine replies.

"Good. And please be assured that your grievances will be heard at the appropriate time, okay?" Cox offers.

"Yes, I understand," Catherine agrees.

"Unfortunately, Lieutenant Winters cannot leave at the moment. I will send down our colleague, Sam. She will meet you in the square and bring you up to him, okay?" Cox tells Catherine.

"Yes, but how will I know who she is?" Catherine questions.

"Don't worry, she will find you. I'm afraid that I won't be here when you arrive. I have other matters to attend to, but I hope to meet you when we are both available. I will hand you back to Lieutenant Winters now. Goodbye, Ms Hamilton." Cox finishes and hands Winters back his phone.

While Winters finishes up with Catherine, General Cox gives Sam her instructions. Sam is to meet Catherine, bring her to the command centre and then make her way to the lab, where Cox will be.

Winters' head goes into a bit of a spin with all the goings-on. General Cox and Sam leave. Cox reiterates her orders before she goes. Winters takes the opportunity to dial Andy again, but the line is still dead.

While Winters waits for Catherine to arrive, the prime minister reappears. She has Prince Albert walking next to her, who she must have left to meet and update. They both stop when they reach Winters. Rainsford asks if he has managed to contact Andy. Winters performs a small bow to Prince Albert as he tells the prime minister that he hasn't had any success. Her disappointment is clear as she tells Winters to keep trying. She then ushers Prince Albert towards General Byron.

Soon after, Sam and Catherine come into the room. Winters waves to them, although he has barely moved from the position he was in when Sam left.

"Any news, Robert?" Catherine asks urgently, as soon as she reaches Winters.

"No, still no phone signal in that area," Winters replies. "The military are moving mobile communications into Wembley, so it shouldn't be long. Did Sam find you alright?"

"Yes, straight away," Catherine says.

"Thank you, Sam. You had better get to the lab," Winters suggests.

"Yes, I'd better," Sam agrees. "Nice to meet you, Catherine."

"You too, Sam," Catherine replies, as Sam turns to go.

"How was Emily when you left?" Winters asks.

"She's fine. She was asleep," Catherine replies. "Sam seems nice."

"Yes, she is," Winters agrees, without saying any more.

"Is that Prince Albert over there?" Catherine asks, startled.

"Yes, and the prime minister. They are taking finding Andy very seriously, as you can see," Winters replies.

"I hope they are still okay," Catherine says.

"Me too. We just need the phones working again. They should be soon," Winters reassures.

"Lieutenant Winters!" General Byron bellows, summoning him to the front.

226

"Follow me, but stop when I say, okay?" Winters instructs Catherine.

Just shy of the front of the command centre, Winters tells Catherine to wait for him there. She stops immediately and watches Winters join the dignitaries.

"The network should be active at any moment, Lieutenant," Byron informs Winters.

"Understood, Sir," Winters confirms.

"Who is that with you?" Rainsford asks.

"Catherine Hamilton, Ma'am. She is Captain Richards' partner," Winters replies.

"How did she get in here?" Byron demands, scowling at Winters.

"She spoke to General Cox, Sir. She is very worried," Winters defends.

"I'm sure she is, but this is no place for friends and family," Byron insists.

"Now, now, General," Rainsford says, in a calming manner. "We are all here for the same thing. To see that Captain Richards is returned safely."

"Yes, Ma'am," Byron reluctantly concedes.

"Please ask Ms Hamilton to join us, Lieutenant. I would like to meet her," Rainsford asks, as Byron rolls his eyes in frustration.

Catherine looks confused as Winters steps back towards her. *Is she concerned that her clearance has already been revoked?* Winters thinks.

"The prime minister would like to meet you," Winters tells Catherine, to her surprise.

Catherine straightens her top and follows Winters forwards. Just as he is about to introduce Catherine to the prime minister and Prince Albert, Winters' hand begins to vibrate.

"It's Captain Richards!" Winters almost shouts in amazement.

Catherine gasps from beside Winters as he answers Andy's call.

Chapter 18

"Which way?" Dixon asks, when I step forwards to join him.

"We either go west or back the way we came. We don't know how far the bombing spread. The car could possibly still be there. We might need it if Lieutenant Winters can't arrange anything," I reply.

"We'll be lucky if the car is still there. Surely the bombs reached that far?" Dixon says.

"I don't know if they would have. It's hard to tell," I say.

"Anyway, Winters won't let you down. And the brass will want your arse back in a sling, sooner rather than later. Why don't you give him a call?" Dixon suggests.

Why don't I indeed? Why haven't I already? Perhaps I am just enjoying being back in the action with skilled operators and my son.

If only that were true. Actually, it couldn't be more untrue because I am not enjoying myself. On the contrary, I am dead tired, my body and feet are killing me, my lungs burn from the smoke. Plus, I've got a splitting headache.

Add to that the loss of two fine, brave men in Simms and Turner and, yes, even the loss of my old foe, Briggs, and it equals another hideous day from hell.

The answer to the question is contained in the second part of what Dixon said, the bit to do with my arse being in a sling. A ridiculous excuse, I know. My arse will inevitably be right back there if I get out of here in one piece.

Whatever the reason, my delay is putting my team's lives in danger. Including Josh's, when he is the main reason why I am here. I should put Winters' number on speed dial, I think, as I quickly find it and press call.

"Andy, where are you? You've got a lot of people worried here," Winters jabbers into my ear. His subtle warning of interested parties not going unnoticed.

"Are Catherine and Emily okay?" I ask, before we get down to business.

"Yes, they are fine. They are waiting to see you. Catherine is with me now," Winters tells me.

"Well then, is there any chance you can pick us up? Getting a cab in Wembley is proving a bloody nightmare, mate," I ask, hoping that he is ready to come to my aid once more.

"A team is standing by. Where are you?" Winters replies, prepared as always.

"Do I have your assurance that we are coming to you and the girls?" I ask, suddenly suspicious.

"Yes, you have my assurance. I'd tell you if it were any different, bud," Winters tells me, earnestly.

"I know you would, mate. It's not you that I'm worried about. It's just that past experiences, you know…" I reply.

"I know, tell me about it. You're coming to Porton Down and Catherine and Emily are here. You have my word," Winters insists.

"Thanks, mate, that's good enough for me. We are outside the stadium, or what's left of it. Extraction point on the north side, bearing east. There are five passengers waiting for evac," I inform him.

"The team is on its way. ETA fifteen minutes," Winters replies.

"Tell them to pull their fingers out. I'm getting the jitters here," I tell him straight.

"Is there an immediate threat?" Winters asks, suddenly worried.

"No, nothing imminent. Ignore me. I just want my bed," I backtrack.

"Understood. They're inbound and won't be long. We'll be tracking you, so see you shortly," Winters tells me.

"Okay, mate, and thanks. Thanks again," I reply.

"Glad to help. Oh, and Catherine sends her love," Winters says, before he hangs up.

I definitely owe Winters a drink, or three, I think, as I put my phone away. *That's if we ever get the chance again*, I warn myself, before I get too thirsty.

"They're on their way. ETA fifteen minutes," I tell everyone.

"I told you Winters would be waiting by the phone for your call. I think he has a man-crush," Dixon grins.

"Very funny. But, yes you did, mate. I don't think he's the only one who was waiting by the phone though. And I'm not talking about my family," I reply.

231

"We will deal with that when we land," Dixon assures me, and I can only hope we can.

"Are Emily and Catherine okay?" Josh asks.

"Yes, they're fine, Champ. Looking forward to seeing us, you can bet," I tell him.

"Emily will go ballistic, having us both back," Josh smiles. I can't bring myself to warn him that it may not all be plain sailing when we land, not right now anyway.

"She will," I smile back at my son.

All at once, things quieten down. I become horribly aware of the tragic destruction there is in every direction I care to look. The carnage stretches as far as the eye can see. The surrounding tower blocks have been smashed in two or completely crumpled to the ground. Smaller buildings have been obliterated into nothing but burning piles of rubble that send plumes of acrid smoke funnelling into the air.

I know that this area was once criss-crossed with roads. They are all now buried beneath scattered rubble, debris and soil that has been churned out of the ground. Every bomb that didn't hit a building has still left its scar on the landscape by forming deep craters that sink deep into the earth.

It is not only the moon that hangs high above our heads that reveals the extent of the destruction. Countless fires create a bright-orange hue in the smoke haze, ensuring that we can see the destroyed Wembley vista. The hellscape is worse than any I have witnessed at first hand before, despite my extensive travels to war-ravaged cities around the world. I doubt that the devil himself could have done a more atrocious job of creating hell on earth than the military has achieved in such a short amount of time.

Was it pure luck or, indeed, a miracle that we five managed to survive the onslaught that has smashed an entire London borough to ruins? Whichever otherworldly force decided to watch over us, it didn't do it alone. My aching back tells me that much.

My eyes become transfixed by the stump of a building that remains in the near distance. Flames dance off one side of the building's carcass, giving it a mesmerising glow, while smoke moves mysteriously on the other side, which has become a flat roof for the floors below. I focus in on the smoke, which drifts across the roof in a peculiar manner, my heart sinking horribly as I peer deeper into the haze.

A distant howl of death echoes into the night sky to accompany my dreaded realisation that the haze contains something far more sinister than smoke alone.

"Contact," I hear myself murmur, as the first shadow drops through the air, falling off the roof and onto the ground in front of us.

"Impossible. Are you sure?" Dixon questions, urgently, his ears not as attuned as mine to the howl of the undead.

"Contact. Eleven o'clock," I confirm without shouting, my eyes fixed on the multiple shadows raining down off the building.

"I see them," Alice says, confirming that I am not losing my mind.

"Me too. Multiple X-rays heading this way," Josh agrees.

"Got them," Dixon confirms, arriving late to the party.

"We need to run," Carter says, in a panic.

"Hold your station, soldier!" I bark under my breath, even though our position is already compromised. The last thing we need is Carter losing his shit again.

"Options?" Dixon asks, urgently. "They'll be on us in minutes."

My head shoots back towards the stadium, urgently searching to find a defensive position. There are no other buildings in our immediate vicinity, and I don't want us to be forced to retreat away from our extraction point.

"They're coming!" Dixon insists. "We need an option now!"

On my right, nestling in the very bottom of the stadium's wreckage, I see an opening under a twisted roller shutter. I have no idea if there is a space behind the shutter, or if the wreckage may collapse on us if disturbed, but there are no other options. We're out of time.

"I've got one!" I shout, as Dixon's rifle erupts into life.

"Go, go, go. I'm right behind you!" Dixon shouts over the side of his rifle.

Shadows are closing in fast. We need a diversion to give us some valuable seconds. One after the other, I pull the pin on three grenades and launch them into the air, in an even spread.

"This way," I order, turning to run towards the opening.

Dixon continues to fire as Josh, Alice and Carter fall in behind me. *Move it, Dixon*, I shout in my head, as I reach the twisted roller shutter. Explosions erupt away to my left, but I ignore them completely.

I skid to a stop next to the opening and shout for Carter, who is closest, to get inside. He peers at the opening in terror, shaking his head from side to side. I grab him to pull him closer and force him down towards the opening. Carter pulls away from me with such force that he breaks my grip on him. Before I can stop him, Carter turns to flee in the opposite direction.

With no other choice but to let him go, I order Alice to get in. She overcomes the fear that is written across her face to bend down and crawl underneath the roller shutter.

Josh bends to follow Alice inside when a chilling scream pierces the air from the direction that Carter hightailed it in. I glance to look as Josh crawls into the gap and see Carter picking himself up off the ground, holding his leg in agony. Carter's fall has crippled him, but he is now beyond my help. He made his choice and, this time, he will have to suffer the consequences.

Josh disappears into the darkness and I bend down, getting ready to follow him, just as soon as Dixon arrives. *Where is Dixon?* I think, panicking. My eyes follow the sound of gunfire and I see him. He hasn't moved from his initial firing position. What is he fucking doing?

"Dixon!" I shout. "Over here. Move!"

Dixon keeps firing, even as Rabids close in on him. So many shadows fill my view of the ground directly in front of the sergeant. *Why doesn't he retreat?* I cry in my head, willing him to turn and run towards me, my rifle back in my hands, ready to cover him.

"Get in, Dad," Josh's voice sounds from around my feet, but I can't. I can't take my eyes off Dixon. A creature leaps through the air, directly at my comrade. I aim at the beast but resist the temptation to fire. I have no chance of hitting the target from this distance. All that would be achieved by me firing would be to give away our position, and bring the horde down on us.

Smoothly, Dixon eases to the side and fills the creature with bullets. It slams into the ground beside him. Only then does Dixon turn to try and make his escape. His heroics have given us plenty of time to make ours. He looks in my direction and I raise my hand to signal him in, but he will never cover the ground between us before he is enveloped by the undead.

I watch in horror as Dixon swerves left, his change of direction taking him back towards the wreckage where we climbed out of the stadium. He cannot possibly survive the peril of the deadly wreckage at such speed and with a pack of Rabid creatures in close pursuit.

A horrific sound of gunfire and crashing steel echoes in the air as Dixon disappears from my line of sight. The sound of gunfire is short-lived, as Rabids pile onto the wreckage after Dixon. Then, horribly, only the sound of crashing remains.

Dixon, you bloody fool, why did you wait so long to run? I cry inside at the loss of my brother in arms. Deep down I know why Dixon made his stand as I duck down to crawl into the gap. He fought on for me. He shot his last bullets to allow Josh's escape. He didn't give up so that he could save Alice. He sacrificed himself for all three of us.

Chapter 19

"Where is Sergeant Dixon?" Alice asks, as I crawl in beside her and Josh.

"He didn't make it," I tell her, solemnly.

"Oh, my God," Alice's voice cracks.

"He made a stand to allow us to escape," I tell them, grimly. "The bloody fool," I add.

"Josh, Alice, help me, please!" a whimpering cry sounds from outside.

I can just about still see Carter through the gap in front of us. He is sitting on the ground some distance away, nursing his injured leg. A moment ago, he attempted to stand but, as soon as he put pressure on the leg, he fell back down.

"We can't help him now. We tried our best," I whisper to Josh and Alice, trying to put their minds at ease.

A silhouette moves across in Carter's direction and a terrified scream assaults our eardrums. The Rabid is on Carter in a shot as more chilling screams ring out. The sound nauseates me and I beg for it to stop. Another Rabid moves in to join the feeding frenzy and, with a whimper, the screaming ceases. My guilt at wishing the sound to stop rises as more and more creatures move in Carter's direction and begin to swamp the area outside our hidey-hole.

How are we going to get out of here when the helicopters arrive? I wonder, as a scraping noise sounds above our heads. It stops but leaves an awful creaking noise in its wake. The hideous sounds remind each of us that we could be crushed at any moment. How stable is the wreckage above our heads? How long until it all comes crashing down onto our little bubble?

"The evac will be here soon," I whisper assurance, despite us having no way out.

"We'll be trapped in here when it does," Josh whispers back, confirming that I am not fooling anyone.

"We will find a way," I whisper in reply.

Outside, Carter's screaming, together with his flesh, has attracted what appears to be the whole horde of Rabids in the vicinity. Shadows stumble around in every direction, looking for the prey. Carter will have been devoured in minutes, however, judging by the number of creatures we see.

The haunting sounds of creaking from the wreckage above us become less distinct as they begin to be overpowered by the sounds of the undead. Their feet shuffle in the rubble, kicking up dust. Snarls and grunts reverberate from the back of the creatures' throats to fill our heads, reminding us of our ominous predicament.

I attempt to block out the entire spectrum of threatening noises from my brain to allow me to think. There must be a way of us escaping our hole before the helicopters arrive.

The evac team's arrival can be no more than a few minutes away, at most. I don't have to imagine what their reaction will be when they arrive to find the enemy in such large numbers in the extraction zone. They will light up the undead. Come at them with all the firepower in their armoury. Small-arms fire, .50-calibre door guns, grenades and missiles are sure to be thrown into the mix.

Nobody will take the time to consider where we are; they will only see the enemy. Even if they do, will anyone even contemplate that we have taken refuge under the wreckage of Wembley Stadium? They would think us crazy to take such a risk. The gunfire and explosions will rain down and, if they don't slaughter us directly, the wreckage will certainly collapse to crush us where we hide, never to be seen again.

Something that Winters said in our conversation a few minutes ago suddenly strikes me. The solution is instantly obvious to me, but there isn't a moment to lose.

"Don't argue. There's no debate. I'm leaving," I whisper, just loud enough to allow Josh and Alice to hear me. "When I'm clear I'll cause a diversion and draw the pack away. Get out of here as soon as you can. Stay close to the stadium's wreckage, if possible, on the north side, and I will come back for you. Understood?"

Even in the darkness, I can see Josh's eyes glare at me, the whites catching the orange glow of the distant fires. Before he can say a word, I turn away from him and shuffle forwards on my chest towards the opening. I cannot afford to pause or to wait to see if the beasts react to my appearance. I expect the helicopters to swoop in imminently. I must get as far away from this position as possible before they arrive.

My head emerges from the hole, the noise of the undead immediately becoming crystal clear to me. I look up to see them shuffling close by, some even turning in my direction, but I don't stop moving forwards.

As soon as I am clear of the twisted roller shutter, I rise to my feet and hang my rifle on my back. The weapon would be useless to me should the pack decide that I am fresh enough for dinner. There are too many of them for me to defeat with the firepower I am carrying. All that the rifle would do is to draw unwanted attention to the stranger in their midst.

My first step is the most nerve-racking. I feel like my heart will burst out of my throat, but I take that step. A nearby creature ferociously snarls directly at me, threatening to attack. I turn away from the fearsome beast and take a second and then a third step. I haven't got time to play 'Rabid creature' with the beast, as I did when I ran with the pack through the streets of the City of London.

Winters said they are tracking me, which can only be through my phone. I must therefore gain as much distance from Josh and Alice as I possibly can. Then, I can only hope that the evac team follow my signal and will be drawn away from the hiding place in the wreckage.

Step after step I move, looking for gaps in the baying horde to slip through. Each one takes me further away from Josh and Alice but then, in the distance, I hear the unmistakable sound of helicopters and I am too close to the wreckage. The risk of the evac team opening fire next to the wreckage is still acute.

I need a diversion and pull a grenade off the front of my combat vest. Keeping it low, I pull the pin, release the lever and then, casually, throw the grenade as far as I can muster.

My actions cause creatures to look at me, their snarling mouths ready to feed, but as soon as I return to walking normally their excitement dies down. Seconds later, a good distance away, the grenade explodes.

The explosion causes a second of stunned silence within the horde, but then all hell breaks loose. A chorus of fever-pitched cries rings out. Ear-splitting screeches tear into my eardrums, piercing my brain, and then the pack surges forwards. They surge towards the location of the explosion and the mushroom cloud rising from it. I break into a run in order to be carried along with the pack, running as fast as my tired body and the hazardous terrain will allow.

I stumble over rubble and skirt round the edges of deep craters, constantly searching in front of me, looking for obstacles. The creatures around me are not so careful in their frenzy to reach the new feeding ground. Their legs smash against large pieces of rubble and their feet trip over the smaller blocks, sending them crashing to the ground. Others take no heed of the craters, running into thin air. They tumble down into the deep holes, only to jump up to try to scramble back out, clawing at the soil and rock. Arms are snapped in half, but arms are of little consequence. Legs are shattered, but even that only slows the creatures down to a crawling speed.

Four helicopters power overhead, surveying the horde as well as the terrain, sending the pack into an even higher-pitched frenzy. The transport helicopters fly into the near distance before hovering up and around to circle back to begin their detailed reconnaissance of the area. They search for their prize.

Each pilot slows their aircraft down considerably, hovering slowly over the pack. Rabids reach up, some leaping into the air in their misguided desperation to capture fresh meat. The helicopters have stemmed the flow of the pack away from the wreckage, the grenade's explosion a distant memory, if these creatures possess that particular brain function.

I come to a stop with them, my plan beginning to fall apart. My head stays down just in case and an eagle-eyed squaddie spots me from above in amongst the pack. I need to think of my next move but, if I am spotted, it might release an onslaught to exterminate the enemy.

How closely are they able to track me? I debate with myself. *Is my signal pinging on a screen above my head as I stand here thinking? Can they see that I am just below them, lost in the mass of the Rabid horde?*

There is no easy option. If I were to separate myself from the pack and make myself known to the closest helicopter, the pilot would certainly swoop in and pick me up. The good news would be communicated to the other crews before I could stop it and they would go to work annihilating the enemy. I cannot be sure if Josh and Alice have been able to escape the wreckage. They may still be there waiting, under thousands of tons of steel and concrete.

I must press on, gain distance from the wreckage, cause another diversion to draw the pack to me. That is the only way to be certain that Josh and Alice are given the chance to escape.

Not far away is a mound of rubble, possibly the remains of a destroyed building. That is where I will perform my diversion, I decide. The mound is close enough to reach, but far enough away from the stadium's wreckage to give me confidence that Josh and Alice will get their chance.

I begin to walk towards my Alamo. Running is out of the question now that the Rabid horde have stalled to a stop. My progress is good: the surrounding creatures are too interested in the helicopters above to bother with me, their fevered, snarling faces raised to the sky. I wonder if anyone in the crew looking down has spotted the figure casually walking through the rest of the pack. If they have, I am unaware of it, and it doesn't really matter unless they decide to test their targeting skills.

The pack thins as I move until I leave it behind entirely. I am out in the open by myself when I approach the mound of rubble. I pull out my last remaining glowstick and crack it, shaking it as I walk. The pink light pleasantly surprises me. I was expecting green. After hanging the glowstick on the front of my body armour, I pull my M4 around off my back and into my hands.

When I reach it, I find that the mound of rubble is solid: my foot confirms it. Carefully, I shin my way up the low slope until I reach its plateau, only a few feet above the ground. At the peak I peer over the opposite side, becoming accustomed to the terrain and looking for cover. The terrain is one of mutilated buildings and devastation but there is an array of dark holes and shadows to give me cover.

Satisfied that there is an exit, I prepare to turn round, psyching myself up to go back into action as I prepare yet another grenade. Just as the grenade's pin falls to the ground, I am suddenly bathed in white light. *Thanks, lads*, I think, for throwing a spotlight on my performance, as I spin round on top of the rubble.

The horde of the undead are spread out before me. Their arms reach up to the sky, baying for the helicopters to land and feed them. The closest helicopter doesn't land but begins to manoeuvre sideways in my direction, the pilot following the instruction of the crew member who has caught me in his spotlight. The scene is set, with the wreckage of Wembley Stadium crowning the battlefield.

Other helicopters manoeuvre in, the pink light radiating on my chest calling them closer. Their movement is away from the wreckage, just as I planned. The hovering aircraft help to move the horde, but it would be remiss of me to let them do all the work.

My body twists left and I launch the grenade into the air behind me. My hands take hold of the M4. I point it into the air and depress the trigger. Bullets spray out of the M4's muzzle, lighting it up so that it flashes brightly against the night sky. *Come and get it, motherfuckers!* my head screams like a crazed warmonger, as the grenade explodes behind me and I continue to fire.

God only knows what the crews of the four helicopters must be thinking as they close in on my position. They must be asking themselves if I've completely lost my mind and tipped over the edge. Gone all Marlon Brando in *Apocalypse Now*, a film that every soldier worth their salt has watched more than once. Wondering to themselves why four helicopters have been despatched to rescue a crazed nutjob from the battlefield.

They can think what they like. It is of no concern to me. All that matters is Josh and Alice's escape and the herd of rabid zombies in front of me is on the move.

The M4's magazine exhausts itself and clicks empty. I only have seconds before the pack of Rabids will reach the bottom of the rubble. I must execute my escape immediately and I turn to run, assured that Josh and Alice now have their opportunity to escape.

Downdrafts from the helicopters buffet me as I make my break for it. The grenade explodes on my right as I turn round and I feint to go right to draw the creatures in that direction. As soon as I disappear down the mound's back slope, I switch direction to head left, grabbing the glowstick from my chest. Pink light spins through the air as I throw the glowstick to the right, in the same direction as the explosion, to further fool the pack of Rabids. Now I can only hope that my ruse has worked and that the pack will follow my misdirection.

Unfortunately, the helicopter above isn't so easily fooled and the idiot in control of the spotlight keeps it burning directly on me. *For Christ's sake, give me a chance to escape,* I cry in my head, as the Rabid horde burst over the mound. *Switch the goddamn spotlight off!*

Far from switching the spotlight off, the beam of light and the helicopter trace my every move. Every twist and turn that I make to traverse the hazardous terrain is illuminated for my deadly foes to see. A quick check over my shoulder shows me that they have seen me running. Beastly shadows have changed direction and are coming straight for me. I have no chance of outrunning them and, thanks to my nemesis in the sky, no chance of hiding from them either.

This would be the ideal time for the helicopter's firepower to intervene and eliminate the enemy. But not a single bullet shoots down from the sky. The only help I am given is the light illuminating my way, which is exactly what I don't want. My legs are frazzled and my lungs are clogging up from the smoke damage coupled with the exertion. I can only imagine that I have completely confused the crews above and that nobody can decide what action to take.

I make the decision for them. I stop running and use the closest pieces of rubble for cover before my legs give out completely. In an instant, I reload the M4, aim at the closest threat and open fire. My first target down, I fire again and keep firing until the magazine is empty, but still I get no assistance from above. *What the hell is going on?* I ask myself, as I rush to reload. *The enemy is out in the open. Exterminate them!*

I begin to fire again but there are too many. They are only metres away and they're coming straight at me. Unless I get some help in the next few seconds, I am doomed.

Finally, and not a moment too soon, the crew of the closest helicopter decide enough is enough and burst into action. Bullets and tracer fire erupt from the lead helicopter, strafing through the night sky to cut into the front of the undead horde. I breathe a sigh of relief as I watch the awesome firepower of the minigun obliterate anything in its path. Rabid heads and torsos are scythed into, exploding and splattering into the air to soak the ground below. I hold my fire, saving my ammo, watching the extraordinary slaughter of the pack. The M4 remains pointed at the slaughter, in case anything strays, but nothing can. The power of the minigun is unstoppable.

As the minigun slows its rate of fire and begins to use better targeted bursts to clear up any stragglers from the horde, I slump down behind the rubble. I need to catch my breath in case my torment begins again. Breathing heavily, my legs on fire from their excursion, I wonder where Josh and Alice are. Have they been watching the drama from afar, or are they holed up somewhere waiting for my call?

My call, I think, and hastily pull my phone out while the minigun finishes its work. I see straight away that I have missed calls but, before I get a chance to check who they are from, my phone's screen lights up with another call. Winters' name is displayed.

"Hello," I answer, groggily.

"What the hell is going on there? We are getting some very concerning and bewildering reports," Winters asks, urgently. He must think that I've gone mad.

"We've had some trouble, mate," I tell him.

"Really, I'd never have guessed. What's going on?" Winters demands.

"Oh, you know, the usually Andy Richards' dramas," I joke. "I think we're getting it sorted now though."

"Seriously, mate, is everyone okay?" Winters insists.

"I think Josh and Alice are, but everyone else is dead. Including Sergeant Dixon," I reply, solemnly.

"What do you mean, you think they are okay? What happened?" Winters asks in frustration, skirting round the bad news.

"We were attacked while we waited for the evac. We became trapped and I had to create a diversion to allow Josh and Alice to escape. Don't worry, mate. I haven't taken leave of my senses. Not yet anyway," I tell him.

"Where are Josh and Alice?" Winters asks, concerned.

"I don't know yet. I had to leave them to cause the diversion. I'm going to get picked up now and try to find them. Hopefully, I'll speak to them on the phone after this conversation. So, I've got to go. I'm okay though, tell Catherine that for me," I reply.

"Will do," Winters replies, and we both hang up.

A quick check shows me that none of my missed calls has come from Josh. I hastily find his number. Josh's phone rings and rings and then, worryingly, the call switches to answerphone. Alice's does the same. *Why aren't they answering?* I think in panic, rushing to my feet.

"Call me, Josh! I'm about to be picked up and need your location!" I say into the phone, urgently, whilst looking up to the sky and after dialling Josh again.

Two helicopters have risen to a higher altitude, presumably to scan the surrounding area now that the main threat has been eliminated. The other two have remained low to bring their armaments to bear, and each of them is still firing intermittently at the ground.

I wave my arms above my head to try and attract the attention of either of the lower helicopters so that they can land and pick me up. Neither seems to take much notice of the raving madman frantically waving at them from the ground. My frustration grows as both aircraft continue to go about their business. Despite that fact, I am the real target of their mission.

Bloody hell, I think, and give up waving, instead getting my phone out once more to call for Winters' assistance yet again. He answers almost immediately.

"Andy, is there a problem?" he asks, urgently.

"Yes. Can you get one of the buffoons up there to land and pick me up?" I reply.

Winters asks me to hold while he relays my request to the relevant person.

"Done, mate," he says, as he comes back on the phone.

"Thanks. It's like amateur hour here," I tell him.

"Really. That's two evac teams and two special-ops teams you've got for company," he informs me.

"You could have fooled me," I respond to his interesting information.

"Any news on Josh and Alice?" Winters questions.

"Neither of them is answering and these dickheads are too busy taking potshots to bother picking me up," I tell him, frustratedly. Just as I say that, the helicopter closest to me begins to lose altitude whilst hovering over in my direction. *Finally*, I think, as I tell Winters I've got to go.

Expertly bringing his aircraft down, the pilot hovers just off the ground to allow me to board. A gloved hand reaches down to help haul me into the hold and, as soon as I am on-board, the pilot takes us up.

I am faced with five men. One will be the door gunner and I can see immediately from the combat gear and weapons that the other four are Special Forces. A quick check of their insignia confirms that the team is SAS.

"Who is in charge?" I bark, as soon as I have a headset fitted.

"I am, Sir. Sergeant Roy," a strong, confident voice tells me through his combat paint.

"A good answer but wrong, Sergeant. I'm in charge," I inform Roy, bluntly. "We have two more on the ground waiting for evac. Understood?"

"Yes, Sir," Roy answers, without a hint of offence in his voice.

"Pilot," I say.

"Yes, Sir," the pilot answers into my headset.

"Put us down near the northeast corner of the stadium," I order.

"Affirmative," the pilot responds, as the floor of the helicopter tilts.

"We were told to expect five passengers, Sir," Roy questions, quite legitimately.

"Two have expired, Sergeant. Let's keep it to that number. Agreed?" I reply.

"Yes, Sir. That's if I have anything to do with it. Can I just ask your name, Sir?" Roy enquires.

"Captain Richards, Sergeant," I tell him.

"An honour, Sir," Roy tells me. He then touches a separate radio on his chest. "Alpha one, secured. Receiving, over." Roy informs his command that I have been secured.

"When we land, secure the perimeter," I order, as the pilot brings us down.

"Sir," Roy confirms, while he checks his weapons.

Roy's team are on the ground in the same instant as the helicopter's wheels. They have secured the perimeter by the time I have ordered the pilot to hold position on the ground and have followed them out. Their rifles scan the perimeter as I hit the ground and rush around the helicopter towards the wrecked stadium.

Disturbing memories flash across my mind as I approach the stadium's wreckage even though I have only just left its carcass. The sight of the wreckage that we clambered over and that I saw Dixon desperately aiming to reach brings me particular torment.

I look away from that harrowing area, instead concentrating on the gap at the bottom of the wreckage. Taking heart at seeing that the wreckage looks like it is still standing above the twisted roller shutter, I speed towards it. Dust swirls into the air from the downdraft of the helicopter's rotors to sting my eyes, making tears form.

More dust flies into the air when I grind to a halt next to the roller shutter. I fall to my hands and knees to peer into the tiny cavern to find my son and Alice. Confused, I blink to clear my eyes of dust and water. Either my eyes must be playing tricks on me or I have come to the wrong roller shutter. I scramble to my feet to search for the correct roller shutter, which must be close by. How could I have made such a mistake? This can't be the right one because it is jam-packed with rubble and steel.

Terror courses through every sinew of my being as it dawns on me that I have made no mistake. There is no other roller shutter. The wreckage has collapsed into the void, just as I feared it might. The only harrowing question now is, were Josh and Alice still inside when the wreckage crumbled?

Chapter 20

"He will be okay. I'm sure of it," Alice whispers to Josh.

"He had better be," Josh replies quietly, peering under the roller shutter.

"We just need to be ready to move," Alice says.

"I can't see him any more," Josh observes.

Josh searches for a sign of his father but he doesn't see him again. All he sees are the dark shadows of Rabids silhouetted by the glow of a burning Wembley. Yet again he must sit tight whilst his father walks into the danger zone. It is so frustrating for Josh, a feeling Alice can definitely sympathise with.

They wait in anticipation of the diversion happening and the Rabid horde moving off. Neither of them is comfortable beneath the straining weight of the unstable wreckage and crave the moment when they can crawl out of its clutches.

An explosion erupts in the distance, causing Alice to jump. A grenade. Josh is certain of it: he is very familiar with an exploding grenade's unique characteristics. *This could be*

CAPITAL FALLING 6 - BREAKOUT

it; Josh tells himself. *But be patient, wait until the horde move a good distance away.*

Angry, fevered snarls and grunts sound from the pack of creatures nearby, raising the tension. A roaring, howling screech in the distance cuts through the air, a call to arms for the army of the undead. Surely the pack will now heed the call and take off, finally vacating the immediate vicinity, to give Josh and Alice their chance to slip out and make their escape? The creatures loiter though, only shuffling a few feet further away from their position, which is not far enough by half to give Josh and Alice a chance to sneak away unseen.

A chopping sound begins to beat into their sheltered crevice, the sound of helicopter rotors cutting through the air. The vibration causes something unseen to move in the wreckage hanging over their heads. A metallic crash rattles into the sides that trap them and the ground beneath them.

Alice grabs Josh's hand in the darkness, the horrible sinking feeling in her stomach becoming unbearable. The helicopter's rotors get louder, the vibrations stronger. More strange noises bang from above, encompassing them.

Dread stifles Josh and he squeezes Alice's hand, his heart racing. It can only be a matter of moments before the wreckage comes crashing down to crush and entomb them. He would rather face the undead, and die fighting on his feet. Even if that inevitably means having his guts ripped out and fed upon.

Josh prepares to move, to take Alice with him. He is certain she feels the same way that he does. He would be proud to die by her side, fighting the enemy. There is no one he would rather have with him than her.

A helicopter roars into view above the heads of the zombie horde. The aircraft's engine, combined with its rotors, shakes the very foundations that are still attached to the collapsed stadium. Another helicopter swoops into view, rattling the wreckage violently. Dust and debris begin to rain down from above to cover Josh and Alice. Crashes sound closer to their heads as yet another helicopter powers over the wreckage.

Calamitous sounds of the wreckage crumbling above them overpower the roar of the fourth helicopter. Josh is already scrambling under the roller shutter though as the aircraft bursts over his head. He couldn't have let Alice out first: his body blocked her path of escape.

Another rumble from inside the shell of the stadium starts a chain reaction of fatal crashing and crumbling sounds. Racked with guilt for leaving Alice behind, Josh kicks and pushes himself free. He pays no heed to the threat beyond, that of the wanton evil creatures that could cut him down at any moment.

A chilling, high-pitched scream spins Josh around in the dirt. He sees Alice's panicked face, her hand outstretched, begging for his help. Josh ducks back under the roller shutter, reaching inside to take hold of Alice's hand. He reaches and touches her fingers as dust billows into his face and pieces of rubble smash into his arm.

Tears stream into Josh's eyes, clearing them enough for him to see Alice's face for one last time before brick, stone, steel and dust pour into the space that traps her. Her eyes plead for mercy from the crushing weight that is engulfing her. Josh stretches desperately to take hold of Alice's hand, a hand that is broken, crushed and lost in the avalanche of rubble and hopelessness.

Forced to pull his battered and bruised arm from beneath the torrent of pain, Josh screams Alice's name, begging for an answer, something that will show a hint of life. Only grinding waves of crushing death and pouring dust call back to him as the void under the wreckage is filled completely.

"Alice!" Josh bellows in a state of delirium, the cascade of falling rubble solidifying. "No," Josh cries at the solid wall now confronting him. No answer comes to him this time, nothing but the sounds of trickling dust that fade into nothing.

"Alice, please," Josh sobs through his grit-filled eyes. He turns away from the wall of rock and metal, unable to look at the haunting tomb of crushing death any longer. His body, weak and distraught, slumps to the side, his back coming to rest against the very tomb that encases Alice.

Sobs of loss and guilt pulse uncontrollably through Josh's body. His rifle is forgotten, discarded in the dirt. Wind from the aircraft above sends more dust into his eyes and throat. Josh doesn't care: let it come, let it choke him. The sight of Alice's petrified face burns into his mind, begging Josh to help her. The sight of her hand outstretched towards him, desperate for Josh to pull her out as the wreckage crumbled down, crushing her.

A flash of light in the distance fights its way through the matted dirt in Josh's eyes. Shadows move against it. The explosion cracks into Josh's ears, piercing through his trauma. The sound causes him to blink and wipe his eyes, to peer at the vision of Alice's pleading face. Her vision floats in front of him, twinkling and dancing with the flames that continue to burn across Wembley. *I am sorry, Alice. Sorry I failed you. Sorry I left you behind to die beneath dirt and rubble.*

Josh sees the shadows moving against the light behind Alice. He knows that the beasts have seen him and are moving to take their revenge for his failure. Alice smiles as the shadows grow larger. Even after he had completely failed her, she smiles, smiles to ease his suffering. Josh begs her not to leave him as he makes his transition. His demise will be different from hers but just as traumatic. It's no more than he deserves. He prays that Alice will stay with him when the undead rip into his body and feed on his flesh. Josh gives into his fateful destiny. He begins to accept the beckoning end.

Three Rabid beasts, stragglers from the pack, remain nearer to the stadium's wreckage. Their brethren have moved off, attracted by the roar of helicopters and the boom of explosives.

The crash of falling wreckage, followed by the squeals of prey, makes them spin back towards the collapsed stadium. Movement piques their interest, their vision homing in on the warm meat.

One creature snarls at the next and the scramble to hunt is on. Two of the creatures bolt in unison, their gnawing hunger undeniable. Racing to be first to feed, their speed across the ground is rapid. Every piece of rubble of consequence is avoided. Their darting skills are impressive, or is it no more than sheer luck?

Inevitably, the fastest, strongest beast takes the lead. Edging ahead, the lead creature is by no means the biggest of Rabids, but it is bigger than the other two weaker specimens it races. Closing in on its prey, the creature's mouth hangs open, its teeth as sharp as those of its bigger counterparts that were tempted to follow the roar of the helicopters. The teeth are certainly sharp enough to sink into the fresh meat on offer. The prey is not moving, or scrambling to escape.

Josh watches the beast that will put him out of his misery chase him. He sees the viciousness in the creature's eyes, the evil of its undead features. Let it feed so that the end comes, Josh challenges, resigned. Alice deserved better and yet she remains with Josh to comfort him. Her smiling face is there, just out of reach.

Fear eventually takes hold of Josh as the fearsome Rabid launches itself directly at him. A scream builds inside him, but he refuses to succumb to it. Just as he refuses to close his eyes in case Alice leaves him to suffer alone.

Blood and guts erupt into the air, the creature's trajectory shifting direction. Josh cries out in defeat, his chance of salvation slipping away. Another burst of bullets rips into the creature, ejecting more fluid and, this time, brain matter.

Josh cries out again as the creature lands in a pile on the ground next to him, unmoving and dead. A shadow moves in front of him, cutting off his view of the two remaining creatures, his last remaining hopes of salvation from his guilt. Alice disappears, erased from his view by the sudden appearance of the shadow, and Josh feels he might burst with anger.

Gunfire bursts from the shadow to attack Josh's death-givers, his chance of peace. He must stop the shadow before it's too late and any chance of peace is extinguished. He fumbles on the ground next to him, his fingers searching for the rifle he discarded, to put an end to the shadow's treachery.

Something grabs Josh as he fumbles. He wills it to be the last remaining creature, the one that will bring him his comeuppance. Tragically, Josh knows instinctively that this is no Rabid grabbing him, come to wreak vengeance. No Rabid would be lifting him to his feet and shouting words of encouragement.

Josh won't allow it. He releases the muscles in his legs to let himself fall back down to the ground. *Leave me here to die*, Josh insists, *I don't deserve to live. Why should I be allowed to carry on living, when I failed to save Alice's beautiful life?*

Josh feels the ground beneath him again. He feels a morsel of contentment at knowing that he will now be left to die. Nobody will bother with him a second time; he simply isn't worth it.

A hand slaps his face hard. Undefined words are shouted. Josh blinks, trying to see who is attacking him. Another slap hits the opposite side of his face and the voice is raised in its determination to make Josh hear.

"Get on your feet, soldier!" the voice cries at Josh, the fog that envelops him lifting enough to hear. "We must move, now."

Blinking hard, Josh's vision starts to clear and a face begins to form in front of him. He blinks again as the face's fearsome features become clearer. Impossible. Surely it cannot be? Surely the face is another vision?

"Sergeant Dixon?" Josh mumbles, unsure if he has completely lost his mind.

"Who the fuck else do you think it is? The Messiah himself?" Dixon barks back at Josh, who is completely dumbfounded.

"You're dead," Josh replies.

"Well, I must be the Messiah after all then," Dixon grins as he tugs on Josh's body armour to drag him to his feet.

"But you're dead," Josh repeats, as Dixon turns to cover their position.

"Don't worry, mate. You're not the first person to make that mistake," Dixon replies over his shoulder. "Where's Alice?"

Josh looks down at his feet, not answering.

"I asked you where's Alice, Josh! Get your shit together: we've got to move. We haven't gone unnoticed over here," Dixon insists, seeing figures moving in their direction.

"She's dead, Sergeant," Josh replies, solemnly.

"Oh, no... I'm sorry, mate," Dixon says, grimly, now understanding Josh's unhinged behaviour.

"I couldn't save her," Josh tells Dixon, sadly.

"But I bet you tried, didn't you?" Dixon asks.

"I tried but failed, Sergeant," Josh answers.

"I know you did," Dixon replies. "I need that spirit now, mate. We've got more incoming. Your dad has missed a few. Are you with me?"

"Yes, Sergeant, I'm with you," Josh confirms.

Dixon rapidly bends down, picks up Josh's rifle and hands it to him. He slaps Josh on the shoulder before he sets off at pace, bearing west. Josh is up and takes off to follow, forcing his grief down, back inside himself. At least for now.

Four helicopters hover in the near distance, above the main horde of Rabids. Josh is confused as to why they haven't opened fire on the ground below. Perhaps if they had the creatures that have detached themselves from the main pack wouldn't have seen him and Dixon. And maybe the creatures would have been cut to ribbons instead of hunting them at speed.

"Run!" Dixon bellows over his shoulder to Josh, the pack of creatures that are pursuing them gaining ground.

Josh increases his speed to stay with Dixon, not wanting to put another comrade in danger. He knows that Dixon is searching for cover, somewhere to stop and take on their vicious pursuers. Options are sparse in the barren destroyed landscape in their immediate vicinity. Josh begs Dixon not to swerve left to use the stadium's wreckage. He couldn't bear that. He'd rather make his stand here in the open than go near the wreckage ever again.

Dixon swerves to the right, away from the haunting wreckage. He wants nothing to do with the death trap either. He also knows that Josh could crumble into a slobbering mess again if he took his young partner in that direction. Instead, Dixon aims for a low building that seems to have escaped the onslaught of bombs that rained down from the sky.

Screeches of death echo from close behind them as Dixon closes in on the building. As he draws near, he sees that the building is no more than a flimsy temporary structure, constructed of wood and glass. Of all the buildings that were obliterated and flattened, it is a mystery how this one survived, is a mystery. The ticket office and its wooden façade should have been engulfed in flames, even though it escaped a direct hit.

Too late to change his mind, Dixon slams three bullets into the door of the ticket office moments before he crashes into it. The door bursts open and Dixon flies inside, closely followed by Josh. Bullets from Dixon's rifle shatter through the closest window to lay down fire even as Josh slams the door closed and pulls a filing cabinet down to block it.

"I count approximately ten to fifteen targets!" Dixon shouts over the blast of his rifle.

Up to fifteen targets, Josh thinks. as he rushes into position next to Dixon. *Shouldn't be a problem.*

"They're spreading out!" Dixon bellows, as Josh opens fire at his first Rabid.

Josh watches as his bullets rip into his target. His head shots miss, the bullets that slam into the Rabid's chest knock the creature's torso back, but the beast soon recovers. Josh fires again, focusing his aim at the Rabid's head. His third shot hits its target and the creature crumples to the ground in a heap before the contents of its head fall out of the air.

Not waiting for congratulations, or a slap on the back, Josh retargets and fires again. Dixon is constantly firing next to Josh. The sound of his rifle is deafening in Josh's ear as the undead close in on their position. Targets fill Josh's view. He is spoiled for choice but, with every target that falls, the enemy gets closer.

Suddenly, a window next to Josh implodes. Glass shatters into the air, a figure flying in with the shards. The body lands halfway inside the ticket office, becoming snagged on the window frame and the splinters of glass it still holds. The Rabid goes wild, scrambling to free itself, its face frantic, its gnashing teeth snapping.

Josh's rifle cuts through the air without a thought, his trigger finger depressing. Bullets burst from his rifle's muzzle, blasting into the creature's head, completely collapsing it. The body's frantic movement ceases in an instant and it slumps, bent it two over the frame, the contents of its head flopping out and onto the floor below.

"Keep firing!" Dixon orders, desperately. "They're going to overrun us!"

Josh spins back to the front, his rifle ready to fire. From out of nowhere, a cloud of dust billows through the glassless window in front of him. A dark shadow bursts through it as the dust covers Josh completely, blinding him. The shadow hits Josh full on, sending him flying backwards off his feet. A heart-wrenching image of Alice being consumed by dust and debris flashes into Josh's mind as he hits the ground, a heavy weight on top of him.

"Fight!" Josh hears Alice scream at him. Is the voice in his head, imagined, or is Alice still with him, watching over him?

Josh forces his eyes open, ignoring the unbearable irritation it brings. He sees the figure looming over him and he raises his hand to defend himself from the threat. His hands struggle to take hold of the creature in his near-blind state as vicious snarls rain down. Weight pushes down against his arms, the beast pressing home its advantage, its desperation to feed overpowering. Josh manages to lock his arms out to hold the creature back.

Dixon's rifle continues to fire. *Hold out*, Josh tells himself, the powerful creature fighting to free itself from his grip. *Dixon will fill the beast with bullets at any moment. Hold out.* Josh's arms begin to buckle under the strain, the creature going berserk on top of him. "Dixon," Josh shouts through clenched teeth, terrified, his grip on the flailing Rabid slipping, the beast's head lowering towards him.

Vile, putrid gunk splatters across Josh's face without warning. His arms win the fight and push the limp body off to the side. Josh knows the victory is Dixon's but he'll take the win. He needs it.

Through the grit and brain matter clogging his eyes, Josh looks for his rifle, his hands feeling for the weapon. Touching cold steel, Josh's hand grabs his rifle, while his other hand attempts to wipe the coarse slime from his vision. *Get to your feet*, Josh orders himself, *get back into position and fight with your comrade.*

Dixon sees the creature fall away from on top of Josh, his bullets having ejected its brains. His body swings back towards the front windows, where the assault of the undead is escalating rapidly. He had counted ten to fifteen X-rays; he must have been mistaken. The fuckers keep coming and they have brought a fucking dust cloud from hell with them.

Peering through dust-filled eyes also, Dixon doesn't see the beast launch itself through the window from his one o'clock position until the last second. He desperately adjusts to bring his rifle around to bear. One shot is all he needs. Flying clean through the glassless window, the creature knocks Dixon's rifle to the side before he can take his shot as it slams into him.

Dixon scolds himself for allowing his weapon to be knocked out of his hands as the creature takes him down. The two bodies crash into Josh as they fall, knocking him back off his feet. Air rasps out of Dixon's lungs when he hits the ground, stunning him. He congratulates the beast for its blow, grinning, as he reaches for an exact point on his right hip.

A cry of joy escapes the creature even as its head whips down to sink its teeth into its prey. Dixon's grin widens as he expertly twists his body underneath the creature, throwing it off balance. Toppling over, the beast only sees a flash of polished steel before Dixon sinks his combat knife deep into the side of his undead attacker's head, killing it instantly.

Swiftly extracting his knife from the beast's skull and re-sheathing it, Dixon takes hold of his rifle, swearing to never let it go again. He turns just as Josh begins to right himself, to take up the fight again.

Dixon's grin is removed from his face in an instant. The dust cloud is finally diminishing and the battlefield clearing. Undead creatures fill his view, multiple targets launching themselves into the air. Determined hideous faces, twisted features and gruesome teeth fly at their front line, ready to devour. Dixon's rifle bursts into life as the first creature crashes through into their confined space. *Fight now, Josh*, Dixon panics. But he knows that even with Josh fighting by his side they will be overrun. They are cornered. The undead have the advantage. Slaughter is upon them.

Chapter 21

"Josh!" I cry out, turning back to the wreckage, "Alice!"

My hands claw at the rubble in my desperation to find my son. Maybe the wreckage has collapsed around them. They could be trapped in an air pocket. Injured, yes, that is inevitable, but, please God, still alive.

A wall of concrete and steel confronts me. The tightly packed rubble rips at the skin on my fingertips, pulls at my fingernails. Dust cascades from between the pieces of compacted rubble and slides off the steel surfaces entwined in the barrier. My fingers and hands become red raw against the solid wall, which I know deep down needs proper equipment to dislodge. Even if I had equipment, any piece of wreckage I remove could do more harm than good. It would risk further collapses, risk further injury or worse for Josh and Alice. Yet I continue feverishly clawing at the rubble. What other choice do I have?

"Captain," a voice says from behind me. "Captain, Sir!" the voice demands.

"What?" I snarl over my shoulder as I dig.

"We are ordered back to base, Sir," Sergeant Roy informs me, calmly. "Do you know where the other two for evac are?"

"They were here. My son and Alice were here. They could still be inside!" I tell Roy, passionately.

"Sir, I'm sorry, but we must evacuate," Roy replies.

I ignore Roy. *He will do as he's told*, I tell myself, as I continue to dig furiously.

"Sir, I have my orders," Roy pushes.

"Yes, you were ordered to cover the perimeter, Sergeant," I bark over my shoulder.

Roy won't accept that. I know it. He doesn't answer to me, despite the respect he has shown. In a matter of seconds, Roy will begin to insist and, if I don't go quietly, I have no doubt he will be forced to use less gentlemanly conduct. *Let him try*, I tell myself, and keep digging.

Gunshots crack into the sky, west of our position. Roy immediately drops to a knee, his rifle pointing parallel to the stadium's wreckage, ready to fire.

I am up and running before Roy can stop me. *The gunshots can only have come from Josh and Alice*, I think, urgently. They must have escaped the stadium's wreckage after all. My relief is tempered by more gunshots. They may have escaped being crushed but that doesn't mean they are out of danger.

"I'm coming!" I shout uselessly, unable to stop myself.

Just as I had expected from the professional that Roy obviously is, he is rapidly at my shoulder, in support. He doesn't try to stop me, not this time. The fight is on, and he can't resist the challenge.

My old, tired legs are no match for his and he easily catches up with me. He even has time to bark orders into his radio with barely a forced breath. Without having to glance over my shoulder, I know that his team will be chasing to catch us up. Their commander is running into battle, they will have his back. There is no doubt about that.

My confidence builds, knowing that I will have a team of four SAS commandos fighting at my side. There isn't much that will defeat such a finely tuned and skilled team of fighting experts, even with an old-timer for company.

Rapid-fire gunshots ring out constantly, giving away their position. Movement at the far north-west corner of the stadium's remains pinpoints our destination. Dark figures are converging on a large Portakabin. Josh and Alice must be holed up inside it, escaping the wreckage before its collapse. The temporary building won't offer much protection from a full-on Rabid assault which, even from a distance away, I can see is exactly what is taking place.

I pick up my speed. There could be a full battalion of SAS commandos racing into battle with me but it won't do any good if we arrive too late.

Roy's team's support helicopter powers over our heads at a low altitude. The pilot has also seen the undead converging on the Portakabin and flies in to try and buy us some more time.

Not daring to open fire near the Portakabin, the door gunner holds his fire as the pilot pulls up just short of the structure. His powerful rotors buzz the Portakabin in an attempt to hinder the undead's attack. Dust billows up from the ground, swamping the Portakabin and the fight. I am sure that this is an unintended consequence of the pilot trying to help. A dust storm will cause havoc with Josh and Alice's defence, blinding them and throwing a cloud over their enemy.

Three SAS commandos appear at Roy's shoulder, battle faces fixed below their combat paint. Roy issues his orders as we run, without saying a word. A short burst of hand signals relays his wishes, his men responding immediately.

Two men peel off to take the exposed right flank. Me, Roy and his other man continue towards the Portakabin head-on. With three in our team, we will make the first assault on the enemy. The other two men will time their arrival to press home our element of surprise and bolster our advantage.

As we close in on the Portakabin, all three of us slow our approach in preparation for beginning our assault. Blazing in at full tilt would ruin the accuracy of our fire and risk hitting friendlies unintentionally. A stray bullet can cause as much damage as an undead Rabid with, tragically, the possibility of it bringing instant death.

Sergeant Roy tries to slow our pace still further, but I'm not having it. The Portakabin is under siege from at least seven creatures. Josh is inside, I am convinced of it, and, worryingly, gunfire has ceased from within. Josh and Alice must be in trouble. Roy can hang back if he likes but it isn't his son in harm's way.

My M4 bursts into life as I press forwards. Bullets slam into a Rabid on the periphery of the pack's assault. The burst of rounds snakes up the creature's back before thudding into the back of its skull. Fragments of skull and brain erupt into the air as the creature slumps into the dirt.

Roy, seeing my urgency, throws caution to the wind. He draws level with me to release his first volley of bullets. I don't see what he hits as my concentration is totally occupied with picking my next target and looking for signs of Josh or Alice.

Gunshots erupt from our right flank to help cull the pack. I fire for a second time, my target a Rabid squirming half in and half out of one of the shattered windows. I take great care with my aim. A stray bullet now could easily strike Josh or Alice.

Creatures launch themselves at the windows, our firepower pushing them forwards. Seeing them enter the Portakabin sends me into a panic. I rush forwards, aiming for the bullet-ridden door. A burst of fire, emanating from inside the Portakabin, spurs me on. *Signs of life*, I tell myself. *They are still alive!*

I throw all my weight against the door, expecting it to burst wide open. I am wrong: it only moves a few inches. Something is blocking its travel and I come to a juddering halt. A fight is under way inside, the gap I have created shows me that much. My heart jumps when I catch a glimpse of Josh, his dirt-caked face desperate and strained as he fights to keep a ferocious creature at bay.

Alice is out of view, surely in trouble and needing help. I push with all my might at the door, a grinding, scraping noise sounds and gradually the door pushes inwards. As soon as the gap is big enough, I slide into the Portakabin, the M4 on my back, my trusted Sig in hand.

A figure flies through the window, just as I enter. Roy lands expertly on his feet, nearly receiving a bullet from the Sig for his troubles. He instantly surges forwards, his combat knife appearing from nowhere. Without flinching, Roy's arm curls around the neck of the Rabid that is attacking Josh. He pulls the creature away from Josh, lifting it clean off its feet. His free hand wields the combat knife and he plunges it through the air, the blade disappearing into the Rabid's head.

Josh gulps in air as Roy dumps the limp body of the Rabid to one side without ceremony. I am already moving to put an end to the other scuffle taking place on the floor. A vicious, large-bodied creature is overpowering Alice, who is pinned down on the ground. I can't see her face because the creature's broad shoulders block my view. I don't hesitate in putting an end to the fight. I step in close, so as to not risk hitting Alice, press the barrel of the Sig to the side of the Rabid's head and pull the trigger.

My bullet whips the creature's head to the side. Blood and brains are ejected out from the other side of its head, the contents spraying across the floor. Josh twitches his foot away when the bullet hits the floor in proximity to his foot but it misses by a safe distance. The dead Rabid keels over, thudding to the ground, dust billowing into the air beneath it.

I focus on Alice, to check if she is okay, and help her back to her feet. Freezing in mid-air as I bend down to help her, shock paralyses me as I see that it is not Alice on the floor but Dixon. My confusion escalates as I realise Dixon is alive. I was sure he'd met his end on the wreckage of the stadium. I was positive. How can he possibly still be alive?

"Surprise," Dixon says dryly, offering his hand for me to help him up.

I take Dixon's hand and haul him to his feet, my confusion going into overdrive. I'm over the moon that Dixon is still in the land of the living. That he isn't crumpled and broken at the bottom of the wreckage or, worse, turned into an undead zombie. He is alive, but then where the hell is Alice, I wonder, looking around the room in case I've missed her. She is nowhere to be seen. I look over to Josh, confused. His face is distraught and then dread hits me.

"Where is Alice?" I ask through gritted teeth, not wanting to know the answer.

Josh looks at me, broken, tears streaming down his face. He is so upset that he can't answer me. All he manages is a shake of his head.

Alice is gone, I know it without him having to say a word. Sadness wells up inside me; I struggle to stop it from bursting out. I have questions, so many questions, for Josh, but I know that this is not the time to ask them. In any case, he is too distraught to answer me and they would only upset him more.

"Are you sure?" I ask. It is the only question that I must ask right now.

Josh nods at me to confirm. His puffy red eyes cannot hide from me the guilt he is feeling. My heart goes out to him, even though it is racked with my own awful sadness.

Around us, the Portakabin begins to vibrate as a helicopter passes overhead, its presence reminding me that we are still in the danger zone. I force my feelings aside, even though I won't be able to keep them there for long. How can we continue without Alice? All I know is that we must, at least for now. Josh is a wreck. He is going to need my support to get out of here.

"Are you injured?" I ask Dixon.

"No, mate. I was just getting started with that brute," he tells me. "You watch out for Josh. He's struggling," Dixon adds, looking over at my son with concern.

Roy has turned his back on us and is covering the windows. I bet he wonders what he has walked into. His team are outside, covering the perimeter and calling in the helicopter to finally carry out their task of evacuating us.

"Better late than never," Dixon says to Roy, as he turns to me and Josh for a moment.

"Getting your arse out of the shit as always, you mean," Roy retorts.

The two Special Forces' operatives obviously know each other and take great comfort from ripping the piss out of one another. Some might call it a professional relationship.

"Are you ready to get out of here?" I ask Josh, leaving the banter to Dixon and Roy.

"I couldn't save her, Dad," Josh snivels.

"I know, son. Tell me all about it when you're feeling up to it," I tell Josh, putting my hand on his shoulder. "We need to go now. There's nothing left for us here. Catherine and Emily are waiting for us. Are you ready?"

My words are hollow, no more than a sticking plaster for Josh's grief, or for mine for that matter. Alice will be sorely missed; she already is. Our team will be empty without her determination, compassion and, last but not least, her formidable fighting skills.

I turn to see dust billowing into the air as the helicopter comes into land a short distance away. Roy's team expertly move in around the aircraft, taking up positions that cover every direction. They wait patiently for us to emerge, their heads constantly scanning the entire area.

"Sergeant Roy?" I ask.

"Clear," Roy replies, after a short pause to signal to his team.

"Are you ready?" I ask Josh.

Josh raises his sleeve to wipe his eyes, nodding to me as he does. I see him reaffirm his grip on his rifle, which gives me confidence that he's ready to move, and then I give the order.

"After you, Sergeant," Dixon offers to Roy, gesturing with his hand.

"Thank you, Sergeant," Roy replies, and slaps Dixon on the back as he moves past.

Roy shoves the filing cabinet away from the door with his foot and then takes us out into the open. I make sure Josh is in front of me as we scamper across the ground, towards the waiting transport. A second helicopter keeps a watching brief in the sky above. The other two aircraft have disappeared, their presence probably urgently required elsewhere.

The downdraft from the rotors washes at least some of the battlefield dirt from us as we duck under the rotors and climb into the helicopter at last. Roy's team don't move until everyone else is on-board. Then, one by one, they spring to their feet and follow us in.

It is a tight squeeze inside the hold with we three evacuees on-board, adding to the passenger list. Thankfully, Roy's team are gentlemen and let us weary soldiers have first refusal on the available seats. I take one by the window, with Josh sitting next to me. Dixon ends up opposite me, with Roy commandeering the seat next to him. Two men end up standing when the music stops but it is of no concern to the young lads. They simply grab onto the nearest handrail and wait for lift-off.

As soon as the hold door is slammed shut, Roy confirms to the pilot through his headset that he is cleared for take-off. Engines above our head power to full throttle and then our stomachs are left behind as the pilot makes a rapid ascent out of the danger zone.

The wreckage of Wembley Stadium zooms away from view as we gain altitude, fires throwing an eerie light across the scene. The iconic stadium is shattered and unrecognisable. Not even the pitch in the centre of the stadium indicates that there was once more than just piles of rubble below. It too is churned into nothing but debris, lost in a landscape of destruction. Destruction that spreads as far as the eye can see and further than I had anticipated.

Neither Josh nor I are in a rush to don a headset. Both of us are lost in our own thoughts. My thoughts are conflicting. On the one hand, I am relieved and forever grateful that we managed to find Josh and, against all the odds, get him out.

But the other hand weighs heavy. The loss of brothers in arms has been heart-wrenching. I barely knew Turner or Carter, but both of their demises were tragic, especially Turner's heroic end. Was I too hard on Carter? He was just a foolish young pup who covered up his inexperience and fear with misplaced bravado. I tell myself that I did all I could for him in difficult circumstances. He took it upon himself to run. I couldn't have done any more to stop him.

My heart sinks further when I think of Simms as I watch his tomb shrink on the skyline. He came to back me up in the face of overwhelming danger. His loss is traumatic. I will never forget the immense soldier and person he was.

My grief inevitably focuses upon Alice. She was a bright star who, from the moment Dan and I picked her up from the roof of the Tower of London, became an integral part of our team and, quickly, part of our family. Her loss has come as a tragic hammer blow to me and even more so for Josh.

I can't help but wonder what happened to her. Josh is in no fit state to tell me. I will have to wait until he is ready and comes to me with his story. Dixon probably knows but to question him in Josh's presence would be like a knife cutting open a fresh wound for Josh. *Patience*, I think, as my head rocks back, thinking sadly of Alice. I can only pray that she didn't suffer.

Too easily I become lost in my thoughts, in my grief. Every day that passes brings more loss and tragedy. Perhaps one day the toll will become too great, and it will consume me, but I can't allow that to happen, not today. There is still business to attend to.

Wearily, I check on Josh and then reach behind for a headset. He is upset and very quiet. *I will need to keep my eye on him*, I think, as I fit the headset into place.

"What is our destination?" I ask anyone who cares to answer, cutting across Dixon's and Roy's chatting.

"RAF Northolt, Sir," Roy answers immediately.

"I have been ordered to travel to Porton Down," I state. "Why are we going to Northolt?"

"Captain Richards, Sir," the pilot interjects, "we are on active duty in the London area, Sir. We don't have the fuel to reach Porton Down either. Our flight plan takes us back to Northolt. From there, as I understand, you will be transferred to alternative transport to make the onward journey to Porton Down. Sir."

"What transport?" I ask.

"I'm sorry, Sir, I don't have that information. You will be met on the ground when we land, Sir," the pilot informs me.

Great, I think. There will be no 'red carpet' laid out when we land. I am sure to be taken into custody. Visions of trundling down the motorway in the back of a military police prison van come to mind. Oh well. There's not much I can do about it. We will just have to go with the flow.

No sooner has the pilot reached his flight altitude than we begin to descend. Northolt is only a short hop from

Wembley as the crow flies. I sit bolt upright, nervous tension returning.

"Sergeant Roy, is Northolt secure?" I ask. When we evacuated, not more than a few hours ago, it was anything but secure.

"Yes, Sir. The small infiltration was quickly dealt with, Sir," Roy assures me.

"It was more than a small infiltration when I left, Sergeant," I press.

"Sir, all force was brought to bear to secure the airport. I was involved. We killed them all, Sir, and reinforced the perimeter. The threat has also been dealt with in Wembley, Sir," Roy informs me.

"The infected are still occupying Wembley, Sergeant, in case you hadn't noticed," I insist.

"Small pockets, Sir. Troops are sweeping through Wembley to clean them up as we speak," Roy replies. "And we are going back in as soon as we drop you off, Sir."

"I see," I say, not entirely convinced by Roy's assurances.

"We expect the quarantine zone to be re-established by the morning, Sir," Roy tells me, confidently.

I raise my eyebrows and sit back, hoping Roy is right. I can tell by Dixon's face that he also harbours doubts regarding Roy's assessment of the situation. He doesn't say anything, however.

We touch down deep inside the airport, well away from any vital infrastructure. The military's precautions in the aftermath of the disaster at Heathrow are still in place. The pilot tells us to remain seated as troops move in around the helicopter, their rifles raised, ready for action.

Eventually, the door of the hold is slid open and each of us has our eyes scanned by a nervous-looking trooper. One after the other we are given the all-clear and the helicopter empties.

"Captain Richards?" a young corporal asks urgently, pushing his way through the troops that make up our welcoming committee.

"Yes, Corporal," I reply, somewhat surprised he isn't wearing an armband with MP emblazoned on it.

"If you would like to follow me, Sir," the corporal asks, saluting. "Your transport is waiting to take off."

"One moment, Corporal," I insist, relieved that it doesn't sound like a prison van will be our mode of transport after all.

"Sergeant Roy," I call. "Thanks for your assistance back there. Thank your men for me, will you?"

"Of course, Sir. It was a pleasure," Roy replies. We shake hands vigorously before he turns to join his men.

"Parting is such sweet sorrow. Or something like that," Dixon says, grinning, as I look at him.

"Don't get all mushy on me," I smile back at him.

"I won't. Don't worry," Dixon retorts.

"Seriously, thanks, mate, I won't forget what you did for me, and I'm sorry about Simms. He was a good man," I tell Dixon, and move in for a man-hug.

"He was one of the best," Dixon replies, as we embrace.

"What now for you?" I ask as we separate, slapping each other's shoulders.

"Report back for duty. Get a roasting for going AWOL again and then back into the fray," Dixon replies.

"Standard procedure then," I point out.

"Absolutely. I wouldn't have it any other way," Dixon laughs. "Look after yourself, Captain, and good luck with the brass when you land. Sorry I can't be there to ensure they don't take the piss."

"You've done more than enough, mate. You'll have to tell me how you managed to escape over a beer one day," I tell him.

"I'd love to bore you to death with it," Dixon smiles.

"Watch yourself out there. Remember only cats have nine lives and you must be nearing your limit," I insist.

"I exceeded my limit years ago," Dixon laughs.

"No doubt. Until the next time then, mate. Look after yourself," I tell Dixon, as his eyes turn to Josh. I step back, knowing he has something to say to Josh.

"Come and give Uncle Dixon a hug then, Joshy boy," Dixon says, smiling at my son.

Josh does as he's told and Dixon clamps his arms around him, pulling him in tight. Dixon doesn't release Josh until he is good and ready, speaking into Josh's ear the whole time.

I have no idea what Dixon says to Josh, that's between them. When Dixon does finally release my son, Josh comes away nodding, looking Dixon straight in the eye for a moment.

"That's my boy," Dixon announces, and slaps Josh heavily on the shoulder. "And remember me to your little sister," he adds, pointing as he turns to join Roy and his men.

278

Chapter 22

The young corporal leads us over to a car he has waiting and opens the back door for Josh and me to get in. Slamming the door behind us, he rushes into the driver's seat, guns the engine enthusiastically and pulls away at speed. Something tells me he has orders to get us on the transport as quickly as possible. Our farewells with Dixon probably weren't in his schedule. We see Dixon for one last time before we speed away, his hand hanging in the air in farewell as he watches us leave.

"You okay, son?" I ask Josh.

"Not really. But I will be, Dad. Don't worry," he tells me.

I leave the conversation there and peer out of the window to see where we are being taken. We are whisked down a side road that runs parallel to the airport's runway, towards the main cluster of buildings. The same buildings where I discovered Catherine and Emily earlier this evening. An event that seems like a lifetime ago now.

We pull up in-between two helicopters, one a military transport, much the same as the one we have just left, and the other an executive type, saved for top-ranking officials.

The corporal is out and opening the door next to me before I have the chance to retrieve my rifle, which is next to Josh's, in-between us.

"You won't be needing those, Sir," the corporal tells me. "I will see that they are returned to the armoury."

"This one doesn't belong to the army, Corporal," I inform him, as I get out and sling my M4 over my back.

The young man goes to protest, but I look daggers at him and he soon backs down. Josh decides to leave his standard-issue weapon behind, which at least gives the corporal half a win.

"This way, Sir," I am told, as I turn towards the transport helicopter, wondering where the pilot is.

I turn around and I am surprised to see the corporal beckoning us over to the executive helicopter, movement in the cockpit of which coincides with the engine whining into life.

"It looks like someone's gone up in the world," Josh says from beside me.

"It would appear so," I say, as the corporal opens the door of the hold for us to embark.

"Have a good journey, Sir," we are told before the door is closed behind us.

"I could get used to this," I tell Josh, as I settle into one of the plush leather seats and put on a headset.

"Me too," Josh agrees, sitting opposite me.

"Pilot, what is our destination?" I ask to double-check that it is indeed Porton Down.

He confirms that it is Porton Down and begins his take-off. Josh and I are silent as we rise off the ground. Both of us look out of the window as RAF Northolt moves into the distance.

"I couldn't save her, Dad." Josh's sad voice pulls me away from the window.

"Change to channel two," I instruct Josh, so that we can have some privacy. "Are you sure you want to talk about it now?" I ask when we've changed channels.

"I've got to," Josh tells me with a tear in his eye. "I need to tell someone."

"Okay, you know you can always talk to me. What happened?" I ask.

"When the helicopters overflew the wreckage, it began to collapse. I had to get out first because I was blocking her way," Josh's voice cracks. "I tried to pull her out, but I was too late. It collapsed right on top of her, crushing her. She was buried alive.

"Her face, Dad. I can't get her face out of my head. She was terrified, begging me to save her. I should have got out earlier, quicker," Josh says, tears now rolling down his face.

My emotions are in turmoil as Josh gives me his shocking account of what happened to Alice. Guilt cuts into me. I was the one who put her into that hole under the wreckage. The wreckage was unstable. I knew it. I heard it groaning under its own weight when was I cowering beneath it, inside the hole. And then I left her there to die, to be crushed alive under concrete and steel. Alice was right there, buried when I was clawing at the debris. How could I have left her encased in rubble? She deserved better. So much better.

"It's not your fault," I tell Josh, trying to keep my emotions in check and be strong for him. "There was no safe option. It was a miracle that any of us made it out alive."

"She was right there and I couldn't save her," Josh sobs.

"It was an impossible situation, Josh. You would have saved her if you could have," I tell him, but my words sound hollow.

Josh falls silent. Only the sound of his sobbing replays over and over in my headset. I lean forwards to put a reassuring hand on his knee, but he moves his leg away. There is nothing I can say to ease his suffering. All I can do is to be here for him and try to stay strong. As hard as I try though, I can't hold back tears from my eyes or erase Alice from my thoughts.

Our journey continues in silence. Try as I might, I can't think of anything to say to Josh to help him. Eventually, his sobbing dies down and he just looks out of the window of the cabin into the darkness beyond, lost in his own thoughts.

His trauma is going to take some getting over. I know from sad experience how hard it is to lose friends on the battlefield. How hard the bitter feelings of guilt, loss and uselessness are to come to terms with. Going over and over their deaths in your head. Telling yourself you should have done more to save them. Seeing their face constantly in your mind's eye or reflected in every window and mirror you glance at. Just as Josh is staring at now in darkened glass of the cabin.

My heart goes out to Josh. Alice was more than just a friend to him. He had deeper feelings for her, and she for him. They had become close, very close. Romance had been in the air. It was obvious for everyone to see.

"Captain Richards." The pilot's voice cuts through my own thoughts eventually.

"Yes," I reply.

"Sorry to interrupt, Sir. We will be landing in approximately five minutes," he tells me.

I thank him for the update as Josh looks away from the window at me and manages a smile. Although the smile is forced and his face is racked with sadness, I feel pride in my son for his courage in trying to put on a brave face at such a difficult time. His courage tells me that he will come to terms with his loss. Not immediately but, given time, he will.

The shining lights of what must be Porton Down come into focus as we descend. There is no welcoming committee waiting when we touch down. Only a secure compound greets us, with pointing guns and eyes scans waiting. I shouldn't be surprised that precautions have been taken for new arrivals. Thoughts of Emily and Catherine waiting excitedly on the tarmac are instantly dispelled.

Josh and I wearily go through the motions as if we have just arrived on a long-haul flight from Timbuktu. We are then ushered onto an electric cart that we are informed will take us into Porton Down Central. The facility is extensive, bigger than I had imagined, and the cart bounces along for around ten minutes.

"Thanks, Dad," Josh says as we go.

"What for?" I ask, confused.

"For coming to find us," Josh replies.

"Don't be silly. There's no need to thank me. I just wish everyone had made it out," I tell him.

"Yes, me too. I'm going to miss Alice," Josh says.

"I know, son. We all will. We were lucky to have known her. Even if it was only for a short amount of time," I reply.

"Very lucky," Josh agrees.

I reach over and squeeze Josh's shoulder just as the cart comes to a stop.

"Dad! Josh!" Emily shrieks excitedly from out of nowhere. "Over here, over here."

Both Josh and I turn to see Emily jumping up and down, waving her hands in the air frantically. She is a few metres away on the other side of a wire barrier that she quickly runs towards to get a better view. My heart fills with joy at seeing my little girl, her face beaming with happiness.

Catherine stands behind Emily, sporting a broad smile. She follows Emily towards the wire barrier to stand next to her. Winters is with them too, smiling. He waits where he is though, giving space for the family reunion.

"Come on, Josh. Better not keep your sister waiting," I smile at my son.

"Definitely not. She might burst," Josh replies with a genuine smile.

Josh exits the barrier first and Emily jumps straight into his arms, squealing with joy. As soon as I join him, Emily transfers into my arms but she doesn't release Josh from her grip around his neck but pulls us both into her. I release one arm from Emily to receive Catherine, her eyes welling up with tears.

"Where's Alice?" Catherine whispers into my ear.

"She didn't make it," I whisper, moving my head out of earshot of Emily.

Catherine gasps in shock uncontrollably and I pull her in tight to me to comfort her. It is only a matter of time until Emily's excitement dies down and she asks the same question, a question that I am dreading.

Winters approaches us, concern etched across his face, wondering the same thing. I simply shake my head at him with a sombre look, telling him all he needs to know. Winters didn't know Alice well, but he knows how close she had become to us and his sadness at the news is plain to see.

"What now?" I ask Winters after a moment, giving Emily back to Josh.

"I expect you're hungry and tired," Winters replies. "I've arranged your accommodation. So, I suggest I take you back there and you can clean up while I arrange for some food to be delivered. After that, I expect some sleep will be in order, for everyone."

"Is that it?" I ask, surprised. "No debrief, or questioning?"

"Not tonight. I've made sure of that," Winters tells me.

"That's a relief. Thanks, mate," I say, still surprised.

"I'll tell you what's lined up for tomorrow while we walk, if you like?" Winters offers.

"Where's Alice?" Emily asks, before I can respond to Winters.

I turn to Emily, looking for the right words to tell her. Before I find them, however, Josh tells Emily the sad news about Alice. Emily buries her head in Josh's neck as Josh also becomes upset again. Josh tells me that he's okay and that we should get going. I offer to take Emily from him, but he says no. He wants to carry her.

"So, you were going to tell me about tomorrow," I say to Winters as we walk.

"Yes, I was," he agrees. "The only thing that's lined up at the moment is that Prime Minister Rainsford has invited you to breakfast with her."

"Really?" I ask, surprised.

"Yes, she asked me to invite you personally," Winters tells me.

"You and her the best of friends now then?" I tease Winters.

"Hardly, but I have had dealings with her today. She is very keen to meet and speak to you," Winters informs me.

"That sounds ominous," I respond.

"Not at all. She is okay, actually. I think she wants to assure you that things are going to be different," Winters tells me.

"She seems like a reasonable woman," Catherine interjects.

"Oh, really? Have you been hobnobbing too?" I ask Catherine, smiling.

"No. I've been worried to death, if you must know!" Catherine snaps, sending me into silence.

"Can I tell her you'll meet with her?" Winters asks, quickly.

"Yes. Tell her Catherine and I would be delighted," I reply, with a hint of sarcasm.

"As long as it's not too early in the morning," Catherine adds, taking hold of my hand.

"I'll see what I can do," Winters replies.

"Thanks, mate. Is there anything else I need to know?" I ask.

"Nothing important that can't wait until tomorrow. You just concentrate on recuperating tonight," Winters advises.

"Oh, I may have been premature when I told you about Sergeant Dixon," I say to Winters. "He's very much still in the land of the living."

"Really? That's good news. He's as tough as they come, isn't he?" Winters replies.

"Tough as nails," I agree, looking to check on my children.

Josh has put Emily down, but she clings to his hand. She is getting too big to carry very far nowadays. They are both sombre, but their tears have dried up, which I find encouraging.

Winters carries on talking as we walk. He tries to familiarise me with Porton Down's layout and occasionally points at a building to tell me what it houses. My concentration wanes, however. I'll be happy just to have a shower, something to eat and a bed. It comes as a relief when he announces that we have arrived at the block containing our accommodation.

He takes us up to the third floor, telling us that I'll be in the same room as Catherine and Emily and that he has managed to get Josh a room on the same floor, just opposite our room.

Catherine tells me that Stacey and Karen are in the room adjacent to ours. They have asked if I would pop in to say hello when I'm ready. I do it straight away, both to put their minds at rest and so that I can concentrate on showering and eating. They are pleased to see me, but I don't hang around too long. I'm simply too tired.

I thank Winters yet again for all his help. He brushes off my gratitude, telling me before he disappears that he will escort Catherine and I to our breakfast meeting in the morning.

Josh heads off into his room to have a shower and put on a change of clothes, which Winters has ensured are already waiting in his room. Once showered, Josh comes across to our room, where we eat together, with Catherine and Emily watching on. We are both dog-tired and, as soon as the food is finished, we opt for bed.

"Good morning," Catherine says, as my eyes peel open.

"Is it already?" I mumble.

"I'm afraid so. You were out for the count as soon as your head hit the pillow last night. Did you sleep well?" Catherine asks.

"Yes, I think so. I was knackered," I reply.

"I bet you were," Catherine says, sitting on the edge of the bed beside me.

"Where's Emily?" I ask, suddenly.

"Stacey and Karen have taken her to get breakfast as we are having ours with the PM," Catherine smiles.

"I didn't hear her go," I say.

"I asked her to be quiet and let you sleep. She's a good girl. She was silent as a mouse," Catherine tells me.

"I wonder how Josh is."

"He seemed okay when I knocked on his door earlier to check on him. He said he was going to sleep on for a while," Catherine tells me.

"Lucky him. What time is it?" I ask.

"Eight-fifteen. Robert messaged me to say he will meet us downstairs at nine-fifteen. We are meeting the PM at nine-thirty. So, you'd better get up," Catherine insists.

"It won't take me long to get ready," I tell Catherine, as I lean forwards to pull her towards me.

"Andy, we haven't got time for that now, and I've just had a shower!" Catherine protests.

"You can have another, and the prime minister can wait!" I insist.

"You're impossible!" Catherine protests again.

"I know," I admit.

"You'd better be quick then," Catherine smiles, as she removes her dressing gown and I pull the bedsheets back to receive her.

There is a knock on the door as I get my breath back and as Catherine is taking another shower. *Who the hell is that?* I think, sighing, wrapping myself in the bedsheet.

"Haven't you even had a shower yet?" Winters questions, as I open the door.

"Just about to. I got waylaid," I tell him, grinning.

"I'm sure," Winters frowns. "Here, I got you this to wear. It's the best I could do at short notice. I couldn't have you meeting the PM in a pair of joggers and a sweatshirt," Winters tells me, handing me a bag.

"Thanks," I reply.

"And get a move on!" he insists, as he turns to leave.

"I'll be ready," I tell him, as he goes.

"Who was that at the door?" Catherine shouts from the bathroom.

"Winters. He dropped me off something to wear," I tell Catherine.

"You need to get that looked at properly," Catherine says, referring to the wound on my stomach, as we leave our room.

"I'm sure they'll be plenty of experts waiting to have a prod at it," I tell her.

"Yes, you're probably right," she concedes.

"I know I am," I tell her, frowning.

"How are you feeling?" she asks.

"Battered and bruised but, other than that, okay, surprisingly," I reply.

Winters is waiting for us downstairs. He looks more nervous than I am about this meeting. I thank him for the new combat uniform he secured for me. I feel more comfortable in it than I would have in the joggers and sweatshirt.

As he escorts us across Porton Down and into one of the large buildings overlooking the main square, he asks about what happened to Alice and how Dixon managed to turn up alive. I fill him in on the sad events of yesterday, not just losing Alice but also the other men. Winters and Catherine listen intently. Winters knew Simms and is shocked by the news of his passing. I find it tough telling them everything, but it is cathartic. I feel some of the weight is lifted off me when I finish my account just as we arrive at our destination.

Prime Minister Rainsford is already sitting at a table in the makeshift dining room that I suspect has been set up just for her use. She is sitting talking to another woman who is sitting with her back to me. I can tell who the other woman is before she turns to look. General Cox's long curly blonde hair gives her presence away.

"Good morning, Lieutenant Winters," Rainsford says, rising from her chair.

"Good morning, Ma'am," Winters replies. "May I introduce Captain Richards and Catherine Hamilton, who you met last night?"

"Hello, Captain. It is good to finally meet you and hello again, Catherine. Thank you both for coming. You have both met General Cox before, I have been informed," Rainsford greets them.

"Good morning, Prime Minister, General," I respond.

"Please take a seat. I think breakfast is ready to be served," Rainsford offers.

Catherine and I take a seat while Winters sits himself down on a chair on the periphery of the room. As we sit, staff appear from a side door with trolleys, ready to serve.

General Cox mostly remains quiet while breakfast is served and Rainsford converses with Catherine and I. She is a clever operator, as you would expect from a woman in her position. She begins with small talk about our families and such and then moves on to more serious business. She has me recount the events of yesterday and I find myself reliving the harrowing events for the second time, having only just done so with Catherine and Winters.

As breakfast draws to a close, and hot drinks are taken, Rainsford moves the conversation on to the real reason I am here.

"Captain Richards," she begins, "we are in your debt. It was you and your team that secured the vital information from the Orion Building that began the work to find a solution to this terrible virus. I also understand that certain people's behaviour towards you and your family since that operation has been less than... how shall I say... proper."

"Some might say criminal, Ma'am," I interject.

"Indeed, Captain. But these are difficult times and decisions that are meant to serve the greater good can sometimes be viewed in a dim light after the fact. You have my apologies for some of those decisions and I can assure you that all will be fully investigated and dealt with appropriately. Lieutenant Winters and General Cox have been very frank with me about these events. Some of which have proved to be misguided, to say the least. General Cox has informed me of the occurrences in Devon, which are now in the hands of the police, who will get our full cooperation. Won't they, General?"

"Yes, Ma'am," Cox responds.

"Devon?" I ask. "Are you referring to the apprehending of my friends and family?"

"Yes, but especially the shooting," Rainsford replies.

"Shooting? What shooting?" I ask, confused.

"I'll tell you after," Catherine volunteers. "It isn't important to this conversation."

"Okay," I say, reluctantly.

"Thank you, Catherine," Rainsford says. "For all our sakes, those of us here must put this behind us and move forwards."

"What is it you want from me?" I ask the prime minister, bluntly.

"I want you to remain here at Porton Down and volunteer to help General Cox find a solution. Her work so far on the biopsies taken at Station Zero is very encouraging. She will tell you what they have found so far, but she needs more samples to work with. Samples only you can provide, Captain," Rainsford answers me.

"Did you know that I was awake when those samples were taken? When my stomach was cut open, and my head drilled into? It was excruciating. I don't know if I can go through that again," I say, honestly.

"General?" Rainsford asks with a horrified expression.

"I was informed of this. There must have been an issue with the anaesthetic," Cox answers.

"I'm confused," Rainsford admits. "What exactly happened?"

"I was paralysed on the operating table when those biopsies were taken. I couldn't move or speak but I could hear everything Major Rees and Colonel Taylor said and I felt every incision they made. That's what happened," I reply.

"Oh, my word!" Rainsford gasps.

"That was not our intention, Ma'am. I can assure you," Cox says, embarrassed.

"Why didn't you tell me this before, General?" Rainsford demands.

"I'm sorry, Ma'am. It honestly slipped my mind. What with everything going on," Cox admits.

"It hasn't slipped mine!" I say, angrily.

"That's terrible," Catherine adds from beside me.

"It sounds horrific," Rainsford agrees.

"I can only guess that the change to Captain Richards' metabolism had an adverse reaction on the anaesthetic and it didn't have the required effect," Cox surmises.

"We can't have it happen again. We aren't barbarians," Rainsford insists.

"No, Ma'am," Cox agrees, before turning to look at me. "We have no plans at present to perform intrusive surgery going forward. The enzyme we need is found in your blood, Captain. We just need to take your blood initially," Cox pleads.

"I've heard that before," I counter.

"There may come a time when we do need to take more intrusive samples. If and when we do, we will of course take steps to ensure it is painless. There are tests we can perform beforehand to make sure of it," Cox insists.

"I wish I could trust you, General. But past experience tells me otherwise," I reply.

"You can trust me, Captain. I won't allow any further mistakes. Is that clear, General?" Rainsford demands.

"Yes, Ma'am," Cox replies, and then turns to me again. "Please, Captain, we need your help, it is vital. Stay and work with us. You are the only chance we have of beating this and I'm confident that, with your help, we can find a solution or even a cure for this horrific infection."

"And if I do agree to stay and help, what about my family?" I ask.

I am no fool. Right now, the prime minister is pleasantly requesting for my help. But if I were to flatly refuse to 'volunteer' then her hand would be forced and my cooperation would be gained by less pleasant means. Either way, I am stuck here for the time being so I might as well play my hand to our best advantage.

"Your family would be taken care of, Captain," Rainsford assures me. "I have already made arrangements for a house to be made available to you on the Porton Down housing estate. It's in a lovely little community. There is a school for your daughter to attend. And, most importantly, it is inside the secure perimeter. Porton Down is the safest place in the country for you and your family at present. I have a house there myself, so we would be neighbours."

"That sounds acceptable," I say, coolly. "I would also expect my son to remain on site and he needs to be kept busy. So, I would expect him to be reassigned to a regiment here. He has been through enough. He has also gone above and beyond in this fight and is definitely overdue a promotion."

"General Cox will certainly take care of that," Rainsford responds, looking at Cox, who nods her head to confirm. "And what about you, Catherine?" Rainsford cleverly asks. "I understand that you are a very capable administrator. I could utilise your skills and offer you a position on my support staff. I think we would work well together."

"Thank you, Ma'am. I think we would work well together too. I would consider a position on your staff. I need to be kept busy also," Catherine agrees.

"Is there anything else, Captain?" Rainsford asks.

"Yes. There are two dear friends in our group, who I am sure you are aware of: Karen and Stacey. They must be given the opportunity to remain if they want to," I reply.

"We will make arrangements for them if they wish to remain," Rainsford agrees.

"Then I think we have an agreement, Ma'am," I say, pleased with my negotiating.

"Excellent. Thank you, Captain. I trust you are willing to get to work with General Cox immediately," Rainsford asks.

"We would just need to take some blood today, Captain. Half an hour of your time. I know you must be tired and you have your family to attend to today," Cox interjects.

"Just tell me where to go," I agree.

"Lieutenant Winters will be your line of communication, if that is acceptable? He will make arrangements with you when we are prepared," Cox offers.

"Marvellous. That's settled then," Rainsford announces, standing. The moment she stands, a man appears from the side door and approaches. He waits patiently by her side. "Now, if you will excuse me? As you can imagine, I have a long day ahead and my presence is needed elsewhere."

Prime Minister Rainsford shakes both Catherine's hand and mine as she says goodbye before the man whisks her off through the side door. *I don't envy her position one bit,* I think to myself, as I watch her leave. She must have the weight of the world on her shoulders.

As soon as Rainsford has left, General Cox thanks us and makes her exit, leaving us in the hands of Lieutenant Winters.

"Well, that went well I thought," Winters says, as he comes over to us.

"So do I, Robert. What do you think, Andy?" Catherine asks.

"Yes, I suppose it did. It looks like we have a new life set out for us. At least for now," I agree.

"What do you mean, at least for now?" Catherine wonders.

"I mean, nothing is guaranteed any more, if it ever was. All we can do is live our lives for the moment and be ready for when it all goes to shit again," I reply.

Maybe my view is a pessimistic one but neither Catherine nor Winters offer an argument against it. General Cox's work may offer a light at the end of the tunnel, but that tunnel is a long one, with many hazards along the way. London is still in turmoil. The undead have already breached the quarantine zone once. They could easily break out again. The future is on a knife edge and the ordered oasis we now find ourselves joining could easily crumble around us.

Epilogue

The enemy approach from the rear. I see them coming but hold my position, lulling them into a false sense of security. Closer they stalk, their weapon primed and ready to fire.

I delay my counterattack too long and, without warning, I am hit in the shoulder. The enemy scream in victory as I go down, hitting the ground hard. I must regather myself and fight back. Twisting on the ground, I manage to get my shot away, but I miss hopelessly, the enemy right on top of me. They fire again. This time I am hit in the chest and another squeal of delight rises from my foe as the snowball bursts across my face.

"I got you, Dad. You're out!" Emily insists, excitedly, before she jumps on top of me, pushing my back deeper into the snow.

"Ha, ha. You got me good and proper," I laugh, as I put my arms around my daughter and twist her over so that it is her buried in the snow, and then proceed to drop a handful of snow down on her.

"Hey, that's not fair. You're out!" Emily protests, laughing.

CAPITAL FALLING 6 - BREAKOUT

"It's Christmas!" I shout down to her, as I grab her arms to lift her back onto her feet.

"Yay, and no more school for two weeks!" Emily announces, as she lands back upright.

We get some funny looks, and a few smiles, from the other parents collecting their children from outside the school.

"What time will Catherine be home?" Emily asks, as we calm down and begin our short walk back to the house.

"Any time now," I reply.

I am still amazed at how quickly we have settled into our new life at Porton Down. Catherine has been away for five days, accompanying the prime minister on a trip to one of the islands of Cape Verde, off the coast of Africa. It was a gathering to discuss the virus and the worldwide response to it. Catherine is back in the country now and flying back to Porton Down by helicopter.

Her new role keeps her very busy, and she takes her job seriously. I have become the homemaker of the family, which suits me just fine. I get to spend as much time as possible with Emily. I am there for my daughter, which I have never had the chance to be in the past. We have become closer than ever.

My work with General Cox consists of reporting for blood samples to be taken and the occasional more in-depth analysis of whatever is going on in my body. I don't understand it really. I just let them get on with whatever they need to do and then go home.

General Cox is still optimistic that the work is progressing, although it is not producing the positive results they were hoping for as quickly as was expected. Labs around the world are working towards a solution. My blood samples are currently residing in laboratory refrigerators in every corner of the globe. I shudder to think how many litres of blood have been drained from me over the last few months.

Luckily, London appears to have gone quieter with the arrival of the freezing weather. The consensus of opinion seems to be that the cold weather has slowed down the infected population of the city. If that is the case, then it will at least give the scientists some breathing room to do their work over the winter. But other opinions differ. Some suggest that the undead are gathering their forces for an all-out attack on the rest of the country. Only time will tell.

"Will Josh be at home when we get back?" Emily asks.

"I'm not sure. I can't remember what time he gets off duty," I reply.

"He'd better not be late for the Christmas party!" Emily insists.

"He won't be," I assure her.

Josh has become an officer in the British Army and holds the rank of second lieutenant. He still struggles often with PTSD and his grief for the loss of Alice, but I am working through it with him, and he has finally agreed to seek professional help. I am confident that, with time, he will learn to manage his demons and move on with his life.

Rainsford wasn't exaggerating when she said we would become neighbours. She has a house on the same road as ours, together with her husband. They have even visited us for dinner on occasions and will be attending our Christmas party later tonight. Who would have thought we would become friends with the British Prime Minister? It's totally surreal.

Security buzz Emily and I through the gate that leads onto our estate. Security is tight, what with the prime minister and others residing on the estate.

Josh is already home when we arrive back. He is in the kitchen talking to Stacey and Karen, who decided to remain at Porton Down when given the option. They live in an apartment in one of the blocks near the main square and both have taken up jobs on site.

"How are the party preparations going?" I ask when I walk through the door.

"Very well," Karen tells me, with a glass of sherry already in hand.

"I can see," I smile at Karen, tempted by a glass myself.

Five minutes later, a car pulls up outside and Emily rushes to open the door, with me close behind her.

"Look who I found struggling through the snow, weighed down with booze," Catherine announces, as she gets out of the car.

"Good afternoon, Captain," I say to Winters, as his head pops up above the car. I can't resist poking fun at his recent promotion.

"Richards," Winters retorts, grinning, making use of his new rank.

"Where's Sam?" I enquire.

"She'll be here later. As soon as General Cox finishes with her," Winters replies, irritated.

"How was your trip?" I ask, taking hold of Catherine on the driveway.

"It was fine, but let's not talk about that now. I'm just glad to be home," Catherine tells me, as she moves in to kiss me.

"We missed you," Emily says, as she joins our embrace.

"I missed you too," Catherine says, breaking off our kiss and lifting Emily up to her. "What about this snow, eh? When did this arrive?"

"Last night. We woke up and the whole place was covered," Emily tells Catherine, as we walk back inside the house. "I beat Dad at snowballs earlier. Didn't I, Dad?"

"You're too good for me," I tell Emily.

"Anything I can do?" Winters asks, putting his bags of alcohol down.

"You can pour me a glass of sherry," I tell my friend. "In fact, sherries all around," I announce, as I look over at my family and friends with a feeling of festive joy glowing inside me.

THE END

If you have enjoyed **CAPITAL FALLING 6 - BREAKOUT**, be sure to leave a review. Amazon reviews only take a minute and are so important in building a buzz for every book. Many thanks, every review is appreciated!

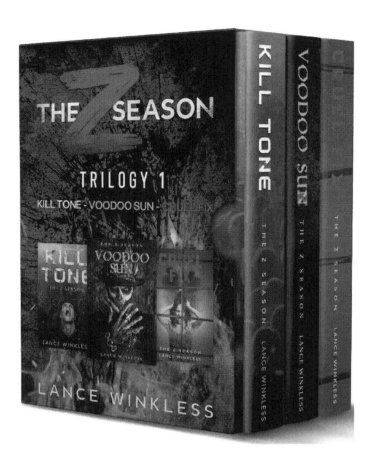

THE Z SEASON - TRILOGY 1

3 Novels - A #1 Best Seller - 650+ Pages -
Infectious to its Very Core

A trilogy of standalone and unique novels that don't
hold back and all with a zombie - undead twist.......
YOU HAVE BEEN WARNED!

KILL TONE

A festival of feverish, exhilarating tension with a rock 'n roll crescendo that unleashes hell itself, this is not for the faint-hearted. KILL TONE proves the perfect blend of decadence and undead carnage, whilst never losing sight of its predominant humanity.

VOODOO SUN

Caribbean Voodoo may have caused this nightmare, and nothing short of a miracle will help Max get out alive.

A tale of undead carnage and mayhem, VOODOO SUN embarks for bliss but lands in true perdition.

CRUEL FIX

CRUEL FIX is a terrifying trip through the labyrinth of loss and lunacy. Bleak and sinister it may be, but spirited humanity retains a twisted shard of hope …. Though all that glitters isn't gold, and all that walks is not alive.

Read these novels in any order, you choose. Each is a tale of its own and completely unique, but be warned they are not for the faint-hearted or easily offended!

Praise for THE Z SEASON TRILOGY

GREAT BOOK ★★★★★

"Just read the Kill Tone what an amazing book. the story had me captivated from start to finish. great author, love his books."

JUST A BRILLIANT AUTHOR ★★★★★

"Another great book by the author Lance brilliant from start to finish kept me on the edge like the others so will have to wait for next one now… hopefully."

ANOTHER GREAT READ ★★★★★

"Action packed from the beginning. So realistic that you could actually imagine this happening! Just wish it didn't end so soon. I would like to see how the virus spreads so roll on the next one."

PAPERBACK – KINDLE & KINDLE UNLIMITED